WISHING ON A DREAM

T0125535

Acclaim for Julie Cannon's Fiction

In *Smoke and Fire*…"Cannon skillfully draws out the honest emotion and growing chemistry between her heroines, a slow burn that feels like constant foreplay leading to a spectacular climax. Though Brady is almost too good to be true, she's the perfect match for Nicole. Every scene they share leaps off the page, making this a sweet, hot, memorable read."—*Publishers Weekly*

Breaker's Passion is…"an exceptionally hot romance in an exceptionally romantic setting. …Cannon has become known for her well-drawn characters and well-written love scenes."—*Just About Write*

In *Power Play*…"Cannon gives her readers a high stakes game full of passion, humor, and incredible sex."—*Just About Write*

About *Heartland*…"There's nothing coy about the passion of these unalike dykes—it ignites at first encounter and never abates. …Cannon's well-constructed novel conveys more complexity of character and less overwrought melodrama than most stories in the crowded genre of lesbian-love-against-all-odds—a definite plus." —Richard Labonte, *Book Marks*

"Cannon has given her readers a novel rich in plot and rich in character development. Her vivid scenes touch our imaginations as her hot sex scenes touch us in many other areas. *Uncharted Passage* is a great read."—*Just About Write*

About *Just Business*…"Julie Cannon's novels just keep getting better and better! This is a delightful tale that completely engages the reader. It's a must read romance!"—*Just About Write*

"Great plot, unusual twist and wonderful women. …[*I Remember*] is an inspired romance with extremely hot sex scenes and delightful passion."—*Lesbian Reading Room*

Visit us at www.boldstrokesbooks.com

By the Author

Come and Get Me

Heart 2 Heart

Heartland

Uncharted Passage

Just Business

Power Play

Descent

Breakers Passion

Rescue Me

I Remember

Smoke and Fire

Because of You

Countdown

Capsized

Wishing on a Dream

WISHING ON A DREAM

© 2017 By Julie Cannon. All Rights Reserved.

ISBN 13: 978-1-62639-762-0

This Trade Paperback Original Is Published By
Bold Strokes Books, Inc.
P.O. Box 249
Valley Falls, NY 12185

First Edition: February 2017

THIS IS A WORK OF FICTION. NAMES, CHARACTERS, PLACES, AND INCIDENTS ARE THE PRODUCT OF THE AUTHOR'S IMAGINATION OR ARE USED FICTITIOUSLY. ANY RESEMBLANCE TO ACTUAL PERSONS, LIVING OR DEAD, BUSINESS ESTABLISHMENTS, EVENTS, OR LOCALES IS ENTIRELY COINCIDENTAL.

THIS BOOK, OR PARTS THEREOF, MAY NOT BE REPRODUCED IN ANY FORM WITHOUT PERMISSION.

Credits
Editor: Shelley Thrasher
Production Design: Susan Ramundo
Cover Design By Sheri (graphicartist2020@hotmail.com)

Acknowledgments

Everyone has a dream. Whether it be win the lottery, take a vacation somewhere exotic, find inner peace, or something as simple as pay off a bill. Everyone that I've worked with to produce this book is, in some aspect, living their dream—producing quality lesbian fiction. To all of you, I continue to say thanks. If not for them and you the readers, we would not be doing what we love for those that love it.

Dedication

For everyone who has a dream

Prologue

I am not a needy person. I own my own home and a year-old Jaguar, and I singlehandedly restored a 1972 Ford Bronco and built a thriving business. I don't need to be surrounded by people, take a plus one to a party or a pal to the movies. I can eat out alone, take a walk alone, and sleep alone. But I do need one thing—desperately, anxiously, almost frantically. I need to get laid.

I need hands, fingers, lips, and tongue caressing every inch of my body. I need to feel the touch of a woman, inhale the scent of arousal, feel the pulse of desire. I need to get lost in sensation, shut out the world around me, and be swept over the edge in waves of release. I need to bury my hands in thick hair, touch soft skin, travel over curves and valleys, and sink into warm wetness. I need to remember to breathe, forget my name, and lose my inhibitions. I don't need to know her life history, her favorite color, or even her name. Actually, I would prefer not to know her name. That's all I need. Pure and simple. But there's nothing simple about it. Not at all.

I'm obsessed with sex. Okay, maybe obsessed is too strong a word, but I think about it all the time when my mind wanders, which, uncharacteristically, has been a lot lately.

I look at people on the street or in the office and wonder if they had sex last night. Or an hour ago. Was it wild and passionate or routine and perfunctory? Did old people still do it? I see a couple in their fifties just about every morning at the Coffee Klatch and just can't imagine them doing it missionary, or any other style, for that matter.

When I see couples, gay or straight, I wonder how they can be that intimate, then sit across from each other and discuss the latest episode of *Scandal* over a BLT at Denny's like it didn't just happen. All I see when I look at people is how they look naked, writhing in ecstasy, sucking on some very private body part, or thrusting deep and hard, exploding in orgasm.

Like I said, pretty simple, right? I'm really good at bullshit and covering up the real truth. I've had lots of experience.

Chapter One

"Oh my, she's hot." Courtney's voice somehow penetrated the music pounding from the massive black speakers thirty feet in front of us. "I'd do her in an instant."

Courtney Saber was the closest thing I had to a BFF. We met in grad school when she saved me from a potentially very nasty situation. I was at a party and she saw a guy drop something into my beer when my head was turned. I'd taken two or three big swallows when she came up to me, pretending to be an old friend. She gave me a big hug and whispered in my ear, "The guy in the red shirt put something in your beer," then released me and grabbed my hand and pulled me away from the bar. I was already starting to feel a bit woozy so I followed her without protest.

"Come on. Susie and Maxine would love to see you. Excuse us," she said, and hustled me out the door and straight to the hospital.

I didn't remember anything after that, but according to Courtney, they drew blood and called the police. The guy was arrested and after a two-day trial was found guilty of aggravated assault. He spent five years as a guest of the California penal system. Courtney was also one hundred percent heterosexual.

"What would Tom think?" I had to scream to be heard over the noise, referring to her husband of eight years and father to her three toddlers.

"I'll tell you tomorrow after I fuck his brains out when I get home."

I pulled my attention from the woman on the stage to look at Courtney.

"What?" she asked, exasperated. "Just because I think she's hot doesn't mean I want to do her. You should, Kiersten. I bet she'd rock your world."

The "she" Courtney was referring to was none other than Tobin Parks, hottest musician of the last few years. Tobin was a mixture of Taylor Swift, Madonna, and Janis Joplin. She was often described as a seductress on stage and a heartbreaker off. She was recognized all over the world, and this was another sold-out performance.

She had no less than eight songs in the last year that had hit the number-one position in every list that meant anything and sellout crowds in every city on her world tour for the past three years.

How do I know this? Because Courtney recited those facts and several more when she was trying to convince me to cough up two hundred and forty dollars for prime seats in the middle of row six.

"Come on, Kiersten. It'll be fun. We'll go out to eat at some trendy little place by the arena, then scream and swoon like we did when we were kids. I guarantee we'll have a great time. Besides, you need to get out more."

Little did Courtney know I had never screamed and swooned as a kid. Cried and sobbed, yes. Screamed and swooned, no. "And you're sacrificing yourself to help out a friend?" I asked skeptically.

"What are friends for? It's the least I can do."

"You just want to get away from your kids."

"Well, there is that, too," she admitted, not seeming the least bit guilty.

So, here we were, two closer to forty than thirty somethings almost within touching distance of the hottest woman I'd seen in a long, long time. I tried not to drool or stare as Tobin moved around the stage. She could shimmy, shake, bump, and grind like nobody's business. She was tall, with a thirty-inch waist and thirty-four-inch inseam, information again supplied by Courtney. And my lord, she didn't hesitate to use every inch of the stage as her playground. She seduced the crowd with romantic ballads and jolted us out of our seats with hard rock and roll. Every woman in the arena wanted to be her, and every lesbian wanted to be with her.

I had stumbled on an interview with her and newswoman Megan Caldwell on *60 Minutes* last month. They were outside in a park, the camera shooting over Megan's left shoulder.

"What's one thing no one knows about you?" Megan asked, as if expecting Tobin to actually divulge something secret, something really juicy.

Tobin laughed and my knees went weak. Her smile was radiant and her eyes sparkled with mischief. I had to sit down.

"Thanks to the media, present company excluded, there's not much people don't know about me, Megan," Tobin replied, dodging the question.

Megan prodded her. "Even more reason to tell us something."

"I don't understand the fascination people have with me. I'm just a singer."

It was Megan's turn to laugh. "Tobin, saying you're a singer is like saying the president of the United States is just somebody's boss. You're far more than just a singer."

The interview cut away to a segment on the early years of Tobin's career. Several videos of her onstage in dark clubs with harsh lighting and bad acoustics preluded more recent ones of her at Madison Square Garden, the Superdome, Central Park, and several venues in Europe. Megan's voice narrated several facts, including that Tobin still traveled in a large tour bus when she could very easily afford her own private jet.

"What about your love life?"

"My love life?"

"You have a pretty active social life."

"Is that what they call it?"

"They say you have a girl in every city," Megan said a little more seriously.

Tobin squirmed in her seat. "Well, don't believe everything you hear," she finally said.

"And what part is that?"

"I don't kiss and tell, Megan." Tobin held up her hands as if to say, "And you'll never get it out of me." When she winked at Megan I stopped breathing until the commercial began.

I have to admit that Tobin Parks was, in fact, hot. However, I'm a bit more verbally creative than Megan so would describe her as incredibly hot. She was in her mid-twenties and wore her dark hair short and spiky. Tonight she had on a pair of jeans and a T-shirt that showed her midriff every time she lifted her arms. Her boots looked like she wore them often, not just for show. Other than a leather bracelet on her left wrist, she had no other jewelry and probably weighed no more than a hundred and twenty pounds and didn't have to kill herself at the gym six days a week to stay there. Whereas most performers had that carefully costumed casual look, Tobin Parks looked like she'd wear those same clothes to the grocery store. However, I seriously doubted she'd have any idea where to find the powdered sugar on aisle six. From this angle her long legs looked like she was much taller than the reported five feet nine inches.

So here we were being jostled by women at least ten, some twenty years younger than us. Courtney danced and sang while I felt completely out of place. I was not a rock-and-roller. Never have been and never will be. I was too self-conscious to move my body like the women around me, and even if I could, I had very little sense of rhythm. So while sixty-two thousand, four hundred, eighty-nine screaming fans sang, danced, and acted crazy, I prayed my eardrums wouldn't burst while I lusted after the woman onstage.

The women in the rows in front of us looked no older than twenty—maybe. How in the hell did they afford the price of the tickets? When I was their age I was eating Ramen noodles and drinking store-brand soda. They were doing everything they could to catch Tobin's eye. If they did, they could claim they had joined the ranks of the Tobin Parks fan club. That was just a euphemism for "I had sex with Tobin Parks." And how did I know that? Courtney, of course. And how did I know Tobin would pick one of these women? Well, besides the fact that she was a very publicly out lesbian—it takes one to know one.

Chapter Two

"Hello, Chicago! I'm Tobin Parks."

The roar from the audience pushed me back a step. We were performing at an outdoor venue, and I could only imagine the roar if we'd been inside. Sweat dripped into my eyes, and I blindly reached for the towel hanging from the mic stand. I took the opportunity to grab a swallow of my special concoction of chamomile tea, honey, and cinnamon to soothe my throat. We were only four songs into the show, and I needed to keep my voice strong. I'd been on this tour for seven months and had another three before it was over.

On my signal Russ started the heavy beat of our next song. We opened big and closed even bigger with a mix of heart-pumping, raunchy lyrics with a little bit of rhythm and blues thrown in for balance. The song *Take Me* was one I had written several years ago as a ballad but with minimal chord changes, a heavier bass and faster beat I had bumped up to pure, raw sex for market appeal. It had rocketed to the top of the charts in record time and stayed there for months. When I sang it alone in my coach, the words were the same, but accompanied by only a classical guitar it was as emotionally raw as it got. No one had heard that rendition, and no one ever would.

When the song ended, I asked my stage manager to raise the house lights so I could see better. I hated singing into blackness, and having the lights up pulled the crowd even closer.

"Well, look at you," I said to the crowd. "Don't you all look nice?" The crowd whooped and hollered again. The thrill of tens of thousands of people coming to see me would never get old. The excitement in the air was palpable, the sense of anticipation in what was to come so thick I swear I could pull a chunk out of the air and swallow it.

"How is everybody tonight?" Again, the sixty-plus thousand made noise, a lot of noise. "How did you like Black Mountain? Aren't they awesome?" I referenced my opening act. They were good, very good, and would be headlining soon. Their lead singer had put the moves on me a few times, and after I told her I didn't mix business with pleasure, she moved on to Cindy, a member of my band. From what I could determine, they were both enjoying themselves. Casual hookups on the road were common when traveling more than three hundred days a year on tour. It was hard, if not impossible, to maintain any type of normal relationship. But what did I know about normal?

My exposure to normality consisted of profanity-laced yelling with more than an occasional slap thrown in, no pun intended, just because. I don't remember ever eating anything green, if you don't include the mold I cut off the end of the bologna or the edge of the stale bread. My diet consisted of whatever was in the charity box that my brothers didn't wolf down the day we got it. My father managed to trade our food stamps for the cheap beer that filled our fridge, and I don't even want to think about what my mother traded for their cigarettes. I was about twelve when I stumbled upon my older sister getting up from her knees in front of the neighborhood drug dealer. She was high for the next three days. Strangers drifted in and out of our trailer, and more than once I had to crawl out the bedroom window to get away from something I intuitively knew would not be good. My brother mimicked our parents, and I escaped into music. Needless to say, "normal" has many different definitions.

I introduced my band, starting with my drummer. Russ had been with me when we started banging out noise in his grandmother's barn. Russ could be a WWF wrestler if he wanted to. His arms were huge, and he reminded me of the cartoon character Popeye. He always wore sunglasses, even inside, not because he thought he was cool but because he had some type of eye condition that made them ultra-sensitive to light. Earlier that evening I'd asked him, "Where are we again?" All the cities we'd been in had run together lately.

"Chicago," he answered, laughing. "Don't worry. I'll remind you."

Chicago? How in the hell did we get to Chicago? "I appreciate that," I said honestly. Normally I slept or had my hands on my guitar when we were on the road, so I had little frame of reference as to our location. The Tobin Parks Band traveled in a convoy of seven Class A motor coaches and three semi-trucks. I had my own coach. Russ and Jones, my bass player, shared, which was comical as Jones was also well over six feet but as skinny as Russ was not. Jones was a diabetic, and even though he was missing three fingers on his right hand from a childhood accident, he was the best in the business and I was lucky to have him. Charity, my second guitar, was all of five feet nothing, with wild curly red hair and blind in her right eye. She doubled up with Cindy, our only female backup singer. The other members of the band shared the remaining three coaches.

Introductions complete, the next five or six songs went flawlessly, and I chatted up the crowd for a few minutes between each. It gave me an opportunity to scope out my after-show-wind-down entertainment. One woman in the fifth or sixth row looked like she would rather be anywhere other than here. She had shoulder-length blond hair and, even though it was hard to tell with this lighting, looked to be in her early thirties. She was cute, but if she wasn't interested in my music enough to dance to it, she wasn't interested enough for me. When our eyes met she looked away. Her friend, on the other hand, was cute but very definitely straight.

A woman a few rows farther to the front was more than a little enthusiastic about our music. Her eye contact never wavered, which I'd always found very sexy. Shy or timid women weren't for me. I didn't have time or interest to persuade a woman to have sex with me. Seduction was not in my repertoire, and I don't believe in it. I looked up the word once. According to the Merriam-Webster's Dictionary, seduction is the act of persuading someone to have sex with you. Where is the *persuasion* in two people wanting to have sex with each other? A cross reference in the psychology dictionary defined seduction as enticing someone astray from right behavior. Well, in my experience, sex was definitely the right behavior.

Twenty minutes later, when Russ started his drum solo, I stepped to the side of the stage. "Fourth row, middle, blue tank top, white pants, dark hair," I said to one of the roadies. It was his job to ask whoever I pointed out if they'd like to come backstage after the show. "Come backstage" was a euphemism for having sex with me. Rarely did the women say no.

It always took me several hours to come down from the adrenaline rush from the crowd, music, and backstage meet-and-greets. The days leading up to the show were filled with interviews and promo spots. After the show was always several hours of the obligatory glad-handing with sponsors and radio and music personalities and those who had won contests to have their picture taken with me. By the time that was over, my face hurt from smiling, my hand from shaking, and spots were blinking in front of my eyes from camera flash. The band wasn't quite as in demand as I was, but they too were pretty thrashed by the time everyone left. Typically the show would end around ten, and I would get back to my coach after one. Life on the road was tough and the music industry fickle, but I was at the top and did everything possible to stay there as long as I could.

We closed the show, and two encores, four beers, and a hundred photos later, the blue shirt and white pants were on the floor in my dressing room, and the woman from the fourth row was writhing on the settee about to come. An hour later I was back in my coach showered and sliding under the covers. I didn't do drugs, I even hated taking Advil, but I did use sex as my drug of choice to sleep. Usually I was dead to the world until the next mid-morning, but tonight I was still keyed up. I lasted only a few minutes before I gave up and pulled a robe over my nakedness and sprawled out on the couch.

My coach was designed so the driver area was separated from the living area by thick folding doors. Frank had been driving me since I could afford him. He was reliable, safe, and, most importantly, minded his own business. We were on the road again, the rhythmic vibration of the big tires rotating millions of times as the Tobin Parks entourage snaked across the interstate highway system in the middle of the night.

I plucked the strings on my guitar, a tune I'd been working on beginning to take shape. I pushed the record button on my phone. I'd write the actual music later, but for now the chords and rhythm were my main focus. I strummed the strings as the lines on the road passed in the dark.

I felt uncharacteristically unsettled tonight. The show was good, one of our better ones as a matter of fact, but the backstage obligatory meet-and-greets had become more than a little onerous. Too many people expecting a piece of me, including Miss White Pants.

She was easy to please, but it took me longer than I expected to get into it, and maybe that was part of the problem. I felt like I was going through the motions and the motions had become repetitive and scripted. I almost said "Just forget it," but the hit to my reputation and image would be ruined if she talked. It wasn't her fault. She tried more than a few ways, but I knew what was or, more accurately, what wasn't going to happen. I wasn't getting anywhere, and, tired of forcing something to happen, I just gave in and faked it.

Jeez, what was wrong with me lately? The grind of the road must be getting to me. I'd played over ninety gigs this tour and had another three months before it was over. Anyone who thinks going from one non-distinct city to another, day after day was glamorous and exciting had never done it. And they certainly had never done it for four years. Sure, I could afford to travel by plane, but that was another hassle I didn't need or want. A private plane would eliminate most of that, but then there were hotels, hotel food, and sleeping in a different bed every night. My coach was my home away from home and my getaway from the world, the hassles of notoriety and the pressures to be Tobin Parks. No one entered unless invited, and when they did they didn't stay long, and I never, and I mean never, brought a woman inside. When I wasn't on the road, my rig was parked and I lived in an obscure senior-citizen mobile-home park on the outskirts of Elk City, Oklahoma.

Everyone at the Hidden Acres Mobile and RV Resort knew who I was. I'd found this little oasis and had worked to get approval from the homeowners association so I could become a part-time resident. The residents valued their privacy as much as I and never told a soul Tobin Parks lived in lot 214. If they had, the paparazzi would have descended like a forty-year flood and never left.

My neighbor to my left, Mr. Justin, claimed to be a retired CIA operative. We shared morning coffee, watched sports on his sixty-inch TV, and drank more than an occasional beer. Mrs. Foster, whose forty-eight-foot ugly monstrosity occupied lot 213 across the street, was a fabulous cook and always had a pot of something delicious on her stove. She also had fourteen grandchildren and talked about them constantly. Thankfully they never came to visit when I was there, or my anonymity would go up in smoke.

I'd spend my days puttering around my little yard, trimming bushes and replanting flowers in the pots that lined my drive. Mr. Justin and Mrs. Foster would take turns watering and tending them until I got my exhausted butt back home. Thus was my life at Hidden Acres. It still surprised me that after swearing for years I'd live on the street before I'd ever live in a trailer park again, this little gem was where I felt most at home. In my little twenty-five-by-eighty-foot piece of paradise I also felt most like myself, whatever that means.

I don't speak for other entertainers, but I think most of us are very different people while doing our jobs versus when we're not. I know I am. My job is to entertain, and according to Thefreedictionary.com an entertainer is supposed *To hold the attention of (someone) with something amusing or diverting.* That is definitely my job, who I am cloaked in Tobin Parks. What comes with that comes with any job. Expectations, responsibilities, and definitely a pay-for-performance position. People pay to see me, and if I don't give them what they want, they'll take their money somewhere else. Thankfully a lot, and I mean *a lot* of people want to see me. But that won't last and I know it. So I retreat to Hidden Acres to return to some sense of normality.

Mr. Justin and Mrs. Foster don't treat me like a multi-millionaire celebrity. They expect me to keep my yard neat and tidy and my garbage contained. They expect me to abide by the rules of the park, join bingo in the rec room the Saturday nights I'm in town, and be a good neighbor. And I do. I live for the time I spend here, and lately I'm finding I want to be here more than on the road. Just a common, every day, twenty-five-year-old woman sitting on her deck in Hidden Acres. But, like most grown-ups, I have responsibilities. People depend on me for their livelihood and I can't let them down. I really do love making music, sitting in the quiet of my coach in the middle of the night in the middle of God knows where telling stories through song. I pick up my guitar and start to pluck a few chords.

CHAPTER THREE

"No."

"You haven't even heard the proposal, Kiersten."

"It doesn't matter. The answer is still no."

"She's perfect for us."

"I don't care if she's Princess Diana or Mother Teresa. The answer is still the same. We do not need her, and we definitely do not want to be associated with her." Good God, how many times did I have to say it? Not that I had to convince Daniel, my chief marketing officer, of anything. I was his boss, Kiersten Fellows, CEO of this company. My company. The company I started with eighteen thousand dollars and a dream. My sweat, tears, and sacrifice. My word was sometimes the first word, but it was always the last. And today, in this conversation, the word was no.

Daniel had stopped in my office twenty minutes ago, bringing two large cups of coffee from the McDonald's down the street. JOLT offices were three blocks east of the fast-food giant and one block west of a twenty-four-hour gym. My office was on the sixth floor, offering me a fabulous view of the park across the street. I allowed myself one trip to Mickey D's once a month and religiously went to the gym every day of the month except Sundays. That day I rode my bike along the twelve-mile path bordering Clearwater Lake, about twenty minutes from my house. Needless to say, I like to keep active. I'd spent too many years of sweat and tears to have it all recede to my hips and ass sitting behind a desk every day. I'd walk to work if I could, but twenty-two miles was, admittedly, a bit far. However, I had pedaled to the office on several occasions on a weekend when I needed to get caught up.

It was Tuesday, a week and a half after Courtney and I spent an action-packed evening with Tobin Parks, and my ears had finally stopped ringing. How could she be exposed to decibels that high every night? I thought about it for a minute before I remembered the speakers faced the audience and she had those things in her ears.

I wondered where she'd performed this past weekend. In the lobby of the auditorium, the vendors had hawked everything from key chains to magnets to multiple styles of T-shirts, one of which had the list of cities on her current tour. I'd noticed Chicago was sandwiched between Cincinnati and Michigan and wondered if her stop in Michigan was at the annual women's music festival. I think I read somewhere that it had been a few days ago. Or maybe it was next month. I wasn't interested so I didn't pay attention. For someone like Tobin, that was akin to a kid in a candy store. Talk about tens of thousands of women to pick from. I wonder if she…

"You okay?" Daniel's voice shocked me back to the here and now. I blinked a few times to focus. "Your face is flushed all of a sudden," he stated, concern in his voice.

"Yes, I'm fine." I wasn't but would be in a second, after I mind-slapped myself to pay attention. Daniel looked at me, the frown between his eyebrows the only lines on his otherwise smooth face. It made me uncomfortable that he'd seen my slip. I was always on, present in every conversation. At least I had been until ten days ago.

I couldn't get Tobin Parks out of my mind. After her concert I'd gone home and spent the next hour reading dozens of headlines and articles about her. I'd spent the next fifteen minutes doing other, more personal things thinking about her.

"Kiersten?"

"What?" I snapped, more than my face feeling heat now.

"Tob—"

I interrupted him, my normally abundant patience rapidly disappearing. "Daniel, JOLT has an image, a brand, one that you and I have worked very hard to cultivate. You know how competitive the energy-drink market is. One wrong move, one small misstep, and we could find ourselves off the shelves and on an end cap at the dollar store. I will not let that happen. She has her own image, and it does not mirror ours." My tone was harsher than normal, but I refused to budge on this, and the sooner Daniel accepted that fact the better.

"But she specifically asked for us."

I hated when Daniel fell into trite reasoning. He was brilliant and fresh out of the country's top marketing school when he came to work for me. That was five years and at least eight boyfriends ago. He was well over six feet tall, with blond hair and the bluest eyes I've ever seen. His skin was tanned from his latest vacation, and he had the glow of new love.

"So because she wants us we should want her? What is this, fifth grade?" I asked a little too harshly. I hadn't been sleeping well and my ankle was throbbing. I'd broken it two years ago playing rugby and had aggravated it in a game last week. I recognized the look on his face and shut him down before he had a chance to get started. "That's final, Daniel. JOLT is not going to sponsor the Tobin Parks tour."

❖

Muttering under his breath, Daniel left my office. I sat down behind my desk, nudged my mouse, and my laptop came to life, the draft of the speech I was writing filling the screen. I was the keynote speaker at the National Beverage and Container convention, this year being held in, of all places, Bozeman, Montana. Last year it was in Boston, the year before that here in Chicago, and next year it would be in Washington, DC. How in the hell did they choose Montana?

When I was asked to speak, I readily accepted. JOLT was a sponsoring member of the trade group and had been since we first opened our doors twelve years ago. For many years I didn't have money for lunch, but I knew the importance of networking, contacts, and allies. My speech would bore anyone that wasn't in the industry, but I was proud of what I'd written so far. My final draft was pretty much complete. I just needed to add a few closing remarks, send it over to Angela, the head of communications for her editing magic, and I'd be done.

I had a great team helping me make JOLT successful. In addition to Angela, who I'd recruited away from Google, there was my assistant Bea Sanderson, a sixty-something woman with seven kids and nineteen grandchildren, who ran my office and my life like an army boot camp. I knew where I was supposed to be when and had everything I needed two days before every meeting. She renewed my season tickets at the symphony, my box seats for the White Sox, picked up my clothes from the cleaners, got me to the dentist twice a year and the gynecologist annually.

In a meeting earlier this morning, Randi, my CFO, had shared that our sales for this year were projected to be almost double what they were two years ago, and millions of dollars from year one. Some days I had a hard time keeping my eyes off Randi's legs when she wore short skirts, but that was neither here nor there.

I never mixed business with pleasure. Never had, never been tempted, and never would. Not only was that bad business, but it was also playing Russian roulette. I would never do anything to jeopardize my professional credibility or the success of JOLT. It was my baby, my company, and hundreds, if not thousands of people depended on it. From the charities we supported to our employees, distributors, and stock boys, the success or failure of JOLT impacted many more lives than just mine. But I could still appreciate a good-looking pair of legs, and Randi had a pair that was outstanding. I wonder if she…

My phone rang, and I hit the send button to whisk my speech across the hall to Angela. "Kiersten Fellows."

"Kiersten, darling, how are you?"

It was my mother, and her greeting always sounded more like "daaling" than darling. Why she called me darling was anybody's guess. I thought that endearment was for lovers, not parent and child, but what did I know. She'd called me that my entire life.

"Hello, Mother." Not Mom, but always, always Mother.

"I called to see if you'd bought your dress for Ray and Judy's party next week."

I hadn't, but I wasn't going to tell her that. "Don't worry, Mother. I'll be there," I said instead. I'd received the invitation to the annual benefit gala in Boston from my parents' closest friends three weeks ago. I'd tossed it on Bea's desk the next morning, knowing she'd take care of everything. I hadn't checked, but I was certain my flight was confirmed, a car service booked, and a hotel room secured for the event. If she could shop for me, I'm sure she'd do that as well. Instead I'd received a call from Joyce, my personal shopper, who had asked my preferences for the event, and two days later a box containing a dress, shoes, and accompanying jewelry arrived at my office. It wasn't necessary for me to try anything on. Joyce had my measurements, but I reminded myself I should just in case. I'd had no appetite for the past few weeks, and my clothes felt more than a little loose.

"Are you bringing a guest?" That was my mother's way of asking if I had a date.

"No, Mother. Not this time." I'd made it sound like on previous occasions I had and this time was an anomaly. That couldn't be further from the truth.

"Now, Kiersten, you know you're welcome to bring anyone to the event." That was my mother's way of telling me it was okay if I brought a woman as my date.

"Yes, Mother, I know, and I appreciate it." I did, really. My parents were completely supportive of my choice in dates, which was the complete opposite of my choice in careers.

The oldest of five, I was expected to follow in my father's footsteps. I was programmed at an early age to study law at Harvard and join his firm as an associate partner, working my ass off filing briefs and muddling through boxes of boring tax documents until I became partner. I never had any interest in the law, other than staying out of jail, and thankfully the heat was off when my brother Marcus took my place.

"Are you seeing anyone?" That was my mother's way of asking when I was getting married. All four of my siblings had tied the knot years ago, and to a woman like my mother, any woman over the age of thirty who wasn't married was, well, it just wasn't right. She was more than okay with the whole gay-marriage thing, but considering I was thirty-six my mother was quite concerned.

"Nobody special." No one actually, but again, I wasn't going to tell her that.

"Kiersten, I worry about you. Do you have your sights set too high?"

My sights set too high? What the fuck was that? Maybe I was living in a fantasy world, but I thought the person you fell in love with, married, and spent the rest of your life with wasn't someone you lowered your sights to get.

"No, Mother. I've just been really busy." I cringed, knowing that was the wrong thing to say.

"You have to make time. Your brothers and sister did. Life is more than nine-to-five, sweetheart." I wish I could remember the last time I worked nine to five, or even seven to seven.

"I know, Mother, and I appreciate your concern, but I'm perfectly happy with where my life is right now. I meet people and go out, but my focus is on JOLT right now." That and the fact that by the time I do get home, I'm exhausted. The last thing I wanted to do after a long day was make small talk to a woman who only wanted to get me into bed, however frightening and exhilarating it might be. I might think about sex all the time and need to get laid, but on most days the effort was just overwhelming. I made a note on my pad to research escort services, then quickly scribbled over it. However easy that would make my life, I certainly didn't need to get caught up in a sting and have my face plastered all over the web.

"It's just that your father and I worry about you."

"I love you, and Father too, but I'm fine."

"Really, darling, you work way too hard."

"I don't really have a choice, Mother. It's my company." The argument was common and old. We hadn't had it in a while so I wasn't surprised. It typically occurred around some sort of family event. The last time was when I missed my niece's christening.

There was a dock-worker strike, and thousands of pallets of JOLT were sitting idle on a ship in Long Beach.

"But can't you assign things to somebody else?" my mother asked naively. She was clueless when it came to business, and that suited her just fine. Her job was to be a wife, mother, socialite, and philanthropist, all of which she performed exceptionally well.

"No, Mother," I replied, much more patiently than I felt. "I have people to do things, specialists in their field, but the overall responsibility of JOLT is mine. I'm sorry, but I have to go. I'll see you next week." I hoped God didn't strike me down for lying to my mother, but I could take only so much of her. And today that glass was full.

Chapter Four

"Tobin, where have you been?"

My back stiffened at the tone of Jake's question. He was my manager, not my mother. One I paid to do things for me, the other to stay away from me.

Jake Richards had been my agent from the day I landed my first recording contract. One of the guys in my band recommended him, and the rest, as they say, is history. And did we have history. Jake bailed me out of jams, set up my concert tours, and negotiated everything from the lease on my coach to the percentage of the concession revenue at each concert. He kept my family out of sight and my name in the headlines. He was my right- and left-hand man. Except for a few key, personal details, he probably knew me almost better than I knew myself. He was five feet three inches tall, balding, and commanded a room like a charismatic politician.

"I was in my coach working on something and lost track of time." I'd had my head immersed in a song that was struggling to get out when one of the stagehands had knocked on my door. "Why are you so upset?" I asked, looking at my watch. "Sound check for tonight's show doesn't start for another ten minutes." My coach was my haven from the chaos of touring, and I hated any intrusion.

"I heard back from JOLT."

Now he had my attention. I'd been after him for a meeting with the nation's fastest growing energy drink to propose they sponsor my next tour. They were the hottest drink on the market, and I wanted to be a part of that.

"What did they say?" I asked, sidestepping a roadie lugging a set of fat, black cables through the control booth.

"No."

I wasn't sure I'd heard correctly. "No?" I had dozens of companies wanting me, practically begging me to be their spokesman, but the one I wanted said no. How ironic was that?

"Yep. Actually, it was more like thank you for your inquiry, but JOLT is not interested in sponsoring Tobin Parks at this time." Jake used air quotes around his clarification, one of his habits that made me nuts.

I have to admit I was surprised and said as much to Jake. "I would have thought they'd want to be with me on my next tour."

"I did too," Jake said. "You're the biggest in the industry, and any company would be lucky to have you. The publicity would be enormous. I told them that but not so directly."

"What was their reason?" I was still trying to wrap my head around this. In the last few years people had rarely told me no.

"They didn't give me one."

"That doesn't make sense. They sponsor all kinds of events. They have their name on a NASCAR car, and I saw their logo on some half-naked volleyball players on ESPN last week. It's not like they don't do it."

"I don't know any more than that," Jake replied, sagging against the control board.

"Don't sit on that," I said sharply. "It cost almost a hundred grand, and we'd be shit out of luck if it broke." The board, as my electronics guru Reggie called it, was the master control of the entire show. With the flick of a switch or a slight adjustment of a knob, he controlled lights, sound, and the video played on the massive screen at the back of the stage. Without it and him, I'd just be a singer with a guitar and a band. Those were the early days.

I was stunned and more than a little disappointed. I wanted JOLT. I wanted my name on their product. JOLT personified the image I'd worked hard to create.

I heard my name called over the walkie-talkie on Gerard's belt. Gerard was my stage manager, a brutish man who towered over my five feet nine inches by at least ten of his own. His hands were like a catcher's glove and his beard as dark as his face. He ran the stage like a choreographed play, and I wouldn't be where I was without him. He was standing a few feet away from me and pointed to his watch, then the stage. I pushed my irritation with JOLT out of my mind when my lead guitarist strummed the first chord. It was time to get to work.

❖

Several hours later, back in my coach, I let my mind wander off the song I'd been working on and onto JOLT. Why had they turned me down? I thought for sure they'd jump on the Tobin Parks gravy train. I reached for my laptop and opened my Google browser.

Eight thousand, four hundred, thirty-nine hits came up, and I started with the most recent. Kiersten Fellows scheduled to speak at the National Beverage and Container Conference in Montana. I read the headline out loud. "Ms. Fellows, thirty-six, the founder and CEO of JOLT, the nation's number-two energy drink, is expected to talk about…" I skimmed the rest of the article and focused on the accompanying image. Even in a flat, one-dimensional photo, Ms. Fellows was stunning. Her blond hair framed her face and was tucked behind one ear. It looked thick and luxurious, and I wondered what it would feel like to run my hands through it. It was obviously a professionally shot photo, and she was looking directly into the camera lens. Her eyes were an unusual shade of blue, and I felt like she could actually see me. My pulse skittered a whole lot more than it had with the woman after tonight's show, or many other nights for that matter.

Kiersten was leaning against a pallet of JOLT, her arms crossed over her chest. Her head was cocked just a little, and her entire body said, "This is me, take it or leave it." This was not a canned CEO head shot. She was wearing khakis and a purple polo shirt with the JOLT logo positioned over her left breast. She wore a large watch and no rings, but a glint of something at her ears alluded to diamond studs. There was beautiful and there was hot. Kiersten Fellows was definitely the latter.

I read several other articles and discovered that she'd had the fairy-tale life I didn't. She had one sister and three brothers, where I had two fewer brothers, thank God. From what I could find, they were all married and had great jobs, or their spouses did. My good-for-nothing siblings would rather scam society or mooch off me than get a job. Her parents were part of the upper crust of Boston society. Not my phrase, but the authors of several articles seemed to like it. My parents were welfare-cheating, trash-TV aficionados and drunks. We couldn't have been more different.

But it was the article about JOLT's charitable contributions that caught my attention. An astonishing thirty-five percent of the profits were donated to various children's charities. I couldn't find any particular reason why that was. Kiersten definitely didn't grow up that way. She had to have a reason other than a hefty corporate tax deduction, and this was why I wanted JOLT as my sponsor. I reached for my phone. It was the middle of the night, but fame has its privileges.

CHAPTER FIVE

"Thank you." I stepped back from the podium and gave a slight wave to the audience. According to the timer on the monitor facing the stage, I'd just spent twelve of my allotted fifteen minutes talking to over eight hundred of my peers, competitors, and beverage suppliers. I loved coming to these events. It kept me connected to the industry, enabled me to keep up on new, innovative products, and let me see old friends and make new ones.

As I made my way down the stairs, several people were waiting for me. The next session wouldn't begin for fifteen minutes, and judging by the number of people milling around me, I knew I probably wouldn't make it to the bathroom before I needed to be somewhere else. The attendees at the conference were primarily men, with a few women scattered here and there. If I did get to the ladies' room, I might just have it all to myself.

Finally, after a very long day, I got back to my hotel room. The door hadn't even closed behind me before I slipped out of my heels, had my suit jacket off, and untucked my blouse. I headed straight for the minibar and grabbed two cordials of Crown Royal and a can of Coke. I'd called ahead to room service, and a bucket of ice and a tuna sandwich and chips were waiting for me. I hadn't had much opportunity to eat much during dinner, or lunch for that matter, my table mates asking me questions practically nonstop. While I talked, they did eat, thus my late-night snack.

I turned on the TV to CNN and tossed my pants and hair clip on the bed. Sitting in front of the handsome Anderson Cooper in my underwear, I ate my dinner, drank one of my cocktails, and started on the second. I pulled my MacBook onto my lap and clicked the little envelope at the bottom of the screen.

After I sorted the one hundred forty-three unread emails I'd received today by sender, I started plowing through them. I started with those from my staff. They often needed an answer or an approval for them to move forward or they had an FYI to keep me out of trouble or from being blindsided. Bea always contacted me by text if it was something critical, and today my phone had been blissfully quiet. Next in the line of priority was one from Daniel.

Kiersten—

Tobin Parks has asked to meet with you Wednesday evening. She suggested dinner at a restaurant just down the street from your hotel—The Stockmen's Club. She'd like to talk with you about the sponsorship.

A flash of anger burned. I didn't want to talk with Tobin Parks, and Daniel should have handled this. Why was he bringing it to me? He was probably an adoring fan who couldn't see beyond her stardom. What was up with that? I read on.

She called me personally when she couldn't get past Bea. And IMPO I think you should reconsider your position. Tobin has the exact fan base that is our target market. We would benefit significantly if we were to partner with her.

Tobin will be at the restaurant at 7:30.

J

Now I was really irritated. First, I hated when Daniel used stupid shorthand. When did people stop using words like "to" and "be" and "in my professional opinion"? Why couldn't he communicate like everyone else? Maybe it was because he was twenty-eight and not in his mid-thirties like me. Second, he sounded like a groupie. Third,

Tobin Parks was pretty presumptuous that I'd agree to meet with her without my RSVP. And what in the hell was she doing in Bozeman, Montana? But most importantly, something about Tobin Parks just made me uncomfortable. I hit the Reply button.

I'll think about it.

I hit the Send button and moved on to the next email but not before changing the channel to a baseball game. The Seattle Mariners were playing the Arizona Diamondbacks and were losing four to two in the top of the sixth inning.

That was another thing that drove my mother nuts, my love of baseball. I attended as many White Sox games as I could and offered my seats behind home plate to fans in my office when I couldn't. I had long ago stopped worrying what my parents thought and, even longer than that, trying to please them. Yawning, I moved on to the next email. It was going to be a long night.

During the workshops the following two days I was uncharacteristically distracted. I couldn't focus and had to force myself to concentrate when I was on my assigned panel. I was embarrassed when I missed a question directed to me.

The conference over, I drove my rental car to the stores that stocked JOLT. As the miles passed I wondered how Tobin Parks traveled from city to city. Did she fly in a private jet? Surely she didn't fly commercial? What a scene that would be in every airport in the world. When I should have been looking at stock levels, shelf space, and promotional displays, I was imagining all the logistics that went into a Tobin Parks show. When I should have been paying attention to the content of the briefing from my district sales manager, I was comparing how the woman seated at the far end of the table looked a little like Tobin. And I won't even mention my dream last night. Or was it a nightmare? I wasn't sure which, but if dreams were reality I'd say the latter.

I didn't finish until after six and was on my own for dinner. I'd had dinner with my sales manager last night and refused to subject her to two nights with the boss. I was driving back to the hotel when a sign on the other side of the median caught my attention.

STOCKMEN'S
QUALITY BEEF AND BREW

For some reason I didn't want to think about too hard, I made what was probably an illegal U-turn and pulled into the parking lot. I exchanged my keys for a valet ticket and opened the heavy front door. It was cool inside, and it took a few minutes for my eyes to adjust to the low light.

"Ms. Fellows?"

I was surprised when the hostess addressed me by name.

"Yes."

"Ms. Parks is expecting you. This way, please."

Ms. Parks is expecting me? I was half tempted to turn around and leave Ms. Parks sitting alone and watching the clock. But I was already here, hungry and curious if she was as confident in person as she was presumptuous.

I saw her before she saw me, and though I interact with high-profile people rather regularly, and much to my chagrin, I hated to admit, I was a bit starstruck. My heart started to beat fast, my pulse raced, and every nerve seemed to come alive.

Tobin Parks was striking in a baby-butch kind of way. Of course anyone under thirty was a baby in my book. Jeez, when did that happen? I might be thirty-six, but starting JOLT and making it what it is today made me feel many years older.

Tobin looked up as we approached her table, and I almost stumbled at the intensity of her gaze. No wonder she had any woman she wanted. Her eyes were a luminescent shade of green and seemed to look right through me. God, she was young. She stood, stepped around the table, and held out her hand.

"Ms. Fellows, I'm Tobin Parks. Thank you for coming." Like she needed the self-introduction, but I appreciated it nonetheless.

I took her hand, and a strong pulse of what I could only describe as energy passed between us. She must have felt it too because her eyes flared with obvious interest.

"Ms. Parks," I replied, equally formal. "I was in the neighborhood," I said, suddenly tongue-tied.

"Please call me Tobin," she said, holding the back of my chair as I sat down. I noticed several people around us whisper to each other when they saw our introductions. Would I see my picture on the Internet tomorrow? Certainly on someone's Facebook page, if the not-so-surreptitious cell-phone maneuvering to my left was any indication.

The waiter appeared out of nowhere and I ordered sparkling water. I didn't dare be anything but absolutely on the top of my game for this conversation.

"Admittedly I wasn't sure you'd show up." Tobin was toying with her half-empty glass of beer.

"I have to admit I wasn't going to."

Her eyebrows shot up. "Why did you?"

I was as surprised as she seemed to be. As famous as she was, I didn't think anyone would not do as she asked, or commanded.

"My marketing guy kept telling me I should hear what you have to say."

"So you're meeting me just to shut him up?"

"No. If I wanted to shut him up, I'd tell him to."

"You're the boss," she said.

"It does have its privileges."

"And its burdens."

I lifted my glass and tilted it slightly toward her. "I'll second that."

"I heard the food here is top-notch," Tobin said, picking up her menu.

"I'm sure the same is true for just about every steakhouse in Montana."

"Probably so. Are you staying for dinner?" She seemed uncertain.

"Might as well."

"Why is that?"

"Because I'm hungry. Besides, you invited me, therefore you're paying."

Tobin laughed, and the water going down my throat got stuck halfway. I tried really hard not to choke and spit it back out. That would be humiliating.

"Well, there is that," she acknowledged playfully.

Tobin opened her menu and I looked at her hands. They appeared strong, which I'm sure they were, due to playing the guitar for as many years as she had. She had a cut on her thumb that was red and looked ugly. I wondered how she got it and if it affected her playing.

"Beef, beef, beef. What a surprise," she said, turning the page.

"What did you expect, sushi?"

"No, but maybe more of a selection." Tobin frowned again.

"Are you a vegetarian?"

"God, no, but I do like variety."

Tobin's eyes pierced mine, and I wasn't sure if she was referring to the food on the menu or the women on her menu.

"So I hear." Shit, why did I make this about sex? Tobin's conquests were legendary, and she didn't need any confirmation or encouragement from me.

"Well, don't believe everything you hear."

"I know better than that." I spoke sharply, remembering how a woman in front of us had been escorted backstage at her concert several weeks ago. She'd looked barely older than jail bait. Thankfully the waiter arrived to take our order.

After he left I was certain everybody in the restaurant was watching us. Who was I kidding? They were watching Tobin.

"How was your speech yesterday?"

I was taken aback by her question. "How did you know about that?" What else did she know about me?

"I do my research," she said, not breaking eye contact.

I thought about her question. "Not quite the adoring fans and thundering applause as you're used to, but it went well."

"Accomplishments are relative," Tobin said evenly.

Her comment surprised me. It was more profound than I expected to hear from her.

"Do you have a show here in Bozeman?"

"No."

"Live here?"

"No."

"Vacation house?"

"No."

I was running out of choices. I tried one more. "Visiting friends?"

"No. I don't know a soul here."

"Then why are you here?"

"Because you are," she said simply.

In another world, someone as gorgeous as Tobin saying that to me would be romantic and make my heart go pitter-patter. But this was not another world, so why was my heart going pitter-patter?

"You came all the way from wherever you were to *maybe* have dinner with me?" The idea was awesome, in that other world.

"Well, it wasn't really that far and I wanted to talk to you. Dinner was an added bonus."

"And if I hadn't shown up?"

"I would have eaten alone, gotten on the next flight, and tried something else."

"Persistent." I stabbed into my salad.

"When I need to be. Neither one of us got to where we are by being a wallflower."

This time when my stomach flip-flopped it was due to a flashback to a time when I was, in fact, a wallflower. A very large wallflower.

"I suppose not," I said, my throat a little tight.

"So tell me about JOLT," Tobin said before lightly blowing on the soup on her spoon.

"I certainly hope you didn't ask JOLT to be your sponsor if you didn't know anything about us. Or was it someone else's idea?"

"No. It was my idea to meet with you."

"Why?" I asked, getting down to it.

"My question exactly. Why not?"

"You first," I said, trying to gain the upper hand in this conversation.

"I prefer it when the lady goes first."

My blood raced, but I didn't know if it was due to the blistering look she was giving me or the fact that she was actually hitting on me. Probably neither.

"That's why."

"I beg your pardon?" Tobin frowned.

"You just hit on me."

"So? You're a beautiful, desirable woman," she replied, as if that was the only reason she needed.

"At the risk of repeating myself, that's exactly why." I studied Tobin's face for a few seconds, and she clearly didn't get it. Was she so self-centered and shallow she thought she could come on to every woman she met? When did that become socially acceptable behavior?

"Do you really expect that sex will get my sponsorship?" This was one conversation I have never had in my entire professional career. But then again I'd never sat across from a totally out lesbian who wanted me. I guess there's a first time for everything.

"I'll do the best I can. However, I've never had any complaints." She sat back in her chair looking smug.

The thought of Tobin doing the best she could made my blood heat and that private point between my legs throb.

"I don't mix business with pleasure." Good God, that sounded like a canned, prudish statement.

"Fine by me. We can do the former, then focus on the latter."

Most of my blood had settled in my crotch, and I needed a moment to dissect her statement. She was unbelievably brash and unequivocally hot. She had the body, attitude, and confidence to carry it out.

"I do not want a spokesman for my company that has the reputation you do."

"Meaning?"

My turn to laugh. "You're not serious?"

"I am."

"I don't mean to be harsh, but are you that clueless?"

"Now you're insulting me?"

"Not at all. I just have a hard time believing you actually think who you are and your image does not factor into a product endorsement. I'm also giving you the benefit of the doubt that everyone says yes to you?" I looked at Tobin closely for a sign that would indicate she had some sense of self-awareness. "Or do they?"

Chapter Six

When had this conversation turned south? More important, who was this gorgeous, classy woman with eyes the color of the clear Montana sky, a drop-dead gorgeous body, and titillating, mind-blowing verbal banter? I'd read quite a bit about Kiersten, but nothing had prepared me for the woman sitting in front of me. Whereas other women flaunted their confidence, Kiersten Fellows wore hers comfortably. Whereas other women often used power as a weapon, hers was understated. Whereas others' brilliance came across as arrogance, Kiersten's was just below the surface. And I was in way over my head. And I mean w-a-y over my head. Also, why was she here?

I'd half expected her to show up, the conceited, I-always-get-what-I-ask-for half. The other half, the normal person's half, thought she wouldn't. Seeing Kiersten in person made my naughty parts spring to life.

"May I call you Kiersten?" I asked in my polite voice. I hadn't grown up knowing manners, but years later I'd paid to learn them and might as well use them.

"Of course."

"So why did you come?" I circled back to one of my original questions.

Kiersten waited for the waiter to refill her glass before she spoke. "Curiosity."

"About me?" I realized that was a big-headed thing to ask.

"Of why you want JOLT. You can have your pick of any product in the world, and you want mine. I want to know why."

"Fair enough," I said. Kiersten leaned back in the uncomfortable chair and gave me her full attention. But, different from most people around me, she seemed to really be interested in what I had to say, not pretending in order to get something from me.

"I like what you stand for," I said simply. When I didn't say any more, her eyebrows rose and her forehead crinkled.

"And?"

"And nothing."

"I'm afraid I'm not following."

"Last year you gave thirty percent of JOLT sales to charity. The year before it was twenty-eight, and the year before that, twenty-five." I recited the statistics I had memorized during my research.

"And you want to be our spokesman because we give to charity?"

"Yes."

"Ms. Parks—"

"Please call me Tobin."

"Tobin." Thank God Kiersten hesitated a few seconds before continuing, because I couldn't hear anything other than the sound of my name coming from her lips. It was soft and melodious, and I suddenly wanted to write a song to describe it. WTF?

"Thousands, tens of thousands of companies for that matter give to charity. Why not one of them?"

"Because they're not JOLT."

She continued to look at me blankly. Obviously I needed to articulate my position better. Articulate, that was the word of the day on my word-of-the-day-calendar on the desk in my coach. I'd been wondering how I could weave it into a conversation.

"It's who you give it to, not how much. Well, it's also how much…but…primarily where. I mean, it's a combination of who and where." I was stammering and not making much sense even to myself. I hadn't stammered since my mother humiliated me in the fifth grade.

"And where is that?"

I named the groups I'd been able to uncover.

"And why do those organizations interest you?"

"Because they're worthy causes."

"Again, there are hundreds of thousands of worthy causes, any of which you could donate to."

It was obvious Kiersten was skeptical. "I would think if you're committed to giving a large portion of your profits to charities, you'd want more profits. Higher sales equals more contributions."

"I know how the math works."

"I can give that to you." As soon as the words came out of my mouth, as true as they were, they made me sound like an egomaniac.

And there we sat, silently staring at each other in a cozy restaurant, complete with white linen tablecloths, candles on the table, and soft music piped over the speakers. We should be having an intimate conversation sharing tidbits about each other's day or flirting as foreplay to the pleasures we both knew would come after dinner.

I held Kiersten's gaze. Normally my eyes wandered around the room, any room. I'd learned very young to know where everyone was in my house. But Kiersten's look was inquisitive, confident, and questioning. It was as if a thousand questions were racing through her mind. She was trying to figure me out. What was my game, my ulterior motive, my hidden agenda?

Our dinner arrived, giving both of us an out without losing face. We chatted about various places we'd traveled, the upcoming presidential election, and the blockbuster movie that had been nominated for twelve Oscars. When coffee came I decided it was my turn to ask the questions. "Why do you support so many groups?"

"Because they're worthy causes."

She'd parroted my answer so I volleyed it back to her. "There are hundreds of thousands of worthy causes."

"Yes, there are, and those are the ones I choose. Now, if you'll excuse me," she said, folding her napkin and placing it on the table beside her cup. "I have an early flight and still have some work to do."

Kiersten stood and I did as well. She was a few inches shorter than me.

She held out her hand. "It was a pleasure meeting you, Tobin. Thank you for dinner. It was delicious. Good night."

And on those last two words, Ms. Kiersten Fellows turned and walked away from my table as gracefully as she'd confidently strode toward it. If I thought my blood had raced watching her arrive, it settled in my crotch as I watched her leave.

Chapter Seven

"Good grief," I mumbled, maneuvering through the crowded restaurant. The patrons that knew I had dined with Tobin were looking at me trying to determine if I was "somebody." I silently told them to mind their own business. God, what a fishbowl Tobin must live in, and no way did I intend to be in the middle of that.

Three couples were in front of me in the valet line, and the longer I waited the more I fully expected Tobin to be right behind me. I didn't think she'd give up that easily. I was disappointed that she had. Obviously when she didn't get what she wanted, she moved on.

The ruggedly handsome valet held the door of the rental car as I slid into the leather seat. I tipped him a five, which I almost grabbed back when he called me ma'am as he closed the driver's door. When had I become a ma'am?

The drive back to my hotel was short. I was so distracted thinking of Tobin I almost passed my exit. If not for the sultry European voice floating out of the car speakers, I'd have missed it completely. Gathering my briefcase and jacket, I left the car with the hotel valet and headed to my room.

For convenience I had reserved a suite. I hated sitting on the bed when it was the only place to get any work done. The desk was always so cluttered with a phone, lamps, directions on how to connect to the Internet, and assorted hotel and local-attraction information it was almost unusable.

It was after ten but I wasn't tired. I was too keyed up from the day and dinner with Tobin, plus my in-box was probably jammed. If I didn't keep up with it I would suffocate in a sea of unread messages.

Thirty minutes later I gave up any pretense of getting anything done. I took a long, hot shower and tried not to think about Tobin Parks and how I'd felt sitting across the table from her.

I had expected a spoiled, rich airhead. I got the rich part, but I saw no indication of the spoiled, and she was extremely articulate. She voiced her opinion on paper over plastic, why John Wayne will always be a better cowboy than Sam Elliott, and the pros and cons of the NCAA. When she started talking about free trade I knew the public and private Tobin Parks were very different.

When she talked she completely focused on me. Her eyes were sharp and inquisitive. She asked questions about JOLT, my vision and how I got started. We had a lively discussion about expansion, and I admit she gave me a few things to think about.

Tobin didn't talk about herself unless I asked a specific question. Then, she answered it simply, without exaggeration. She didn't name-drop or try to impress. I had a few twenty-somethings in my office, and Tobin was by far more mature than they. Maybe because she'd been on her own for many years or had been exposed to more things, but she was much more sophisticated than I expected.

I expected her to be acutely aware of the women around us. Someone with her reputation would be on the prowl for her next conquest, but I had her constant, complete attention. When she looked at me it was as if she could see inside me. When we talked about serious topics she frowned in concentration and scrunched up her mouth when trying to understand. Her eyes lit up and sparkled when she laughed or told a funny story of life on the road. I was completely surprised by her and had grossly underestimated her. She was smart, well mannered, respectful to the wait staff, and very, very good-looking.

During dinner I caught everyone sneaking a peek and some rudely staring. What were they thinking? Were they wondering if it was really her? Did they dare ask for an autograph? Several brave souls had, and Tobin had graciously signed a napkin or a drink coaster and thanked them.

I couldn't help but wonder what she was like in bed. Remember, I'm the one who thinks about sex all the time, and she oozed sexuality. Sitting across from a stunning lesbian did nothing to redirect that line of thinking.

I was curious about what it was like to have that kind of sexual confidence. Was she any good? Even if she wasn't, the women she was with would surely think she was, i.e. the aura of sex with Tobin Parks. Her name alone conjured up an image of pure, raw sex appeal. Was her sexual-technique repertoire enormous? Did she know hundreds of ways to please a woman? Did she like to be tied up or be the top?

All this and many more vivid images popped in and out of my brain all through dinner. Needless to say I hadn't eaten much. Tobin, on the other hand, ate everything on her plate, including her salad and a piece of chocolate cake. Ahhh, the metabolism of a twenty-five-year-old.

What was she doing now? Had she gotten back on an airplane and flown to wherever she came from? Had she made a detour to a bar for some quick, naughty entertainment? Was she with her now? Was she on her back or between a stranger's legs? Did she come only once or as many times as the play allowed? Did she demand submission or active participation? Did she talk dirty or say nothing at all?

"Enough!" I spoke out loud to the empty room. I got up and walked to the patio door on shaky legs. My hands trembled as I fumbled for the lock. Pushing the curtain aside, I slid the door open. A cool blast of fresh air hit my overheated skin, and goose bumps sprang to life on my arms.

There wasn't a cloud overhead, and thousands of stars stood out on a background of jet-black sky. There were very few lights and no pollution, and the air smelled crisp and clean. I could get used to this. I let the cool breeze blow across me for several minutes, hoping I would cool down enough to get some sleep.

I returned inside, turned off the lights, and slid under the covers. Sleep slowly settled over me with the image of Tobin's face dancing in the candlelight as I drifted off.

Chapter Eight

Here's your key, Tobin. Room 1042." Jake handed me a bright-orange card key. My coach had been running hot, and I'd be spending the night in a hotel while it was getting checked out. I had two shows here in Boston so the timing was perfect. We'd pulled into town about an hour ago, so I had time to take a quick nap before sound check.

The lobby was busy and thankfully nobody noticed me. I could have come in through the rear, but that always made me feel like a criminal. I passed an ornate sign giving directions to the Fergusons' party on the second-floor ballroom. I couldn't remember the last time I went to a party. High school, maybe? No, more like middle school. I dropped out of high school to play music in cheap bars around town. There were so many, I could have played in a different one every night. More often than not I recognized someone from my neighborhood, and occasionally they weren't with the person they were married to.

My band and I didn't start in my garage. Trailer parks don't have garages. Besides, we didn't have a car to put in it even if we had one. We practiced in Russ's grandma's barn, which was nine hundred and eighty-two white lines painted in the middle of the asphalt road from mine. I counted them what seemed like at least a hundred times as I walked to and from Grandma Elliott's house. When it was too dark to see, I could tell how much farther I needed to go till I got home. Not that I needed to be home by a designated time. My parents' idea of curfew was just don't have the cops bring me home. Their idea of parental responsibility was very similar.

I left Jake downstairs and slid the thin card into the slot, then turned the knob when I heard the soft click of the lock. The room opened into a large sitting area containing three overstuffed chairs, a couch, love seat, and four tables. I kicked off my shoes and let my toes sink into the plush, ridiculously white carpet. To my right was a bathroom, and four steps into the room was a bar. Chrome and glass glinted off the mirrors behind the neatly lined bottles waiting to be plucked off the shelf and put to work. A silver ice bucket with a pair of stainless-steel tongs across the lid stood in the middle of the counter. I was eleven years old before I learned you didn't just reach in and grab ice cubes with your hands. I still have the scar on the top of my hand as a reminder. Like I needed one.

The walls were white with oil paintings on one and abstract sculpture on another. With the exception of pillows of varying shades of green, it looked like a snowstorm had hit the room. Warm and relaxing it was not. The bedroom was equally sterile and almost blinding when I pulled open the curtains. A small seating area on the balcony was the only place that looked remotely inviting. I unlocked the patio door, and it didn't make a sound when I slid it open.

I stepped outside and inhaled deeply. The air smelled of soot, car exhaust, and history. Boston was one of the oldest cities in the country, its architecture and customs couched deep in history. The city is less than fifty miles square but home to over seven million people. My hotel was downtown in the middle of an eclectic combination of old and new. A building secure as a historical landmark was adjacent to an empty lot, recently razed to build a high-rise office building. Several bridges spanned the Charles River connecting the neighboring communities to the historic city.

I'd read all this the last time I was in town, which was over a year ago. Then I'd been able to get out and roam the city undetected. I'd walked through the Boston Tea Party ships and the John F. Kennedy Memorial Library. I'd even attended an afternoon game at Fenway Park.

I left the doors open and stripped down to my skivvies. My luggage had been brought up by the bellman or a roadie and was stacked neatly at the foot of the king-sized bed. My guitar case was propped against the wall by the window.

I picked up my cell, unlocked the screen, and touched the phone icon. Scrolling down to Favorite #4, I touched the number. While it rang I opened the cap on an overpriced bottle of water sitting on the counter above the mini-bar.

"Hello?"

"Mr. Justin. It's Tobin." My neighbor had not yet entered the digital age, let alone the caller ID of any smart phone.

"Tobin, how are you?" the familiar voice said in my ear. "Where are you?"

"Boston. I'm here for a few days," I answered, looking out the large window and feeling a little bit lonely.

"I love Boston," he replied, his voice rough and scratchy. "Have you been to Betsy Ross's house yet? It's this little bitty thing tucked up on the second or third floor of an old block building. Hard to imagine living in a place that small."

Mr. Justin loved small talk and could discuss anything, anytime. He'd been everywhere and always had an amusing anecdote about my current location.

"No, not this trip, I'm afraid," I answered, the same answer I always gave him when he asked.

"Tobin, you've got to get out more. You travel to some of the most important and magical places in the world, and you don't see anything except the inside of your bus."

I sensed disappointment in his voice. "But I can tell you where every marker is on every stage in the world," I said.

"I'll be sure to put that on your tombstone."

Leave it to an eighty-something-year-old man to tell it the way it is. "How's Frieda?" I asked, turning the topic to his favorite one—his forty-eight-pound greyhound. We were on his porch playing cribbage when the greyhound walked up and sat beside the old man. Frieda had no tags, and when the vet declared she wasn't chipped, Mr. Justin took her home.

"Sitting right here," he answered, and I pictured the gray dog lying in her usual spot just to the left of Mr. Justin's feet. "We tossed the ball for a bit after lunch and she's taking a nap." It was more than likely Mr. Justin was the one taking the nap.

We chitchatted about nothing in particular, and I let him go with a promise to call and check in with Mrs. Foster tomorrow. He said she missed me, and that made me feel all warm inside. I slid under the sheet. Jake would wake me in plenty of time to get to wherever the hell I needed to be.

I closed my eyes, and the image of Kiersten flashed in front of me. I'd been thinking about our conversation a few nights ago. Actually, I'd been going over it in my head almost word for word. Why had she said no? What could I have done or said differently to change the outcome? I had no idea. What I did know was that Kiersten Fellows was a stunning, attractive woman. I wondered what she was like in bed. Was she as cool and composed as she looked, or did she unravel when she came?

I had noticed her hands. That's usually the first thing I notice. Were they big and strong to hold and caress boldly or small and delicate to caress with a feather touch? I make music with my hands by stroking the strings on my guitar or the skin of a beautiful woman. I pluck strings or a nipple. I slide my fingers down the neck of my guitar or a smooth inner thigh. I make beautiful music with my guitar and beautiful music with a woman. Music can be romantic, soothing, or hard and explosive. Sex can be described exactly the same way. I fell asleep imagining Kiersten in all of them.

Chapter Nine

"Kiersten?" I stopped so suddenly Jake ran into me. Kiersten turned at the sound of her name, and my throat went dry. She was wearing a sleeveless royal-blue dress that dipped low in the front, lower in the back, and fell just above her knees. Her hair was up, accentuating her long, graceful neck and her tanned back. A sparkly watch on her left wrist and a couple of silver bangles on her right, along with a delicate necklace around her neck with a small pendant lying tantalizingly above just a hint of cleavage, complemented her outfit. The transformation from businesswoman to *all* woman stunned me. She was breathtaking.

She looked at me for a few moments before recognizing me. My body responded like it was more than a little happy to see her.

"Tobin?"

The way she said my name was both a statement and a question. She looked from me to Jake, then back to me.

"What are you doing here?" I asked stupidly. I was still dazzled with how beautiful Kiersten was. Until seeing her, I always categorized women as either hot or gorgeous. My vocabulary had just increased with words like stunning, striking, and lovely.

"I'm attending a party," she said carefully, looking between Jake and me again.

"I'm not stalking you," I said quickly, the second stupid thing to come out of my mouth in as many minutes. "I have a show at… uh…" I had no idea where it was. I looked to Jake for help.

"The City Performing Arts Center," he supplied. Jeez, how messed up was I that I couldn't even remember where we were playing tonight.

"Jake Richards," he said, extending his hand. "Tobin's manager."

Kiersten shook his hand. "Kiersten Fellows." My breath caught at the way her dress moved when she shook Jake's hand. It reminded me of water flowing in a shallow stream.

"Yes. I know who you are," he said in that we-can-do-something-for-each-other tone I recognized. Kiersten heard it too because her expression went from polite but cautious to polite but wary.

"Jake, I'll meet you at the car," I said, not taking my eyes off Kiersten.

"Tobin—"

"I'll meet you at the car," I repeated.

"We have to go," he said firmly.

"They can't start the show without me, Jake," I said jokingly. The tension around us was suddenly thick. "Go on. I'll be right there."

He took one last look at Kiersten, then me, then back at Kiersten.

"I'll be fine," I said, my hand on his back pushing him toward the front doors of the hotel.

When he was out of hearing range I said, "You are absolutely gorgeous." I probably should have said something less personal, but I had no idea what. My mind wasn't consulting my brain at this moment.

In addition to the blue dress, Kiersten had on heels that put her eyes at least two inches above mine. A pair of diamonds dangled from her earlobes. Her makeup was subtle but clearly intended for evening. I wouldn't personally know, but I'd been around enough makeup artists to recognize at least that. For some odd reason a pang of jealousy rumbled in my stomach. Who was she meeting to make her take extra time and effort to look like this? This was certainly not a dinner meeting.

"Thank you," she answered politely.

I didn't know what else to say. When we'd met over dinner that was business, and she'd looked nothing like this. Suddenly I wanted her. Every delectable inch of her. It was a vaguely unfamiliar feeling, one I hadn't experienced in some time. Lust, yes, but this was more than a physical reaction. It both excited and startled me.

"Did you want something?" The instant Kiersten said the words, blood roared through my head. What a loaded thing to say in such a sexually charged moment.

"Well, now that you asked," I said hopefully.

Chapter Ten

Tobin's eyes made a slow perusal of me, from my freshly cut and styled hair to the top of my Blanchard shoes. She didn't hurry, and when her eyes came back to mine they were darker than ever. I should have been offended by her blatant cruising, but for some reason I wasn't. She liked what she saw, and I felt good that she did. I'd worked my ass off, both literally and figuratively, to have a woman look at me the way Tobin was now. But I wasn't going to do anything about it, certainly not with Tobin Parks. My God, she was, what…at least ten years younger than me. My pulse jumped a few more beats per second at the expression of raw desire in her eyes. I might not know what to do with it, but I certainly recognized it.

"No."

"You don't even know what I was going to ask," Tobin said.

"I have a pretty good idea, and the answer is still no."

"Can we at least talk about it?"

"No, I'm late, and your manager was not happy that you didn't go with him."

"He'll get over it. Can we meet later?"

The way Tobin was looking at me, "later" was more than a reference to time.

"I'm sorry, but…"

"Please. I just want to talk to you."

I looked at her skeptically. I might be naive but I was no dummy.

"Well, okay, I admit I'd like to do more than talk, but I promise to be on my best behavior." She stepped back and gave me a salute. "Scout's honor."

"Why do I not believe you were ever in any sort of scout troop?" I said, fighting the smile tugging at the edge of my lips. "Other than to be around all the girls," I added.

"Ugh…busted." Tobin slapped her hand over her heart, pretending to be hurt. "My secret's revealed."

I suddenly wanted to reveal all her secrets, very, very slowly. I swallowed to regain my equilibrium. "I'm sure your late and mine are hours apart." Now why did I say that? She would probably take that as a weakening of my "no."

"I'll be back here no later than eleven thirty. We can meet in my room," she said eagerly.

My eyebrows shot up, and before I could say no fucking way she added, "Or in the lounge. Wherever you say."

If I wasn't mistaken, it looked like Tobin was expecting me to fall all over myself and say yes. I bet she'd never had to ask twice for anything in her life. If I gave in now I'd just be one more in a long line in the Tobin Parks's harem because we were not talking about business.

I have to admit I was tempted. Tobin Parks was hot with a capital H-O-T. I'd be crazy to turn her down, especially the way my pulse was racing and my other parts were tingling. But as much as right here, right now was personal, it was also professional, and I still didn't mix the two.

"I don't think so. Now, if you'll excuse me, I'm late for an event upstairs." The look of disappointment on Tobin's face almost undid me. I hoped my knees would carry me to the elevator before I turned around and said yes.

Luck was on my side when the doors opened immediately after I pushed the button. My hand was shaking so bad it took two times to hit the button for the third floor. I entered the car and turned around. Tobin was standing exactly where I'd left her, her eyes burning when the doors closed behind me.

More than my eyes were burning when I stepped out of the elevator. I took several deep breaths before entering the crowded ballroom.

"Kiersten, darling. What took you so long? I thought you'd be right behind me."

"I'm sorry, Mother. I got held up. I ran into a business associate in the hall." Not quite the truth, but not a lie either.

"My goodness," my mother said, fretting around me. "Don't those people know it's after hours and Saturday as well?" She sounded as offended as if they'd stopped to negotiate a merger as I was walking down the aisle.

"It's nothing, Mother. They were just saying hello. Where are Judy and Ray?" I asked, hoping to appease my mother's disgust and end the conversation.

I'd just greeted the hosts of the event when my brother Harrison caught my eye from across the room. He excused himself from the group he was talking with and walked toward me, his gait like a man going to the guillotine. He'd put on a few pounds since I saw him last, and if he kept that up he'd need more than one larger suit size. He didn't hug me or show any sign that we were family.

"Kiersten, how have you been?" he asked politely.

Harrison was the senior partner in one of New York's largest brokerage firms. I loved him, but he had grown into a pompous ass with the requisite Windsor knot in his tie and thousand-dollar wingtips. He had a chip on his shoulder the size of my portfolio because he didn't have my portfolio.

"Good, Harrison. And you?" I sipped my drink. I should have asked the bartender for a double.

"Fine. Investments are up twelve percent this year."

It was sad that my big brother, whom I'd idolized as a little girl, judged his success by the return on his investments. I braced myself as Brittney, Harrison's wife, approached. She gave me the expected, not-so-subtle once-over. When her face didn't scrunch up into her normal scowl, I assumed she approved of what I was wearing. I didn't care.

"Kiersten, I'm surprised you could make it."

Brittney was at least eight inches shorter than me, and she tried to make that up by being politely nasty to me. If written on a sheet of paper, her words were benign, but I always heard a hint or more of sarcasm just below the surface. Her greeting really meant, *I'm shocked that you actually left your high-powered life and made time for your family*. I didn't know if she hated me because I was a lesbian or because I wasn't the kind of woman she chose to associate with. She was forced to be around me because she had married my brother. I could care less, and it burned her butt that I didn't.

"Wouldn't have missed it," I answered. What I really meant was, *I'd never miss the chance to put that sour taste in your mouth.*

I hadn't liked Brittney from the moment Harrison brought her home. I'm a pretty good judge of people, and I read her book more than once. She was a snob, self-centered and manipulative. I kept my opinions to myself. Who was I to talk about relationships? When they married eight years ago, I posed with family photos, said all the right things, went through all the right motions, and beat it out of town as fast as I could. I'd been to their house twice in the intervening years, both times for obligatory family gatherings.

My sister Meredith joined us with the excuse that her husband, Dr. Steve, had an emergency and was at the hospital. He's the lucky one, I thought, and more than once I wondered if it was a convenient excuse he used whenever he had the chance. Steven was a cardiothoracic surgeon and was gone more than he was at home. Meredith was a pediatrician. God only knew how they were able to make three very spoiled children.

Meredith and Harrison chatted for a few minutes with Brittney, adding her two cents when my other brother Marcus joined us. Marcus, married and with three children, was clawing his way up our father's law firm. We stood in birth order, with Meredith directly across from me, Harrison to her left, and then Marcus. My baby brother Maxwell was in his third year as a Lutheran missionary in Nigeria and by far the family favorite. My parents across the room rounded out the Fellows family.

Meredith chatted with Brittney about tennis lessons and shopping, and I saw Marcus clench his jaw when Harrison pitched an investment to him. My dislike of one brother and my admiration of another went up a notch. A few questions were directed my way, mostly about JOLT and nothing remotely personal. I snagged a passing waiter for another cocktail and was looking for an escape route. Somehow I'd found one, and after talking to my parents for a few minutes, I made my excuses and left to mingle.

❖

Three hours, four cocktails, and one plate of lo-cal snacks later, I said my good-byes and made my exit. My feet were killing me, my throat hurt from answering questions about JOLT, and I was slightly buzzed, the latter due to my mother's constant hovering. I was alone in the elevator and leaned against the back wall. I closed my eyes, suddenly exhausted.

The doors opened, and two women barely in their twenties giggled as they stepped inside. They were slim, their skinny jeans so tight I could probably see their who-ha if I dared to look. Their perfect firm asses and energy overwhelmed me. Did I ever not have a care in the world like these two? If I did, I certainly didn't remember. When I heard Tobin's name I paid closer attention but pretended not to.

"I can't believe we just had sex with Tobin Parks," Bimbo Number One said.

"I know. I almost peed my pants when that big guy asked us if we wanted to come backstage." Bimbo Number Two practically swooned.

Good God, I thought. Of all the elevators in all the hotels in this city, I get the one with Tobin's latest sexual conquest. I couldn't catch a break tonight.

"He was scary, but I guess he has to be to protect her," Bimbo One said, checking her makeup in the mirror on the back of the elevator door.

"It's like that Whitney Houston movie where Kevin Costner was her bodyguard." Bimbo Two sighed.

"I know what I'd do if I was her bodyguard."

"You could protect her front and I'll protect her rear." Bimbo Two giggled at her double entendre. She adjusted her cleavage so that it was even more exposed than when she'd stepped in.

"I tried to get her between us, but she wasn't interested," Bimbo One said.

"Who cares. She was hot, I was ready, and she got me there."

"She said my skin tasted good," Bimbo One said, as if trying to one-up Bimbo Two.

"She told me I was hot."

Both girls giggled. Giggled! Then Bimbo One smacked Bimbo Two on the arm.

"Ow," she whined. "What gives?"

Bimbo One didn't even try to hide her motioning toward me. They remained blissfully silent the remainder of the short ride to the thirty-eighth floor.

Bimbo Two snickered as they exited the elevator and turned left. "She's just jealous because Tobin will never say she tastes good."

I exited and turned right, knowing that an already long evening was turning into a very long night.

I undressed, took a quick shower, and slipped on my boxers, a JOLT T-shirt, and a light robe. I usually slept naked but never in a hotel, at least not anymore. I was in Singapore several years ago when the fire alarm and sprinklers went off. It was the middle of the night, and I was jet-lagged and exhausted from meetings and negotiations. When I woke I was completely disoriented, but I was with it enough to comprehend what was happening. I grabbed my phone and briefcase and opened the door. Dozens of people were in the hallway making their way to the stairwell when a cold draft hit my body. It was then I realized I was totally naked and halfway out my door. I was able to grab it before it locked behind me, and I threw on a pair of shorts, a shirt, and shoes and dashed out of the building with hundreds of hotel guests. I still have dreams where I'm caught naked locked out of somewhere.

I tried watching a movie and reading, but neither kept my attention. Even the briefcase full of work I'd brought didn't keep my mind from wandering. Images of Bimbo One and Bimbo Two draped all over Tobin kept popping into my brain. I snickered. Bimbo One and Two sounded like the characters Thing One and Thing Two in a Dr. Seuss book.

Giving up on trying to sleep, I lay on the bed in the dark. The girls in the elevator were exactly why I did not want Tobin Parks connected to my company. JOLT was second only to Monster, but if Tobin graced our media campaigns, our cutting edge would end up being a bleeding, if not hemorrhaging, edge. Yes, she was the most sought-after ticket in town. Yes, she was hot. Yes, she didn't care who knew she was a dyke, and she didn't care what people thought of her. But I did.

JOLT had several sponsorships already, and those had been carefully vetted. It was critical that we have JOLT's name out there, especially in the consumer-fickle energy-drink market. We had two very different target markets and were successful in both. First was males seventeen to twenty-five years old. They were all about image and style, what the guys looked like holding a can of JOLT. Drinking our product symbolized they were hip, cool, and had the world by the balls.

What set JOLT apart from the other drinks on the market was that inside one sixteen-ounce can were all the daily vitamins and minerals an adult needed, disguised by a carefully crafted formula. My marketing team and I had spent countless hours debating how to, or in this case how not to, advertise that fact.

I wanted JOLT to stand out from the others for just this reason, and the team said if we didn't, we would be lumped in with the other hundreds of "protein drinks" on the shelf. That market was saturated, and not only would we not get shelf space, but our target market would default to weight control. I agonized over this decision for weeks.

When I was just getting started I carried three prototype cans with me everywhere. I asked everyone I knew—friends, family, and the guy on the street—for their opinion. My neighbor's nephew used them in his freshman marketing class at Arizona State University. According to his kid-in-college, unscientific research, ninety-seven percent of the two hundred fifty-two people he surveyed on campus preferred can #2. One hundred and ninety-six of those didn't even look at the FDA-required label on the back, and of those who did, eighty-nine percent had no clue what it meant. I finally gave in and trusted my gut.

Am I selling out? No. I advertise in serious health-conscious magazines. Not the frou-frou women's magazines that promise you'll lose ten pounds in a week and drive your man crazy every night. Our message to the serious health-and-fitness market is the nutritional aspect of JOLT, the image secondary.

JOLT sponsored women's pro beach volleyball and several youth sports leagues in at-risk neighborhoods across the country. We bought football jerseys for a struggling school, new uniforms for an inner-school marching band, and even a bus to transport kids to after-school events. We funded a program for middle-school girls and boys to help give them a sense of respect for themselves and the opposite sex that seems to be missing in our youth today. We sponsor programs in several youth correctional facilities to help kids get back on track. Sure, we have our name on a NASCAR, two LPGA pros, and the Chicago Triathlon. We have to pay the bills. But when I started JOLT I wanted to make enough money to help better society.

I must have fallen asleep because I woke to the phone ringing. Groggy, my eyes crusty with sleep, I reached for the room phone. It was my wake-up call. I flopped back on the bed and laid my arm across my eyes. The sun coming through a crack in the curtains sliced through the room like a samurai sword.

I am not a morning person. I inherited that trait from my mother. I can barely get out of bed and into the shower without running into a wall or banging my elbow on the doorknob. I would never cut it as a fireman or in any job that required me to wake from a deep sleep and be able to function. If I could have an IV-drip of black coffee in my arm when I woke up I'd be the happiest woman in the world. A spanking new Keurig coffeemaker sitting on my gleaming counter in my kitchen at home is my new best friend.

I dragged myself out of bed, cursing the fact that I'd let myself get caught up in the sideshow of Tobin Parks. For the few short hours

I did sleep, I tossed and turned to images of Tobin performing—her sultry voice and more than a little provocative moves onstage telling the world exactly what sex with Tobin Parks would be like. And it would be pure and raw.

My dreams were usually murky, with faceless people in places I couldn't quite recognize. But last night Tobin was crystal clear and left no doubt as to exactly what she was doing and to whom.

In one scene she had a woman pinned against a large speaker onstage. In another she pulled a willing participant into a coat closet or storage area, and in a third they were behind a sand dune on a beach. Each time Tobin was the aggressor, and by the look on the woman's face and the way her body was responding, it was clear that Tobin knew exactly what to do and the woman liked it—a lot. What shocked me the most was that I was the woman. I never, and I mean never, have dreams about sex. Even when I thought about sex, it was never about me. Never about me doing it, me losing my mind, me grabbing the sheets as I came.

Is this the time to say I'm a very visual person and I like porn? Not the hard-core, ball-banging, fucking kind. That's not for me, but I have found several sites that appealed to me, and I have more than a few DVDs on my shelf that are more reflective of my tastes, so to speak. The women are smart, attractive in the real sense, not enhanced with fake boobs and scripted moans. Amateur porn is my favorite. The women aren't paid actors and generally appear to be into what they're doing. Okay. I admit I have more than a few DVDs in the bottom drawer of my dresser and some other tools in my nightstand. Am I kinky or perfectly normal—whatever the hell that means these days? I have no idea. It's not a topic of conversation, even with Courtney.

One night after three too many glasses of wine she did, however, bring it up, saying that she and her husband—how did she phrase it—added some spice in the sheets. Of course my sex-obsessed mind immediately went to what they looked like doing it. Let me clarify. I do not have any sexual attraction to Courtney or her husband, but I do wonder what sounds she makes, if she's on top and the aggressor, and how in the world she sits at the breakfast table with her husband and kids after completely letting loose the night before.

I either need to get a grip or get laid. This was getting borderline creepy.

Skipping back to the here and now, I felt like I'd been hit by a bus. I was lethargic and knew I'd need more than a few cups of coffee to get me going.

I don't mind being a caffeine junkie. I love coffee and think I'm one of the few people on the planet that doesn't like Starbucks. Another anomaly is that I drink it black, no sugar. No venti latte, no caramel macchiato or whatever other pretentious, fussy concoction the barista at the corner can whip up. Plain, black coffee. If I'm feeling really bold I'll toss in some cinnamon for a little flavor.

I started the coffee in the machine on top of the minibar and glanced at my reflection in the mirror. I didn't even have the energy to groan. Not only did I feel like shit, but I looked like it too. It'd take some work to put myself together for brunch with my mother. I stepped in the shower, and the scalding hot water soothed me. I stood there completely still for several minutes before reaching for the shampoo. Showered, shaved, and patted dry, I stepped out of the bathroom twenty minutes later.

I pulled my brunch-with-Mother clothes out of my suitcase. If I were at home I'd put on a pair of raggedy, comfortable shorts, a JOLT T-shirt, and some deck shoes. Brunch for me consists of a trip to Einstein's Bagels for the morning paper and an everything bagel with cream cheese. Oh, and a large black coffee. I'd eat my breakfast, devouring the news of yesterday beginning with Dear Abby. My mother can't understand how a college-educated, successful, professional woman would even dare to read the advice columnist. It grounds me to know that there are very stupid people in the world.

Dressed, coiffed, and made up, I grabbed my wallet and key and headed out the door.

Chapter Eleven

As I headed toward the bank of elevators where I last saw Bimbo One and Two, my pace stuttered when I saw Tobin walking toward me. How did we keep running into each other? Some sort of carefully crafted plan on her part? Coincidence? Karma? What the hell?

Tobin saw me, smiled, and her steps quickened. My heart skipped a beat or two, and my pulse picked up. I mean it was Tobin Parks, and she was incredibly hot, even at nine fifty in the morning. I was about to reach for the button to call the elevator to our floor when she stopped in front of me.

"Hey, good morning," she said, a little too cheery for me even after two cups of coffee and a long shower.

"Good morning," I managed to reply. I looked her over for any signs of Bimbo One or Two.

"I didn't know you were on this floor." She must have seen skepticism in my face because she quickly added, "Honest. I had no idea. I didn't book this hotel or the room. Jake did."

God, she sounded so young. I pushed the down arrow, glancing at my watch. I had ten minutes to meet my mother in the lobby restaurant, and you were never late for a meeting with Joanne Fellows, even if you were her daughter.

"Heading down?" Tobin asked.

"Yes. I'm meeting my mother for brunch." I could kick myself. Why did I say that? I didn't have to explain my comings and goings to Tobin. She took in my outfit, and I was surprisingly glad I wasn't in my normal weekend wear. I had on a jade-green scoop-neck T-shirt tucked into a pair of black capris. My thin, black belt was buckled into the same notch it had been for the past eighteen years. Not the same belt, of course, but the same size. My toenails were polished a dark burgundy and peeked out from the end of my favorite flat sandals. My outfit was dressier than I normally wore, and I'm sure my mother would make some comment about its casualness, but this morning I didn't care.

"She must be very proud of you."

"I suppose." Damn, where was the elevator? There were four, and none of them had yet to arrive to rescue me from myself.

"That was an unusual answer," Tobin commented.

"Well, my mother is an unusual woman," I replied dryly. Where was the elevator? But then again I didn't know why I was so eager to be in a small enclosed box alone with Tobin. I was doing such a great job of embarrassing myself standing there in the middle of the large hall, I could only imagine what I'd say trapped in the elevator. I'd probably recite my life story, starting with when I learned to ride a bike.

"How was your show?" I found myself asking. I was polite if nothing else.

"Good. It was a great crowd. I was back here by eleven thirty, like I said I'd be." She practically glowed, as if I should be proud of her or something.

Finally the bell rang and the doors opened. Tobin held out her hand, signaling me to enter first. I did and pushed the button for the lobby. "Where to?" I asked, since I was in front of the only indicator panel.

"All the way down," she said, referencing more than just the floor button to punch.

I broke out in a sweat, and my hand shook when I pushed the button again needlessly. *I'll just bet she goes all the way down.*

"You don't live here, do you?" Tobin said after the doors closed. Hopefully the ride down would be shorter than the one up last night.

"No. I live in Chicago." *God, Kiersten, shut up*! My mouth was working overtime, and my mind was still in bed.

"How long are you in town for?"

"I leave tomorrow." Thank God I didn't volunteer any more information, like my plans for the rest of the day.

"Hey, I do too," she said enthusiastically.

Again, God, she was young—and refreshing. And did I mention sexy? She was wearing a pair of hip-hugging jeans, boots, and a black long-sleeve T-shirt with the sleeves pushed up to her elbows. Her hair was arranged in its customary messiness, and I caught myself looking for any sign of a hickey or bite mark on her neck.

"Since you're here and I'm here, we can—"

The doors opened and we were on the ground floor. People were milling about waiting to get in the car we'd just vacated, and more than a few heads turned when they recognized Tobin. I saw my mother get off the elevator directly across from us.

"Kiersten, darling, good morning." She pulled me down so she could buss my cheek. I was at least seven inches taller than my mother, but she could still manhandle me like I was three years old.

"Good morning, Mother," I replied automatically. Out of the corner of my eye I saw Tobin still standing beside me. When I saw my mother glance at Tobin, then back at me, I knew this was going to be awkward.

"Kiersten, where are your manners?" My mother was scolding me.

"Mother, this is Tobin Parks. Tobin, my mother, Joanne Fellows."

"You look so familiar," my mother said, looking at Tobin hard. "Have we met?"

"No, ma'am, we haven't. I guess I just have one of those faces," Tobin answered graciously. I had expected her to introduce herself and wait for my mother to fawn all over her. Little did she know my mother didn't fawn over anything, including her own grandchildren.

"I'm sure I know you from somewhere," my mother said, frowning. She hated to lose at anything, and if she thought she knew Tobin she wouldn't rest until she figured it out. I decided to end her quest.

"Mother, Tobin is a singer and musician. I'm sure you've seen her on TV or a magazine cover somewhere." I'm positive she hadn't seen her on the cover of *Curve* magazine, stark naked and draped over her guitar. That issue was one of my favorites.

She thought for a moment, and then recognition filled her face. Then something else not quite so nice appeared. "Ah, yes, that's where it is. Nice to meet you, Ms. Parks." She turned to me. "Kiersten, are you ready?" she said, effectively dismissing Tobin.

"Yes, of course," I replied quickly. Once a dutiful daughter, always a dutiful daughter. I turned to Tobin.

"It was good to see you again, Tobin. Enjoy your day." I followed my mother into the restaurant.

❖

"Kiersten, how do you know that girl?"

I have to admit my mother has the term rich snob perfected. She asked her question with as much distaste in her mouth as if she'd just bit into a mealy apple. This morning she was wearing an impeccably tailored Donna Karan yellow dress, and her shoes and bag were equally coordinated. My mother was never anything other than perfectly put together, and I couldn't remember if I'd ever seen her with a hair out of place, a chip on a nail, or, God forbid, a run in her hose. Her hair had just enough very expensive attention that she didn't look a day over fifty, even though she passed that big-o birthday more than a decade ago. Her plastic surgeon had magic skills, and her personal trainer was demanding.

The waiter had come and gone, and we were sipping our coffee. "I've only met her once or twice, Mother. She wants to be a spokesman for JOLT."

My mother dropped her spoon, and it clattered loudly on her saucer. I felt a dozen pairs of eyes look our way.

"Now, Kiersten, I don't ever tell you how to run your little company, but do you think that's wise?" she said, quickly gathering her composure.

First of all, my mother has never given a rat's ass about my little company other than to wonder why I ventured out on my own in the first place. Second, she has absolutely no clue what is best or not, and third, my *little* company had sales last year of eighty-eight million dollars, ten times the revenue of my father's firm. I was still angry for the way she'd dismissed Tobin.

"Why do you say that, Mother?"

"Why?" she asked, obviously confused.

"Yes. Why would I not want to consider Tobin?"

"Well, she's a lesbian."

I almost laughed but held it in. That would not be good. "Mother, *I'm* a lesbian," I reminded her.

"Yes, but not like that." She waved her hand in the direction we'd come.

"Like what?"

"She's so…out there."

"And?"

"And you read the same papers I do."

I didn't but wasn't getting into that conversation this morning.

"You know what she does, how she lives. I've heard she has a different woman in her life every week. Probably more often than that."

Lucky girl, I thought.

"Her image is not…oh, I don't know…wholesome." She tossed her hand as if ridding it of something slimy.

This time I couldn't hold back a laugh. "Wholesome?"

She frowned at me. "You know what I mean. She has a reputation, and you don't want to get mixed up with that." She looked at me squarely in the eyes. I'd seen that face. It was the you-better-listen-to-me one. "Do not get mixed up with that."

"Don't worry, Mother. I'm not interested in Tobin Parks in any way."

As we waited for our meal I wondered why I had phrased my response like that. It sounded like there was more than one avenue of interest I could travel on the Tobin Parks highway. But I wasn't headed in that direction either.

I spent the next thirty minutes listening to my mother fill me in on the latest in her life and old friends. I nibbled on my eggs and moved the rest of my brunch around my plate, making it look like

I was eating. I didn't have much appetite this morning, which was fine, because I watched my weight very closely.

My mother finally called for the check, and relief flooded me that I was almost paroled from this meal. Her American Express card contrasted sharply against the white of the bill just before she closed the dark, conservative leather folder it came in.

"Are you sure you can't stay another few days?" she asked hopefully. "Meredith, Harrison, and Marcus would love to spend more time with you."

"Mother, we talked last night." And our conversation was not something I cared to repeat. At least not right away. I doubted they wanted to hang out with me.

"Did you all get a chance to catch up?" My mother had certain expectations of how her family should interact with each other, which included knowing what was going on in each other's lives. She wanted it to be that way because it was expected, not because it would make us closer.

"Yes, we did." I regurgitated a few of the snippets of conversation I'd overheard, and she seemed satisfied because she didn't ask anything else about that.

"Are you taking care of yourself? Are you still jogging?"

My mother tried to sound genuinely interested, but I know she thought any form of exercise that wasn't performed under the watchful eye of a trainer or yoga instructor wasn't appropriate. The fact that she called it jogging was almost insulting. I don't jog. I run a six-minute mile and had finished six triathlons in the past eight months.

"Are you seeing anyone?" she asked, biting into her slice of dry toast and not giving me a chance to answer her first question.

I held in a sigh. We were going down this path, *again*. "No one special," I lied, preparing myself for the requisite rebuke of the emptiness of my life.

"You need to settle down, Kiersten. You're not getting any younger, you know."

"I'm happy with my life, Mother. I have a company that I love, good friends, and I'm happy." All four things were true.

"But you're alone."

"And that doesn't make me unhappy," I replied, trying not to become too defensive, which was difficult. This line of questioning was old—very, very old.

"But you need someone in your life. Someone to take care of you."

There it was. My mother never failed to deliver. Just because my mother, sister, and obviously Brittney were not complete without someone to take care of them did not mean that I needed a guardian as well.

A commotion to my right caught my attention. My heart jumped and the blood in my veins grew suddenly very warm. A group of people surrounded Tobin and were thrusting papers, pens, and even napkins at her. She calmly signed every one and said a few words to people as they approached. Finally she was free of them and continued through the dining room. I heard my mother tsk, tsk the entire scene. I followed Tobin with my eyes until she walked out the side door onto the patio and took a couple of deep breaths to calm myself before returning my attention to my mother.

"Mother, I can take care of myself. I *am* taking care of myself."

"I know, but…"

"But nothing. I'm thirty-six years old and doing exactly what I want to do. Can't you just be pleased for me?" That was the crux of my relationship with my mother. Her idea of happiness was radically different from mine. She was a very smart woman, but she just couldn't grasp my life. We finished our breakfast, my eyes drifting to the patio doors more than once.

CHAPTER TWELVE

If I wondered what Kiersten would look like in another thirty years, all I'd have to do was look at her mother. The resemblance was remarkable. I'd known this was her mother before Kiersten even introduced us. They had the same bone structure, facial features, and crystal-blue eyes. But there were subtle differences between the two. Kiersten's smile showed in her eyes, her mother's not even close. Kiersten carried herself relaxed, but her mother had a stick up her butt. Kiersten's voice was warm and inviting, her mother's cold, almost shrill. At least those were the impressions I had from the two minutes we were together.

Mrs. Fellows eyed me with a look I recognized. It had been a staple of my childhood every time I went to the store or to school or any place outside of my trailer park. That look said you are the child of trash, and since the apple doesn't fall too far from the tree, it's only a matter of time before you're rotten as well. I hadn't seen that look in years, but I hadn't forgotten how much it hurt.

I knew Kiersten and her mother were in the dining room and purposely asked the hostess to seat me in the opposite direction on the patio. I definitely didn't look their way on my way in. I hadn't planned to eat in the restaurant, but since I wasn't in my coach I really didn't have much choice. I didn't want room service because it made my room smell, and I couldn't very well go down the street to the local Denny's.

I sipped my coffee, thinking about the difference between Kiersten and the two women in my dressing room last night. Talk about complete opposites. They were all giggles, jiggle, and little else. Kiersten was smart and could carry on a conversation. During our dinner she'd talked about current events, politics, and the financial trouble in the European Union. I doubted if those girls knew who the president was, let alone where Europe is.

I couldn't remember their names. Was it Candy and Brooke? Heather and April? It didn't really matter because I didn't need to know their names. Not long after meeting them I simply thought of them as Tweedle Dee and Tweedle Dum. The most disconcerting part of the evening was the fact that I wasn't the slightest bit interested in having sex with one or both of them. That was a first, especially when they looked like they were the models for a Hooters ad.

They were all over me all night, and I kept sliding away from their wandering hands and persistent mouths. Finally I went through the motions, giving them what they wanted, and told Jake to get rid of them. I left the arena and went to my room shortly thereafter. I didn't immediately go to bed but sat on the couch with my feet on the table, looking at the stars blinking on the other side of the large window.

My waitress brought me my breakfast and refilled my coffee cup. She asked if I wanted anything else in that tone that said anything meant *anything*. I politely declined.

"No, thanks. I'm good for now." She walked away looking disappointed. Too bad.

I knew several people in the restaurant were looking at me; they always did. Usually a few brave souls and a few rude fans ventured over and asked for my autograph. Most were polite, and after I signed their napkin, scrap of paper, or coaster, they left me in peace. Others weren't quite as considerate. That's why I usually ate in my room or Jake accompanied me.

Life on the road is not glamorous. It's hard, exhausting, and lonely. Traveling from place to place in the span of sometimes twenty-four hours didn't leave much time for socializing or sightseeing.

I was living the dream, the one I had from the moment I lifted that old guitar out of the trash bin. It was almost bigger than I was and was missing two strings, but I'd strummed that thing like I was a rock star and dreamed of being famous.

My dad had laughed at me, saying, "You'll never amount to nothing," his words, and told me to "Get that piece of shit out of the house," again his words. I did as I was told, having learned long before not to disobey him, but I hid it under the trailer where the skirting had torn off in the last storm.

I went to the local library, and since it didn't cost anything to get a library card, I checked out every book I could on learning how to play the guitar. There were videos, but since we didn't have any way to play them, I watched them in the privacy of the small desk area in the back corner of the library. I used the library's yellow pages to look up a music store. I'd go by the store and stand on the sidewalk and look through the window. It took several tries before I finally got up the nerve to walk into the store.

As soon as I entered, it was like the gates of heaven opened. I swear I could hear a harp playing as if beckoning me in. I'm sure I looked like a zombie walking into the store, my mouth hanging open in awe at all the shiny new instruments. I rarely went into a store that sold new things. Goodwill and the church thrift box were our Neiman Marcus, and I was stunned by what I saw.

Drums, cymbals, trumpets, and trombones adorned one side of the room, and guitars and pianos the other. I knew the clerk was watching me so I was very careful not to get too close or touch anything. A gleaming red electric guitar in a stand drew me closer. Six strings ran the length of it, starting at the saddle and wrapping around the tuning heads. I'd never seen a guitar that fancy, and through my voracious readings I knew the name of every part.

"Can I help you, young lady?"

The deep voice behind me made me jump. I took a few steps back, my eyes never leaving the guitar.

"N...n...n...no sir."

"She's quite a beauty," the man said.

"Yes sir, she is," I replied politely. I think I actually whispered my answer because I was so enthralled at what I was looking at.

"Would you like to try it?"

My head shot around and looked at the man. He was old, like my next-door neighbor Mr. Bruce, but this man had kind eyes. "No sir, I can't."

"Why not?'

"It's too nice. I might break it." And if I did, there would be hell to pay for sure.

"Here," he said, lifting it off the stand. He pointed to a bench to my right. "Have a seat." I couldn't resist and did as I was told. He handed it to me.

It was heavy and cool against the top of my thigh. The body was thin, the fret board long, stretching out almost as far as my eight-year-old arms could reach. I couldn't believe I was holding the most beautiful musical instrument I'd ever seen.

"Do you play?" the clerk asked.

Somehow I managed to nod.

"Play me something."

My eyes shot to his again. "Oh, no sir, I couldn't," I said, terrified just holding it on my lap.

"It's okay," he said, sitting beside me on the bench. "People do it all the time. How else will they know how it sounds and if they want to buy it?"

"Oh, no sir, I can't buy it," I said like it wasn't already glaringly obvious.

He chuckled. "Someday you will," he said with the kindest smile. "Go ahead, give it a try."

It took a few more words of encouragement and permission, and when he handed me a pick, my hands shook. I placed a chord on the strings on the neck with my left hand and dragged the pick over the strings with my right.

My heart leaped in my throat, and I was so startled the guitar almost slid off my lap and on to the floor. The sound was amazing. It was strong and deep, and it echoed in the room. The strings reverberated under my fingers, and I was in love.

The clerk persuaded me to keep playing before he got up to wait on another customer. I played every song I knew and made up a few I didn't. I stopped when he returned.

"You play pretty good. Do you have one at home?" he asked, pointing to the sleek guitar.

"Yes sir, I do, but not like this," I answered, still completely in awe of the instrument I was holding.

"How much is a guitar string?" I asked, pointing to a classic wooden guitar with nylon strings.

"It depends," he said, stepping behind the counter. "Which one do you need?"

"A and D," I said with confidence.

"Let's see now," he said, rummaging around on the shelf behind him. "Normally they're two dollars and sixty eight cents each."

My heart fell. I'd never have that much money for one, let alone both of the strings I needed. All the excitement I felt playing the electric guitar leaked out of me like a balloon losing its air. I used extra care and returned it to its display location.

"But," the old man said quickly, "for some reason we have some loose ones back here that we can't sell because they're not part of a set." He took them out and laid them on the counter. They were wound up tightly, looking like gold snakes ready to strike. "You're welcome to these if you'd like."

My eyes shot to his, my danger signals blinking at full speed. Nobody gave me anything and didn't want something in return. He must have seen the wariness in my eyes. Or the fear.

"No, really, you can have them. No charge," he added.

"Won't your boss fire you for giving me something that I should buy? Isn't that kind of like stealing?" I knew all about stealing, thank you very much, Dad.

"I can't get fired," he said, his smile big, his eyes sparkling. If he had a white beard he'd look a lot like the pictures of Santa in the books at the library. "I'm the boss," he added.

He wrapped the two strings in white tissue paper, placed them in a bag with the logo of the music store on the front, and handed them to me. I took it, my hands shaking like a leaf in a wind storm.

He held out his hand. "My name is Micah Solomon."

Tentatively I placed my hand in his. "My name is Tobin Parks." I'd already decided on a stage name, and it was the first time I'd used it.

"Tobin Parks," he said, nodding and repeating it a few times. "I'll remember that name when I hear it on the radio."

Eleven years later I returned to that store and bought that red guitar. Well, not that one, but one very similar to the one leaning against the stand by the old worn bench years ago. Unfortunately Micah Solomon had died the year before, but his son, Micah Junior, was just as nice.

At times when the crowd was roaring or I was alone in my room plucking at the strings, I would say out loud, "Thank you, Mr. Solomon."

I finished my coffee and signed the check, which, by the way, had a phone number under my waitress's name. Then I glanced up and directly into the eyes of none other than Kiersten Fellows.

CHAPTER THIRTEEN

"I beg your pardon," I said to my mother, who, with her bi-monthly Botox treatment, surprised me by being able to frown her disapproval.

"Whatever are you looking at, Kiersten? You're barely paying any attention," my mother said.

"It's nothing, Mother. I'm sorry. What were you saying?" I pulled my attention back to her. She'd caught me looking at Tobin.

"I said Brittney is meeting us in a few minutes. She said she wanted to talk to you about something, and I told her we'd be down here this morning. She should be along any time." My mother glanced at her Bulova diamond-faced watch.

Oh God, what now? I did not need the sister-in-law from hell this morning. I looked around for a chance to escape but didn't see any excuse that would be acceptable to my mother. I forced myself not to look at Tobin again as I waited impatiently for my sister-in-law to make her grand appearance.

Brittney breezed in a few minutes later and practically commanded our waitress for coffee and freshly squeezed orange juice. She studied my plate, trying to determine what I'd eaten. She was always giving me food advice, just to help out, she'd say. I knew she did it to dig at me.

I struggled with my weight for over twenty years. When puberty arrived it brought along with it one hundred and eighteen pounds that crept up on me like the fog rolling in. One day I was a size eight, the next a size twenty-eight. It took me four years, hundreds of hours at the gym, thousands of miles pounding the pavement and swimming in the community pool. I weighed myself every Tuesday, and my daily exercise routine was now a vital part of my life. I vowed I would never go back to that lonely, self-conscious place again. Obviously Harrison had shared this information with his lovely wife, who was probably the same size at forty-four that she was at fourteen.

"Kiersten, you look like you didn't sleep well." Translation: *You look like shit and you should have at least made a better effort to pull yourself together*.

"Actually, I slept great." I had no qualms about lying to her.

"Hmm, well," she said, looking at me critically.

"Mother said you wanted to talk to me this morning. I don't mean to be rude, but I don't have much time before my flight." I got a disgusted sigh and an eye roll for that.

"I'm throwing Harrison a surprise birthday party next month, and I know he'd want you to be there."

"Of course," I answered politely. No way in hell did *she* want me there. I doubted Harrison did either.

"The eighteenth, seven o'clock. I've reserved the Club Royale," she said, as if just saying the name made her richer.

"No doubt," I said with just a hint of sarcasm.

"It will be fabulous," my mother said. "I just love the Club Royale."

Of course you do, I thought. Members of the club were the who's who of Boston, and the get-in ticket was six figures. No thanks. I'll take my corner coffee shop and the pool in my backyard instead.

My mother and Brittney were talking about the arrangements, caterers, and music, and I couldn't sit there any longer. "Mother, would you excuse me for a minute?" I said to be polite, but it was obvious that neither woman was paying any attention to me.

I was almost to Tobin's table before she looked up and saw me. She stood immediately.

"Kiersten?" Tobin asked, obviously surprised to see me at her table.

"May I sit for a few minutes?" I hated the fact that I needed an escape and Tobin was it.

"Uh, sure." She shifted and held out the chair across from her, the one with my back to my mother and Brittney.

"Thank you," I said nervously. I had no idea why I had escaped to Tobin's table and even less idea what to say.

"Is everything okay?" she asked carefully, her eyes dancing from mine to something over my shoulder. She was probably looking at the table I'd just vacated.

I let out a deep breath and sat back in the chair. "Yes, my mother and sister-in-law were driving me crazy, and I just need a minute." I hoped that would appease her curiosity. It didn't.

"Anything I can do?"

"No, thank you. I love my mother but can only take her in small doses. My sister-in-law on the other hand…" I let Tobin draw her own conclusion.

"Only like her because she's married your brother?" she offered as an option.

"Nope, not even that."

"Tolerate her?"

"Barely," I supplied, drumming my fingers on the white tablecloth. "Do you have siblings?" I immediately regretted my question when her face hardened.

"None that I claim publically."

"And privately?" I didn't expect her to answer, but she did.

"One sister, one brother."

"Any of them married?"

"Not that I know of."

"Not close?"

"Not until my first record hit number one." I heard more than a little anger and bitterness in her voice.

"Sorry," I said. "None of my business."

"It's okay. What's the saying, You can choose your friends but not your family?"

"Something like that, I think."

"I'm no expert, but your sister-in-law's shoes probably cost more than the trailer I grew up in."

Ouch, that was nasty, and telling. "I'm sorry," I repeated. "I didn't come over here to touch on a sore subject. I just needed a minute. I should go back." That was the last thing I wanted to do, but I wasn't comfortable sitting across from Tobin either. I pushed my chair back to stand but stopped when Tobin laid her hand on my arm.

"Stay," Tobin said softly, her eyes drilling into mine. My heart raced, and I suddenly found it difficult to breathe. I wasn't sure I could stand up even if I wanted to. And after that one simple request I didn't want to.

"I'm intruding." My excuse was halfhearted.

"If I didn't want you to stay, I wouldn't have asked."

Tobin's voice was smooth and full. No wonder she was the number-one entertainer in the world. Her eyes held mine and I couldn't look away. The longer she looked at me the darker they grew, and it felt like I was sliding down a funnel headed straight toward her. She released my eyes and looked over my shoulder again.

"I don't mean to hurt your feelings, but I don't think they know you're gone." She lifted her head, signaling me to turn and see for myself.

She was right. Mother and Brittney were deep in conversation, their heads bowed as if sharing state secrets.

"How was your party?" Tobin asked.

"My party?"

"Last night. You were on your way to a party. A fancy one if your dress was any indication."

My skin heated where her eyes traveled over my body as if remembering what she saw last night.

"You were very beautiful."

I had trouble swallowing and even more difficulty finding my voice. "Thank you," I finally said.

"Who were you all dressed up for?"

"A family friend has an annual fund-raiser."

"What was the cause?"

"The National Center for Missing and Exploited Children."

"Wow, that's serious stuff. They do that every year?"

"They started it twenty-nine years ago when their son disappeared on the way home from school. He was nine. We walked home together every day, but on that day I was sick with the chicken pox."

"Oh, Kiersten, I'm sorry," Tobin said sympathetically.

It took years and many more hours of therapy before I finally made peace with the circumstances of Danny's disappearance.

"I was only seven."

"Was he ever found?" Tobin asked gently.

"No," I said flatly, signaling the end of that topic. Surprisingly I had never had that conversation with anyone before.

"Is that why you donate to them?"

"If it can bring one child home it's worth every penny."

The ensuing silence made me uncomfortable, and I was just about to get up when Tobin spoke.

"Have dinner with me."

"What?" The shift in subject caught me off guard. Obviously I was still hanging on to Danny.

"Have dinner with me," she repeated firmly.

"Have dinner with you?"

Tobin nodded. "You said you weren't leaving until today."

I did say that, but no way was I going to have dinner with her. "Thank you, but my flight leaves at three."

"I promise I'll behave. You can trust me."

I wasn't so sure about that. I decided to change the subject, again. "How was *your* party last night?"

She frowned, then smiled. "I was in bed by twelve thirty."

"I'll just bet you were."

"What does that mean?"

"I rode up in the elevator with two Daisy Dukes who were talking about how they'd been in your dressing room." I mimicked their ridiculous voices. "Small world, isn't it?"

Tobin looked at me for a few moments. "Jealous?"

"Of them?" I was surprised. "Not hardly. I never looked like that, and I certainly never acted like that, nor do I ever want to."

"I meant that I invited them."

"No," I said, lying to myself and Tobin. "I don't share." Actually, I've never had anyone to not share, but if I did, I knew I wouldn't.

"A one-woman woman?"

The smoldering look in Tobin's eyes told me I could be her one woman—for right now.

"I have to get back. My mother's probably having a stroke."

Tobin looked over my shoulder.

"Well, her back is to me, but your sister-in-law looks like the cat that swallowed the canary."

"Oh, God, I'll never hear the end of this," I groaned. Brittney wouldn't hesitate to bring up this entire event in subtle and not-so-subtle ways every chance she had.

"And speaking of the cat, she's on her way over here."

Brittney didn't even acknowledge Tobin before saying, "Your mother is ready to leave."

"Tobin Parks," Tobin said, extending her hand and introducing herself and calling Brittney on her rudeness.

"I know who you are," Brittney replied, more than a little snotty and ignoring Tobin's offered hand.

"Then you should know better than to be rude, Brittney," I said, my anger starting to burn.

"Then you should raise the bar on the company you keep."

I was stunned. Brittney was mean but never blatantly like this.

Tobin stood and took a half a step into Brittney's space. "Since you know who I am, then you know I can have you thrown out of here with a wave of my hand."

"Brittney," I said.

"Who do you think you are, interrupting a business meeting with your piece-of-shit attitude and your rude behavior?" Tobin asked. Her voice was calm but her tone was angry. "Kiersten will leave when she's ready to leave."

I stood and touched Tobin's arm. Her muscles were tight, and a current pulsed under her hot skin.

"I just stopped by to say hello, Brittney, not that it's any of your business who I do business with." I turned to Tobin. "I apologize for the rude behavior of my family." I used that word loosely. "Enjoy the rest of your meal."

I grabbed Brittney's arm and yanked her away from Tobin's table.

"Ow," she whined, trying to pull her arm away. "You're hurting me."

"Shut up," I growled through clenched teeth and practically dragged her across the room.

"Don't you dare tell me to shut up!"

I stopped in the middle of the room, not caring who was witnessing our family squabble.

"I'll tell you to shut your goddamn mouth anytime you're rude to anyone involved in my business. That was beyond rude. It was despicable and reprehensible, and if you ever do that again, I will rip you to shreds."

I walked back to my table and picked up my bag. "I'm sorry, Mother. I have to go."

As calmly as I could with dozens of eyes on my back, two in particular, I walked out of the restaurant.

Chapter Fourteen

I sat back down not quite sure what had happened. One minute Kiersten and I were having a conversation, and the next I was being spat on, euphemistically, of course, by some bleached-blond bitch with fake tits and false eyelashes. What the fuck did I ever do to her? I'm pretty sure nothing, but it wasn't the first time my reputation had preceded me.

Kiersten looked mortified at what her sister-in-law said. I bet if we weren't in a public place Kiersten would have belted her. She looked that mad. As it was, it appeared that she gave her quite the dressing down by the salad bar, if I read her body language correctly. Kiersten held her head high as she walked out of the room. God damn, she had a nice ass.

Several people were looking my way, and it wouldn't surprise me if I didn't read about these last five minutes in some gossip rag tomorrow.

The next morning my phone rang, and even before I answered it I knew it wasn't going to be good news. Jake's voice boomed out of the speaker. "What the fuck is going on?"

"And I pay you to talk to me like that?" I asked, annoyed. I'm not a morning person and certainly didn't enjoy being woken with that greeting.

"You pay me to keep your face in front of your fans, so why didn't I know about this?" he asked, almost accusingly.

I sat up too quickly and the room started to spin. I took a few deep breaths before standing and heading for the kitchen and some much-needed coffee. "Know about what?" I normally didn't fire on all cylinders before two cups of coffee.

"The headline story in *The Informer*. That's not what I'm looking at," he said smugly.

The Informer was the most famous gossip web site in the country. It was also the most inaccurate. They had been sued for slander more times than I could remember, and somehow they were still publishing lies, innuendos, and bullshit. I was a regular on their page.

"Tobin Parks and gal-pal lovers' spat?" Jake said.

He must have been reading me the headline. Gal-pal? Where in the hell did that stupid term come from in the first place? If the woman was a friend, then call her a friend. If she was her girlfriend, then call her that. If she was just a lover then…well, anyway, you get my drift. If they'd stop taking pictures of me, they wouldn't have to figure out who the woman was on my arm, or occasionally in my lap, or in this case sitting across from me on the patio of a nice restaurant enjoying a beautiful morning.

"There's nothing to tell, Jake," I said, bypassing the coffee pot and opening the lid on my laptop. My fingers fumbled on the keyboard, and it took me three tries to get the right letters in the right order for the URL.

I ignored what Jake was saying and scanned the article. It insinuated that Kiersten was my new love or the other woman. God, what a mess. Didn't people have enough in their lives to do instead of making up shit about mine?

"Tobin? Are you listening to me?"

"Yes." I lied.

"You didn't hear a thing I said, did you?"

"Yes, I did." Two lies before breakfast is not a good way to start the day. "I need Kiersten Fellow's phone number," I said, interrupting whatever he was saying.

"Why? I've been dealing with her marketing guy," Jake said almost dismissively.

"Then get it from him," I said abruptly, my patience nonexistent this morning.

"What's going on, Tobin?"

It was Jake's job to manage my career, not my personal life. He wouldn't agree, often saying they were one and the same. "I need to talk to Kiersten."

"Tobin," he said in his what-the-hell-are-you-going-to-do warning tone.

"Jake, just get it for me." I could tell he wanted to say something else, but I hung up before he could. I leaned back in the chair.

"Oh God," I said as I read the article thoroughly. It gave quite a few details that were, for once, pretty accurate, but there was more innuendo than fact in some places. The author couldn't decide if Kiersten was my lover, Brittney was my lover, or we were a threesome. Sex sells, scandal sells, and the combination was a guaranteed sellout. The advertisers on the side of the page were definitely reaping the benefits of this story.

At least they hadn't yet identified either Kiersten or Brittney, but it would be only a matter of time. Cyber time. I half expected the page to refresh with their names in the revised headline.

Kiersten was not going to be happy. She certainly was not going to be happy when her name became attached to this. Her phone was probably already ringing with her friends and family calling. Did they, like Jake, want to know what was going on between us, or did they want the inside skinny on me?

"Don't fuck this up, Tobin."

I was hoping I already hadn't as I waited for him to call back with Kiersten's number.

Chapter Fifteen

Kiersten Fellows."

"Kiersten, it's Tobin Parks."

My heart skipped and my stomach tingled more than a little. Damn. I didn't normally answer my cell at work, preferring to keep my personal life personal. "Good morning," I said, for lack of anything more intelligent than that traveling from my brain and out my mouth.

"How are you this morning?"

I sensed something more than polite small talk in Tobin's voice. The butterflies in my stomach went from fluttering to full-blown flapping.

"I'm well, thanks," I replied, equally cautious. I had no idea why she was calling. I didn't even ask where she got my number. Tobin Parks probably got anything she wanted—or anybody she wanted. I was not going to be the next statistic.

"Have you seen *The Informer* this morning?"

I usually started my day reading on-line news sources. I skimmed the headlines and dove into the business section. "No. I don't know what that is." Now my gut was telling me I obviously had missed something important. I touched my mouse to wake up my computer and went straight to Google.

"Did you see the headlines in the entertainment section?"

"No." I clicked the icon to the page she referenced.

"You better, and I'm really sorry."

I didn't hear anything else she was saying, my attention fully on the teasing headline below a photo. TOBIN'S LATEST GAL-PAL? TROUBLE IN PARADISE?

Pictures obviously taken by one of the patrons at the restaurant yesterday accompanied the article. The first was of Tobin and me seated at her table, her hand on my arm. My body reacted as it had when it happened, and I looked at the place, expecting to see it there. The angle of the shot made it look like an intimate morning-after breakfast. The second showed Tobin and Brittney facing off against each other after Brittney had insulted her.

"Oh, no." I wasn't sure if I said it out loud or just thought it.

"I'm so sorry, Kiersten. I know better. I should have kept my mouth shut, and I never should have got in her face, definitely not in a public place."

I was listening to Tobin as I skimmed the article. I didn't see my name or Brittney's, which was a relief, if only momentarily. They'd ID me and Brittney by lunch.

"Tobin, don't worry about it. Nothing we can do about it now." I had no idea why I was so calm about this. It was going to turn into a major shit storm with my mother.

"But—"

"But nothing. Brittney was way out of line, and it serves her right for her unforgivable behavior to have her name trashed." My mother, on the other hand, would be horrified and mortified, and I'd hear about it by the end of the day.

Daniel stuck his head in my doorway, and I waved him in. I swiveled my monitor around and pointed to the screen.

"I'm sorry, Kiersten," Tobin said again.

"And I'm sorry for the way Brittney treated you. Now enough apologizing for something neither one of us did." I glanced at Daniel, who was rubbing his temples and frowning. I could practically see the damage-control wheels in motion.

"What do you want me to do?" Tobin asked.

"Do?" I asked.

"To help with this."

"Nothing."

"I have to do something. This isn't right that they're going to drag you through the mud."

"Nothing, Tobin." Daniel's head shot up. I nodded. "There's nothing to do. You have your own PR person, who knows best. They'll tell you what to do. I would just appreciate honesty and not spin."

"I'd never spin about you, Kiersten, and I'd fire anyone on my crew who did."

"I appreciate that, but what you do with your staff is your business. I have to go. I've got someone in my office."

"Oh, okay, I understand. Kiersten, I'm really sorry."

"Good-bye, Tobin."

I pushed the end button and tossed my phone onto a pile of papers on my desk. I closed my eyes and rubbed the back of my neck. When I opened them, Daniel was patiently waiting for my explanation.

"I was having brunch with my mother in Boston yesterday when Tobin came in. We said hello, and she went her way and we finished eating. My sister-in-law came in, and when she and my mother started cackling about something I had to get out of there before I pulled my hair out right there at the table. I was sitting with Tobin when Brittney came over and completely insulted her. I mean her words were like a slap in her face. Tobin was just standing up for herself. End of story. Obviously somebody in the restaurant wanted to make a few bucks at our expense and sold the photos."

"I didn't see your name anywhere, but you know it won't take long before they ID you."

"I know."

"I texted Marcia to come over so she can get right on it. We need to issue a statement."

"No."

"No?"

"No. This is a personal matter between me and my family. Tobin just got caught in the crossfire."

"But this implies you're the other woman." Daniel hesitated. "Are you the other woman?"

"No. I am not the other woman or *the* woman."

"I hope I didn't walk into what it sounded like I walked into." Marcia Lindstrom, my public relations director, came into my office and closed the door behind her.

Marcia, a petite redhead, stood no taller than five feet zero but was a powerhouse PR expert.

"No," I said, and three minutes later Marcia was up to speed on the situation.

"I agree with Kiersten," she said. We need to be prepared with a statement, but we don't need to justify the article with a response. We'll say something about a business discussion and nothing more. You, however," she pointed her well-manicured finger at me, "are going to be in deep shit from your mother."

"Your father and I will expect you by seven."

Even though I was thirty-six years old, college-educated, and a successful businesswoman, my mother still had a way of making me feel like I was twelve.

Her words echoed in my head as I pulled into their driveway. My stomach clenched when I saw Harrison's Mercedes parked in front of the door. It was too late to turn back, so I locked my car and walked up the front steps.

Dinner at my parents' house is always a formal affair, meaning nice pants or a dress for women and khakis and a collared shirt for the men. Since I was coming directly from work that was one less thing I had to worry about.

I heard voices in the front room, and they didn't sound happy. It had taken the media less than thirty minutes from the time Tobin called to identify me and another five for Brittney. Always needing to face the unpleasant head-on, I squared my shoulders and walked confidently into the room.

Conversation stopped and four sets of eyes turned my way. My parents were sitting in matching Queen Anne chairs, and Harrison and Brittney perched on the couch across from them. Brittney wore a self-satisfied smirk, Harrison looked resigned, my mother furious, and my father fidgeted in his chair.

"It's about time," Brittney said sarcastically.

"Were you expecting someone else, Brittney? It's only six fifty," I said, not looking at my watch.

"Sit down, Kiersten," my mother commanded. She pointed to a flower-print chair sitting alone to the side. It looked like an inquisition chair.

In a fit of defiance, I sat in the overstuffed love seat to her left. Her eyes narrowed, and I knew my action wouldn't help my case.

"What do you have to say for yourself?" my mother asked, never one to mince words.

"About?"

"Don't be smart," my father said harshly, surprising me. Rarely did he scold or reprimand. That was my mother's job.

"I have no control over what the media chooses to print."

"But you do have control over who you associate with."

"Yes, I do, and I choose who that is."

"That woman—"

"Is Tobin Parks, and she is a business acquaintance to whom I was simply saying hello." I interrupted my mother before she could malign Tobin.

"You had no right to insult me like you did by telling me to shut up," Brittney said angrily, jumping in.

"You had it coming. You were horrible to her when she did nothing to you."

"You made a scene," my mother said, which was the crux of this entire summons.

"And you humiliated me on the Internet. Now everyone thinks I'm queer." Brittney looked horrified.

I had to laugh at the absurdity of her statement. Daggers shot across the room, and I mentally sidestepped them. "First of all, Brittney, I didn't do anything. You," I said, pointing my finger at her, "brought this on yourself. Second, no lesbian, and I mean *no* lesbian would claim you. Maybe you'll think twice before you open your mouth and spew hate, especially to people you know nothing about. Now if you'll excuse me," I said, starting to get up.

"We're not finished," my mother said.

"Well, I am," I said, and every mouth dropped open. I don't think anyone has ever spoken to my mother like I did, and never, ever, one of her children. Well, I always was the odd one in the family.

"Brittney was despicable, and I don't care if she is married to your son. I will not let her get away with it. She embarrassed me and humiliated Tobin, and if the tables turn on her because of it, then so be it."

I looked at Harrison. "I love you, Harrison. I always will, and I will always support you no matter what, because I do love you. But the woman you have chosen to spend the rest of your life with is mean, ugly, and homophobic, and I will not sit quietly any longer." I looked at each of my parents, then Brittney.

"Good night." I walked out the front door calmer than when I walked in.

Chapter Sixteen

"Oh, man, Kiersten, you are really not getting a Christmas gift this year," Courtney said, signaling the bartender for another round. I'd called her after I left my parents, and we'd met at Caruso's, our favorite gay bar on 52nd Street, where we could have a drink or two and not get hassled.

"I should be so lucky. Maybe that means I won't be expected for Christmas dinner either."

"What were you thinking?" Courtney asked. She'd been to my parents' house several times and had heard more than a few dozen other stories.

"I wasn't," I said, confused.

"That's not like you, Kiersten. You never do anything without thinking it through."

"The whole thing just pissed me off." I took another swallow of my drink. Was this one stronger than the last? "How dare they think they have a say in who I see or do business with? And Brittney was nothing short of a completely inexcusable bitch." I shook my head, the familiar anger starting to boil in me again. "No way is she going to get away with it. She can't stand me, and I know she thinks being a lesbian is a capital sin and contagious, but she had no right to do that to Tobin."

Courtney was looking at me, a strange expression on her face.

"What?"

"I've never seen you like this, K."

"Well, I've never been here before," I answered, finishing my drink and signaling the waiter to pour faster. I'd already decided I'd be calling a car service to take me home.

"Is she as hot in person as she was onstage?"

"Yes, both times I saw her," the two cocktails inside me said.

Courtney choked on her beer and gasped for breath. I patted her on the back a few times and signaled the bartender that there was no need to call 9-1-1.

"What both times?"

"I had dinner with her."

"When?" Courtney asked, shocked.

"When I was in Bozeman."

"That was two weeks ago, and you're just now telling me? You're supposed to let me know these things. It's in the BFF handbook. What the fuck, K?"

Courtney was pissed at me for not telling her and hurt for the same reason. I told her how we came to have dinner and about our conversation. I don't think she blinked during my entire monologue. Finally, she said, "And you walked away? You were in a place where nobody knows you, in a hotel with a hot tub in every room, with Tobin Parks hitting on you, and you walked away?"

"Well, when you phrase it that way," I replied sarcastically. "Yes, Courtney, I walked away."

"And yesterday at brunch you walked away again?"

"Did you actually expect me to leave my mother and bitch Brittney and go upstairs and have sex with Tobin?"

Courtney looked at me with an expression on her face that clearly said DUH!

"I am not going to have sex with Tobin Parks."

The bartender set my drink down in front of me. "I'd have sex with Tobin Parks," he said, fanning himself with this little white bar towel. We scowled at him.

"Why not?" Courtney asked after the bartender moved to the other end of the bar.

"Why not?" I mimicked. "I don't even know her."

"So, it's Tobin Parks."

"And because it's Tobin Parks I'm supposed to just jump into bed with her?"

"Well, yes," Courtney said seriously.

"Well, no."

"Why not?" Courtney asked again.

"I am not going to be another notch on Tobin Parks's guitar."

"Why not?"

"Did you hit your head, Courtney? You're starting to repeat yourself."

"I just can't understand why you don't jump at it."

If she only knew. "Can we change the subject?"

"No, we can't," Courtney said forcefully. "K, when was the last time you got laid?"

I didn't answer because that was the answer.

"Obviously it's been too long," Courtney said, and I didn't bother to correct her. "She's perfect."

"How so?" I found myself asking.

"No need to wine and dine and all that foreplay shit you don't have time for. And no strings after. I mean it's not like she's going to call you the next day."

I looked at Courtney like she was an alien. "What the fuck, Courtney? You make her and me sound like sluts." I should probably be insulted, but I wasn't.

"I didn't mean it like that, K. It's just that that's the excuse you use every time I ask who you're dating. No time or not interested in a relationship. So if Tobin fits that description, why not?"

Courtney was the most pragmatic person at times, and this was one of them. "It wasn't the right time."

"What does that mean? Were you on your period?"

"What? No. Jeez, Courtney, just let it go, will you?" I said shortly, my patience wearing thin. That and it was getting harder to dodge her questions. Courtney, my BFF, had no idea that, other than a few clumsy, embarrassing gropings, I was still a virgin.

It started out innocently enough. She just assumed I had an active sex life, like any normal, adult, attractive lesbian. The thing is, up until the year before we met, I was anything but attractive and, truth be told, still had a hard time seeing myself as such. When puberty hit, the weight piled on, much to the horror of my mother. She tried to guilt me into what she called a balanced diet, and when that didn't work she resorted to near starvation. The more she pressured, the more I pushed back and the more the weight also refused to budge. She never said as much, but I knew I was an embarrassment to her. Braces were the first in my mother's carefully planned makeover. Then came contacts and a hair and makeup stylist. But all that on a frame that carried at least an extra sixty pounds just didn't work for her. She was, and still is, all about image and is proprietary, so an overweight adolescent was just not acceptable. I melted into the background and made myself as invisible as I could.

I didn't join any clubs in school, go to sporting events, and certainly never had a boyfriend. That part didn't bother me because, in addition to being overweight, I knew a *boy*friend was not in my future. The direction my weight was going, a *girl*friend wouldn't be either.

My senior year in college I had finally had enough. I pawned my grandmother's brooch that my mother gave me on my sixteenth birthday and hired a personal trainer. Eighteen months and one hundred and twelve pounds later, the new me made her debut. Courtney never knew the old me, and I was very successful in leaving that girl behind when I entered grad school. What I couldn't leave behind was my insecurity. I hated it and considered that element of my transformation as a work in progress. So I blustered my way through that part of my life, letting people believe what they thought they saw.

"Are you happy, K?"

Either her change of subject, the third drink, or my trip down memory lane had slowed down my brain. "What?"

"Are you happy?" She held up her hand, stopping me from answering. "I mean, really happy. I know you love your job, it's your dream, but there's more to life than JOLT."

"Now you sound like my mother," I said sharply. She ignored that comment.

"I have Tom and the kids. As much as I bitch about my boring middle-class life, I don't know what I'd do without them. I thought I had it all, was happy, till I met Tom. I didn't even know anything was missing until then. And my boys. I'd give my life for them. I want the same for you, K."

Now she was getting maudlin, and it was making me nervous, because she was getting close to what I wanted too. And I was tipsy enough to confess it. They say confession is good for the soul, but if I did, then that would make it real. I took the offense instead.

"And I'm going to find it by fucking Tobin Parks?"

"No, but it'll be a hell of a lot of fun until you do." Courtney started giggling and I reached for my phone.

Chapter Seventeen

I waited until the Uber driver backed out of my driveway and drove down the street before keying in the code to my garage door. As a woman living alone I was more than a little safety conscious. I always drove with my doors locked and windows up. When it came to my house, I lived in a pretty nice neighborhood, each house sitting in the middle of a three-acre parcel of wooded land. Great for privacy but not so great for running next door in case of an emergency.

From my phone I could check the status of my alarm and quickly scan the four video cameras that kept watch on the exterior surrounding my place. The cameras were motion-activated, which saved me hours of fast-forwarding through hours of nothing just to check if I had had any unwanted visitors. In the last few years all I saw was the UPS, FedEx, and the occasional Girl Scout cookie troop.

I had checked both as my driver weaved his way through the street to my house. I double-checked again and keyed in my code and stood back as the door silently rolled up.

My garage is brightly lit, with nothing anyone can hide behind, so after a quick look behind me I stepped inside and hit the close button. Only after the heavy door sealed itself to the floor did I unlock the door leading into the house.

The familiar, comforting chime of the alarm greeted me as I punched in the silence code. I immediately reset the alarm to Stay mode, which allowed me to move freely inside the house without setting off those motion detectors, while the exterior doors and windows remained armed. Why do I live in what Courtney called Fort Knox? Because I'll never forget the sight of my neighbor's body being wheeled out of her house wrapped under a black tarp with the letters CORONER neatly stenciled on top. I was ten years old, and it scared the living shit out of me. What was the classic cliché, better safe than sorry? Yep, that was me when it came to me.

Sitting patiently beside her water bowl was Rockette, my sixty-nine-pound German shepherd. I named her Rockette after the Radio City Music Hall Rockettes because when I scratched her belly, her legs kicked. Between K-9 Companions and many, many hours on my part, Rockette had been well trained, including to sit quietly when I came home. The only muscle that moved on her big, hairy body was her tail, and that was wagging so fast, I could barely see it. I gave her the release command, and she sprang forward like a dog one quarter her size. She came to a sliding stop and sat politely no more than two inches from the tip of my shoes.

"Hello, Miss Rockette," I said, kneeling and ruffling her head and shoulders. She dropped to her back and rewarded me with her exposed belly. My best buddy, my fierce protector was a belly-scratch whore. After a few minutes of attention, Rockette followed me through the house to my bedroom.

My shoes clicked on the wood floor as I walked through the kitchen, across the great room, and into the master bedroom. The plush carpet silenced any noise except the heavy, excited breathing from Rockette at my heels.

After I changed into a pair of purple LSU basketball shorts and a yellow tank top, Rockette followed me through the patio doors and outside. She grabbed her ball and nudged my hand with her wet nose. As soon as she felt my fingers at her mouth she dropped the ball into my open palm. I tucked the bright-orange ball into the Chuck It, and, well, chucked it far into the yard. That simple gizmo had made someone filthy rich, saved my shoulder from rotator-cuff surgery, and made Rockette a very, very happy dog. Twenty minutes and God knows how many throws later we were both relaxing on the couch. Rockette was devouring a treat, and I was flipping through the channels.

I needed to eat something to soak up the liquor sitting in my stomach, and after hitting the play button on a recording of yesterday's White Sox game, I went in search of something quick and easy. I was a pretty good cook, but it was a pain in the ass to cook for one. Too much trouble and too much work. But the alternate was eating out, and that would add ten pounds without even thinking. I scrambled some egg whites, tossed in a whole egg for flavor, added a few secret ingredients, and presto—dinner.

Four innings later, Rockette nudged open the doggie door and went outside without a backward glance. The neighbor girl a few houses down the street usually came over after school to play with Rockette. Her mother was allergic to dogs so she lived vicariously by playing with mine. Rockette got some much-needed attention while I was at work, and Becky got to have a dog without actually having a dog. She refused to take any money, but periodically I gave her "movie money." I wish somebody had given me fifty bucks to go to the movies when I was seventeen.

Rockette returned and effortlessly jumped onto the couch next to me. This was the only piece of furniture she was allowed on, and she snuggled close to my leg. She dropped her big head in my lap, dislodging the report I was reading. She sighed, obviously content.

A familiar voice drew my attention to the TV, and I looked up and right into the dark eyes of Tobin Parks. Other than my heart beating faster I hadn't moved, but Rockette lifted her head and looked at me with a WTF expression. I patted her head a few times, my attention on the sixty-inch screen.

It was a promo for an interview Tobin was doing for the *Today* show. There were a few clips of the interview with just enough tease to get people to tune in, followed by the date and time of the segment. I looked at the date on my watch. Damn, the interview had been this morning. I grabbed the remote and scrolled down to until I found the On Demand selection. In a nanosecond I lost interest in whoever was beating the White Sox and hit play.

I had to fast-forward through at least eighty percent of the show until I finally saw Tobin in the interview chair. I turned up the volume.

"When did you first realize you could make a living singing?" the interviewer asked. The camera was on her face, and she beamed at Tobin. From what I could tell they were sitting in a Starbucks appearing to chat like two people who'd just met. A pang of jealousy shot through me and I frowned. That was ridiculous.

"I was in a bar sitting in a wobbly chair on a stage put together with plywood and two-by-fours when an old man dropped a wrinkled dollar into the tip jar on the corner of the stage. I'd begged the owner to let me sing, but since I didn't have any experience he was hesitant. I told him I'd do it for free, like an audition."

"Obviously he agreed."

Tobin laughed, and my heart skipped and my stomach jumped a little. "No, not at first. It took weeks to get him to let me play." Tobin's face was wistful, as if she were experiencing it all over again in real time.

"What was the first song you sang?"

"'Breakwater Baby.'"

The interviewer frowned. "I don't think I've ever heard that one."

"I've never recorded it. It was really bad, but it worked at the time…and every other time I sang it. I performed every night, and at the end of the first week I counted the money in that tip jar and never looked back."

"How much did you make?"

"Fifty-six dollars," Tobin answered proudly.

"Fifty-six dollars?" the interviewer asked, clearly trying to sound impressed.

"Yep, and at that time that was more money than I'd had in my entire life."

"How old were you?"

Tobin hesitated a moment. She winked at the blonde, and I choked on the iced tea I was swallowing. The dark liquid dribbled down the front of my shirt. Rockette raised her head, sensing something wasn't right, and I gave her a few reassuring words before Tobin replied.

"Let's just say I looked a lot older than I was."

The rest of the questions were pretty light: highlights of the three local shows she had scheduled and some background on her next single. This was clearly a puff piece, not the tough interview of *60 Minutes* a few weeks ago. I guess sex, lesbians, and rock and roll didn't mix well with morning coffee.

I hit the rewind button and watched the short interview three more times. Something about Tobin grabbed me. And judging by her millions of adoring fans, it snared them as well. She was direct, didn't pull any punches, but wasn't obnoxious or full of herself. What you saw was what you got. I found that hard to believe. No one was that transparent, especially an artist whose entire livelihood was based on the fickle tastes and whims of fans.

Don't get me wrong. Tobin was controversial. She worked hard and played harder, that was evident. She was young and was going to squeeze out everything she could while she could, and who could blame her? Not me. The average tenure on the top of the charts was fleeting at best, and she'd been there a few years. Surely dozens of others were just waiting for her to stumble, some probably plotting ways to trip her up and take her place.

Entertainment was a business. A BIG business with big paychecks and fragile self-confidence. I'd heard about it and was unfortunate enough to see it a few times. When athletes or personalities, or anyone high in the public eye, falls from grace they fall hard. One negative review, one song that doesn't hit the top ten, one book that doesn't sell a million copies, and their faith in their talent starts to crumble. Did Tobin suffer from that same curse? What made her famous could also crush her.

I turned off the TV, checked the alarm, and doused the lights. Rockette, who followed me, did her usual three circles before flopping down on her bed, which happened to be right next to mine. She settled in with a sigh as I set my alarm and crawled under the covers. I closed my eyes and started my own nighttime calisthenics to shut down my brain. After I inhaled deeply several times, I exhaled through my mouth slowly. Starting at my toes, I tensed, then relaxed them five times. I moved on to the arch of my foot, then my ankle, calf, and knee. The isometric exercises and deep breathing made me forget everything that had happened that day and the list of things I needed to do next. I'd tried yoga several different times but was always distracted by any little sound. Yet this routine ultimately caused me to relax and fall asleep. Occasionally it took several trips up and down my body before drifting off, but most nights I never made it past my shoulders.

Tonight, the last thing I remembered was the way my body responded when Tobin smiled.

CHAPTER EIGHTEEN

How did you get this number?" My heart raced and my anger soared and my blood pressure skyrocketed. Lights flashed in front of my eyes, and I felt ready to explode. We were at a rest stop somewhere between Boston and Des Moines when I made the mistake of answering my phone. I didn't recognize the number and thought it might be Kiersten. Wrong on so many counts.

"Now, Carol, is that any way to greet me? We haven't talked in a month of Sundays."

With the Southern drawl, Sunday sounded more like Sundee. Even though the familiar voice was raspy from cigarettes and cheap booze, only four people in this world still called me Carol. I'd gone by Tobin Parks since my first gig, and when I was eighteen I legally changed my name. That had kept my family from finding me for a few years, but they eventually tracked me down.

"What do you want?" I looked over my shoulder in both directions, making sure no one was within earshot. This was nobody's business.

"Why do you always ask that when I call, sugar?"

"Because that's what you want."

"You don't invite us to any of your concerts."

And I never will.

"How've you been, sugar?"

The endearment wasn't dear, just a word used in habit in just about every conversation. There was never anything special about the word, or any of the others she used, like *baby* or *honey*.

"I doubt you called to inquire about my health." I wasn't quite as blistering mad as I was when I first heard her voice. I'd learned the hard way that I had to calm down. The first time she contacted me, I did something stupid and have paid for it ever since.

"Can't I call just to see how you are? If you're getting along all right?"

"No, you can't. We have an arrangement, and the fact that you are talking to me violates your part of it. I could shut you down."

"Now, Carol, honey. Oh, wait. I forgot it's Tobin now. Well, anyway, *Tobin.* There's no reason for you to be mean and ugly like that."

I hated the sound of my name coming from my mother's mouth. I held the phone away from my ear as if the germs in her cough coming out of the speaker could somehow float through the airwaves and deposit their contagion in me. Shit, with my luck with this woman, they probably could.

"What do you want, Irene?" I'd stopped calling the woman on the other end of the line mom years ago.

"Jimmy's car broke down."

Crashed it was probably more like it. "Maybe he should learn how to save a little instead of spending every dime. On second thought, maybe he should get a job."

"Sweetie, you know he can't work." Another empty endearment.

"Won't work." My worthless brother was only good for one thing, and that was mooching off the state and everyone he came in contact with, including me.

"Nobody's hiring, Tobin. You know how it is around here."

My mother's voice had the same nasal whine I remember hearing my entire life. Other than the Camel-cigarette accent, it still sounded the same.

"He's your brother. Family helps family."

"He can help himself. He's a grown man."

Why I kept arguing with her I didn't know. She would never see reason, just as much as she would never stop calling me for money. The phone calls had started as soon as my first song hit the air waves in Sulphur Springs, Texas. No one in my family ever gave a damn about me until I had something they wanted. And now I do—money.

My father, Jimmy Senior, hadn't been around much when I was little. But then again, if Irene (nee Johnson) was my wife, I'd have been a long-haul trucker too.

They'd married at nineteen, four months after too much partying, too much booze, and not enough birth control. Five months later, Jimmy Junior arrived, and eleven months later I came along. My father must have been gone a lot more after that, because it was another four years before my sister Frances arrived, looking suspiciously like our neighbor's little girl. His love of booze finally caught up with him, and he was fired and became a regular fixture on our couch after that.

I wasn't missed around the dinner table. It was piled high with crap and dirty take-out containers. No one asked where I was, cared about what time I came home or even if I went to school. The truancy officer frequently visited our trailer.

I remember walking in on a man and my mother one afternoon I did go to school. The guy moved faster than I thought anyone could at his age and waistline as he jumped off the couch, tossing my mother on her ass. Her short skirt was up and his belt buckle open, and there was no doubt I wouldn't be getting into trouble that day. Finally, at age sixteen, I stopped pretending to go to school and focused on my music instead.

No one knew that, a few years ago, I hired a private tutor to help me learn how to read better and do more than basic math. With his help I passed my high-school equivalency test and was currently enrolled in an online program to get a business degree.

I was a good student, *A*s and *B*s, but I had to work my ass off to get them. I still had difficulty focusing at times, but I was determined to complete my degree. Not that it mattered that I would be the first in my family to graduate from college. Hell, I was probably the first one to finish high school.

"Are you daydreaming again, Carol?"

This time my mother's voice had that edge to it that I knew so well. It was the one I'd heard when I had a song dancing around in my brain, when a chord or rhythm got stuck like a repeating track, when I had escaped from the reality of my dysfunctional life.

I didn't answer, instead repeated my original question. "What do you want?" I asked, even though the instant I heard her voice I knew.

"A new truck for Jimmy."

Now we were getting somewhere. At least it only took five minutes for her to make her demand. The first time she called she'd kept up the façade of catching up for fifteen minutes.

"No."

"How do you expect him to get around? Take me and Sharon to the grocery store?"

The liquor store or the casino was more than likely their destination.

"That is not my concern. He needs to—"

"Are you sure you want to do this, little miss high-and-mighty superstar?" My mother's nastiness contaminated her question. "All it would take would be one phone call, and the rich and famous life you have would be over."

The first time she threatened me I gave in and wrote a check. The second, third, and fourth I wired the money to Western Union at the local Walmart. The demands and threats came more frequently now. I guess the more they got, the more they wanted. I'd given them more than enough money to buy a nice house, furnish it, and have more than plenty to spare. I wasn't interested enough to find out what they'd done with it. I couldn't care less. It's not like it was a loan, even though my mother had phrased it like that the first few times. But I was older, a whole lot wiser, and completely confident in my talent, unlike the scared teenager I was when I struck out on my own.

Suddenly I thought of Kiersten and how she'd built her company out of nothing but a dream and a few bucks in savings. I admired her tenacity and her willingness to do what she needed to make it happen. A calmness came over me I never had experienced before.

"Then make it."

I pushed the red-phone handset on the screen of my phone, ending the call.

Chapter Nineteen

I was getting pretty tired of losing focus. I'd dreamed about Tobin all night and had woken up so aroused there was no way I could get on with my day without taking care of business. I don't normally do the "I am my own best lover" in the morning, but today was a very pleasant exception. Pleasant if you don't mind solo sex. Solo is the only way I have sex, so this was nothing new. What was new was the intensity of my orgasm and the speed with which it blew off the top of my head. It was better than coffee, and that's saying a lot.

I reached for the stack of colored file folders Bea had laid on the corner of my desk. A red folder contained things I needed to do immediately, yellow was important but could wait a day or two, green signaled FYI, and blue was stuff to read. I worked my way through the red one, occasionally making notes of what I needed a member of my staff to do. The yellow contained several invitations for various social events, and Bea had indicated those she'd already given my RSVP.

My heart jumped when the familiar seal of my high school peeked out from the bottom of the stack. My hands trembling, I pulled the yellow paper from the bottom of the pile. I quickly scanned the letter, the paper shaking so badly I had to lay it on my desk so I could read it. It was an invitation to my twentieth high-school reunion, urging me to join my fellow alumni to "reconnect and reminisce" four weeks from Saturday. On the docket was a formal dinner and dance to be held at the prestigious Kristoff Club, with cocktails and appetizers at six, dinner at seven, followed by dancing and a slide show of the highlights of our *four awesome years at Alhambra High School.*

Flashbacks of my four years at AHS were anything but awesome. I was fat, a complete dweeb, and hated every minute of it. I didn't have a best friend, join a club, or go to football games. Did I mention I was fat and had no friends? Every day felt like a prison sentence, and my parole was graduation. Why would I want to go back there and relive old times? I would need more than a few cocktails to get me through it. I wrote my response in big bold letters and tossed it into my outbox. Bea would send my regrets.

"Tobin Parks is here," Bea stated after knocking on my door and sticking her head in. She was obviously trying to be professional, but I could tell Tobin had the same effect on her as she did every other person on the planet. Okay, maybe that statement was a bit too broad.

I suppressed a sigh. The last thing I needed was to be seen with Tobin again. But she was here, and surprisingly I wanted to see her. "Show her in. But if she's not out of here in ten minutes, come get me." That was the ploy used in hundreds of offices every day to get unwanted visitors out. I wasn't above using it.

Something about Tobin made me nervous and jittery. My insides skittered around and my stomach flip-flopped. I had a hard time thinking clearly. I didn't need this with the likes of Tobin Parks. I had just enough time to take a deep breath before my office door opened farther and Tobin walked in.

I don't remember standing, but I must have, because all of a sudden I felt dizzy. I gripped the edge of my desk to keep from toppling over.

"Thanks for seeing me," Tobin said, stopping in front of my desk. "I know you're busy so I won't take more than a minute," she said, her words coming out in a rush.

For a moment I thought Tobin was as nervous as I was, then scoffed at my silliness. She had been in the company of kings and princes, presidents, and thousands of screaming women. Little ole me was barely a blip on her screen.

"I have a few minutes." I indicated she should sit in one of the chairs in front of my desk. I could have invited her to sit on the small couch in the casual seating area in the corner, but I needed something to deflect the sexual magnetism between us.

"I just wanted to apologize again," Tobin said sincerely.

"How do you live like this?" I asked, still a bit frazzled by everything.

"I beg your pardon?"

"The paparazzi, the fishbowl, under the microscope, however you'd like to phrase it." It was my turn for words to rush out. "I came in the next morning to one hundred and two messages on my desk, and that was after I had to maneuver my car through the hordes of photographers and microphones stuck in my face. I'm not sure I didn't run over one particularly aggressive reporter who jumped on the hood of my car as I pulled into the garage." I dropped my head in my hand, already exhausted, and it was only a little after nine. "My neighbors are going to hate me," and my mother is going to kill me, I thought but didn't add.

"I'm so, so sorry, Kiersten."

"It goes with the territory," Tobin answered.

"Well, that's a landscape I don't want to be anywhere near. Oh, wait…I'm already there." I couldn't mask the sarcasm in my voice. It was my way of coping.

"I'm sorry—"

"Stop saying that. You did nothing wrong. We did nothing wrong, but *we* seem to be getting all the attention."

"What kind of fallout are you getting?"

"You mean other than these?" I asked, picking up the pink phone-message papers and dropping them back onto my desk. I didn't wait for her to answer. "Just my mother and her 'we have appearances to keep up' speech," I said, remembering the scene last night. "And instead of my typical good-daughter, yes, Mother, I proceeded to go ballistic on her and kept going until I insulted my sister-in-law and probably alienated my brother. And I won't even mention the look on my mother's face," I added. I'll never forget it and felt vaguely proud I put it there.

"I am so sorry."

"Stop apologizing!" I said, probably too loud. "You didn't do anything. No, that's not right. You provided me sanctuary from an impossible situation, and I should be apologizing to you."

"Me? Why?"

"You were trying to have a quiet meal, and as soon as I sat down, the flashbulbs started going off—so to speak."

"The cameras are always on me. Oh, wow, that sounded more than a little conceited, didn't it?" Tobin asked sheepishly.

"No, I get it." I waved off her concern. "Nonetheless, I appreciate your concern. You didn't need to come by. I'm fine," I said, surprisingly so.

"I wanted to see you again," Tobin said quietly.

The flip-flopping in my stomach ramped up into a full-blown butterfly attack.

"No," I said, suddenly not sure if I was answering her question about sponsorship or that something else that was reflecting in her eyes.

"Why do you keep saying that? You don't even know what I was going to ask."

Tobin stood and walked toward the window. I glanced at the clock on the wall across the room. Eight minutes until rescue.

"This is a beautiful view," she commented, her back to me. She was silhouetted against the midday sun streaming through the windows. Thin with an almost boy-like figure, she had all the right girl curves in all the right places. Her jeans hung low on her hips and fit perfectly, outlining her butt and long legs. I wondered absently if they were off the rack or custom made to bring out her best features. Seven minutes until rescue.

"I rarely get to see anything like this," she said, more than a little melancholy in her voice. "I'm always either in my coach, driving in the middle of the night, or in a concert venue." She raised her arms above her head and stretched. Her shirt lifted, exposing a few inches of bare skin above the waist of her jeans with just a hint of the band of her underwear showing. Under Armour? Calvin Klein? Jockey? At least it wasn't a thong, but then again Tobin didn't look like a thong girl.

"I don't remember the last time I spent the day outside."

I was still looking at her midriff when Tobin suddenly dropped her arms and turned around. My eyes shot to her face but not before catching a glimpse of her stomach. Oh, my goodness.

Now my face was hot and clearly reflected that I had been caught peeking. It probably screamed that I liked what I saw as well. I was obviously busted so I forced myself to maintain eye contact and not look away. My heart started racing, and my blood skittered through my veins. When two women gaze directly at each other with more than politeness on their mind, it's just downright sexy. It was the "I like what I see, interested?" look. I was about to open my mouth and say something that would probably be incredibly stupid and embarrassing, but Tobin broke eye contact first. I was glad I was sitting down because it was like I'd been released from a tractor beam on a *Star Trek* episode. She stepped toward the chair she'd vacated a few minutes ago but stopped and picked up the white card from my inbox. She read it quickly.

"Are you going?"

"Excuse me?"

"To your reunion," Tobin clarified, wiggling the invitation dangling from two fingers of her right hand.

I reached across my desk and snagged it from her. "Not that it's any of your business, but no."

"Why not?"

I wasn't going to answer her.

"Twenty years?" she asked.

"Yes." I hated admitting it. It made me feel old.

"How old were you when you graduated?"

"Seventeen."

"So why aren't you going? Didn't stay in touch with anyone? Busy schedule?"

I didn't answer because it was, after all, none of her business.

"No date?"

I chuckled. "I haven't needed a date to do anything for years."

"Want one?"

"A date?" This conversation had suddenly turned ridiculous.

"You can take me."

"What?" I was dumbfounded.

"I'll go with you."

"I don't need a date, an escort, or to babysit," I added, alluding to the difference in our ages.

"Okay. I'll go as your arm candy."

"My arm candy?" I asked, incredulous at the thought. God, I felt old.

"Why not?"

"I can think of many, many reasons." Other than the obvious, I really couldn't, but I was trying to make a point.

"Come on, Kiersten. Why not go and show them who you've become?"

"I'm pretty sure they know who I've become," I replied. This assurance had been validated when the invitation had come addressed to me as CEO of JOLT with the address of our headquarters, not my home.

"So let's go and have a little fun?"

"And how would you going as my date be fun?"

"Ouch, that hurt," she said, but I doubt she meant it. "Reunions are supposed to be all about going and showing off who you are, what you have, or, in this case, who you have."

"And you know this how? You're not even old enough to have had a reunion."

"Everybody knows that's what they're for," she answered, looking at me like I had no clue. "Come on. Have a little fun."

"I have fun." God, I sounded pathetic. Tobin raised her eyebrows and confirmed my fear. "I thought you were here to apologize," I said, trying to get this conversation back on track.

"You kept telling me there was no need, so I moved on."

Was it really that simple? Had it ever been that simple? I suppose when you're young, very rich, and have the world at your feet, it is.

Chapter Twenty

"Come for me." The voice in my ear was coarse and sounded way too sure of herself. After all, she was fucking Tobin Parks. Her words were a little slurred, but I attributed that to post-orgasmic lethargy, not alcohol. Her breath had a faint scent of whiskey, but she wasn't drunk. I didn't do drunk, or even tipsy for that matter. That just isn't right. A lot of things were wrong in my life, but that wasn't one of them and never would be. If a woman was with me it was because she wanted to be, not that she'd lowered her inhibitions or wasn't thinking clearly.

"I gotta go," I said, pulling her hands away from me. She was strong and was making a definite play to get her hands in my pants. Little did she know that nobody, and I mean nobody, put their hands on me. Tonight was no different. Even though I was still infuriated by the call I'd received earlier in the day, I hadn't lost my mind.

"But you didn't come," she said, as if just because she did I had to too.

"I've really got to go." It wasn't a lie. I did need to get out of this backstage room, a carbon copy of dozens of others in cities that blurred together on the seemingly endless road to stardom. Everything was the same after a while. The same songs, same sets, same crowds, same venues, same expectations, same women. Most apparent was the fact that I had my pick of women and would invariably bring one backstage for an after-show performance. I'd always leave before it got personal. Like having sex wasn't personal. What kept it impersonal was that it was clearly sex and occasionally fucking. The women I left could brag about the fact that they had been with Tobin Parks, the hottest singer in a decade. I, however, never asked anyone's name.

I didn't want to be here. No, strike that. I don't want to be here, doing this any longer. In the beginning it was great, just the typical after-hours party where I was expected to schmooze with the radio-station bigwigs, smile for the camera, and kiss the girls. But I was tired and just wanted to go back to my coach and go to bed—alone. I didn't like the direction this party was headed and had been trying to make my escape for a while. The last thing I wanted or needed was another photo of me and my gal-pal or another innuendo-laced article of my wild and wicked personal life appearing on the cover of the latest rag magazine or blog. I did, however, fully expect a synopsis of an interview with Irene Brown.

I'd still been angry and a little rattled after I hung up on Mommie Dearest. I barked orders, was short with my answers, and had been a general all-around bitch since then. The show tonight had been a little more raw and edgy than usual, and the crowd loved it. My band, being the professional musicians that they are, kept up with me and followed my lead. By the end of the show I was exhausted, yet hyped. I couldn't wait to get back to my dressing room and release some steam. Unfortunately, after whatever her name was left, I was still as keyed up as I was right after Irene's call.

Back in my coach I popped the top off a cherry Coke and tried to relax. I picked up my guitar and began to strum a few of the chords to a song I'd been working on for the past few weeks. I closed my eyes, willing my brain to empty itself of recent memories of my childhood spent in a single-wide.

I often thought of my life as before and after. Before consisted of everything I could remember before I left home. It contained monochrome images of a broken, dirty front window and sun-bleached fake flowers in a cracked pot on the patio. Outside, dead grass and plastic bags tumbled down the potholed street on hot summer afternoons. A faded red wagon with one wheel missing lay in a rusting heap along with three paint cans. Across the street a Ford Grand Torino, its hood missing and tires long gone, sat on gray cinder blocks. The trunk lid had been removed the day after Michael Flannigan died of heat stroke after he thought the old car was the perfect place to hide from his abusive father. Unfortunately he'd been trapped inside for an afternoon, and by the time anyone thought to look inside he was dead. Stale perfume and cheap beer clung to the threadbare carpet and flimsy curtains inside our humble abode. I could still smell the stink of the rotting garbage, filthy socks, and unwashed males. The welcome mat was never out at my childhood home.

Freedom came when I finally had enough money to leave. Run away was probably the technical term, since I was only fifteen and not old enough to do anything on my own. I doubted my parents would call the cops and report me missing. Hell, it was probably a week before they even realized I was gone. One less mouth to feed, to clothe, and find shoes to wear. Not that any of it ever fit anyway. It was probably good-bye and good riddance, until they connected the dots between Carol Brown and Tobin Parks. Then it was hello, favorite daughter.

Jimmy, the douchebag that was my brother, had called me three or four times. Each time the conversation was disjointed and ridiculous. He stuttered and could barely put three words together, and I had no idea what he was talking about. I also didn't care. The only thing I was ever good for to Jimmy was as the recipient of his verbal insults and a punching bag for his fists.

My sister, on the other hand, was a master manipulator and practiced on me until I was old enough to realize what she was doing. She was much more subtle than our mother and would either end up the wife of some rich bastard or in for ten to twenty years without parole. I had no idea what she was doing now. Irene never spoke of her, and I didn't care enough to ask.

I thought about Kiersten's family and how we grew up on completely different sides of the street. Her family was probably just as fucked up as mine, but in more sophisticated ways, and I didn't know which was worse. The Browns who lived at 15 Stewart Road, space 34 were exactly what you saw—poor-white trailer trash. Kiersten's family probably lived in an affluent white suburb and was picture perfect. At least the part they let everyone see.

Chapter Twenty-one

"Dance or drink?" Tobin asked expectantly.

"Drink, definitely," I answered. "But no more than two."

"Two, max, got it," Tobin replied, and led us across the room to the nearest bar.

Cocktail in one hand, Tobin's arm in the other, I faced the crowd. Just the simple fact that Tobin was beside me confirmed that I must be out of my fucking mind to be here and with her.

"I don't think we need these, do you?" Tobin asked, looking at our name tags in her hand. "I think everyone knows who we are, or they will by the end of the evening."

I grabbed mine from her before she could look at it. It showed my senior portrait when I was at my heaviest. My mother had sent me to a hair and makeup stylist the morning the picture was taken, but the professional could do little to disguise the subject at hand. What was the saying, the camera never lies, and sometimes nothing was uglier than the truth. Thankfully Tobin didn't protest and want to see it. I could do little to keep her from watching it during the slide show, but I could keep her from viewing it plastered on my chest.

A lot of people looked familiar, but I remembered the names of only a few. There were at least two dozen round tables, each with perfectly arranged place settings for ten. Sweating glasses filled with melting ice ringed the inside of the large table. The centerpiece at each one was a stuffed animal of our school mascot.

I suddenly realized I was angry for allowing these people to intimidate me and make me feel small and insignificant—again. I'm better than that now, and I was all those years ago. It's just that my confidence was buried under one hundred and twenty-six extra pounds. Once I shed that, I shed my inhibitions and vowed I would never go back to that dark, lonely place again. I stood up a little taller.

Movement to my right caught my eye just before I heard someone say, "Kiersten, so good to see you again."

While the mystery woman was looking at Tobin, I sneaked a peek at her badge.

"Francie, how are you?" I asked politely. Francie had driven me to school my junior year, but I was just a paid member of her car pool, not one of her besties.

"I'm good," she answered, trying real hard to look at me when she answered. "This is my husband Marty," she said, pulling an overweight, pasty-looking man toward me.

I removed my hand from Tobin's arm and suddenly felt very alone. "Kiersten Fellows." I introduced myself when it was obvious Francie didn't intend to. Marty's handshake was as limp as his suit.

"Francie, this is—"

"Tobin Parks." She was gushing all over herself like she was twelve. "When I heard you were coming, Kiersten, I told Marty we just had to be here."

Somehow I knew that wasn't true.

"Francie, I'm here as Kiersten's guest, nothing more. Now, will you excuse us?" Tobin said, smoothly extricating us from the gawking Francie and her husband.

"Relax," Tobin said, taking my hand as she led me away. "We're supposed to be together," she added, pulling me closer.

"How do you deal with this?" I asked, casually glancing around the room. The lights were low but bright enough to see everyone.

"Like what?"

"Everybody watching you, your every move."

"Ignore them."

I had to chuckle. "Just that simple? Just ignore them?"

"That and don't make eye contact," she said, hiding a smile behind her glass of beer.

"Kind of hard to do when we're at a party."

"Good point, but they're completely focused on you. You're the most beautiful woman in the room."

I stopped so I could look into Tobin's eyes. They were dark, her pupils large with flecks of color.

"What?" she asked innocently. "You are."

"Hmm, not hardly," I said, not believing her.

"Why do you say that, Kiersten? You are."

"I know you saw my yearbook photo."

"So? That has nothing to do with who you are now. I was pretty ugly and gawky at that age too. I was missing a front tooth and was skin and bones. My clothes were from the church give-away box, and I never had a pair of shoes that fit. Good God, Kiersten, look around. Everyone here has changed. I doubt they all were this overweight or bald in high school. They're the ones that should be embarrassed, not you."

"I'm not embarrassed," I protested. "I wasn't twenty years ago, and I'm not now," I lied.

"Okay, wrong word. Let's just focus on having them drool all over the successful CEO and her hot girl-date." Tobin grinned and raised her eyebrows several times. "Let's give them something to talk about, shall we?"

For the hundredth time I questioned my decision to let Tobin escort me to this stupid reunion. What did she mean by that? I'd been embarrassed and humiliated enough years ago. I didn't need it now. If I thought the picture from our innocent conversation on the hotel patio was something, this would be an Internet feast and a shit storm when my mother got wind of it. Oh, well. Too late now, I said to myself, squaring my shoulders and standing up straighter.

"Okay, but within reason. I still have a reputation to uphold," I said, sounding old and stuffy.

"So do I," Tobin said just before she kissed me.

Chapter Twenty-two

Holy cow, could she kiss. Her lips were soft, yet sure of exactly what she was doing. It wasn't too wet or sloppy or indecent. It could probably be described by some as chaste as far as a Tobin Parks's kiss went.

It was over almost as fast as it started, but I felt it to the tip of my toes. My stomach was somewhere below my belt buckle, and it was putting some serious pressure on some serious girl parts. When she lifted her head and I opened my eyes, Tobin was looking at me with raw desire. My pulse was racing, my heart hammering, and my crotch was throbbing in an unfamiliar way. My mind went blank, and my throat felt suddenly very dry. I instinctively licked my lips, and Tobin's eyes grew darker as she watched. My knees became suddenly very weak.

"I think I need to sit down," I managed to choke out.

Four other couples were already seated at the nearest table, and the women gaped while the men stood as we approached. One of the men I recognized as my chemistry lab partner in tenth and eleventh grade. Finally a friendly face.

"Josh." I hugged him. "You look great." He did. He was still trim and had all his hair, which was more than I could say about the three other men at our table.

"Kiersten, CEO of JOLT. You've come a long way, obviously because I helped you learn the periodic table of elements." I heard nothing but friendly joking in his comment and remembered how much I liked him.

"Without you, where would I be?"

"Slinging hash at the diner." We laughed at our inside joke. "Hey, this is my wife, Linda. Linda, this is Kiersten Fellows. We were chem-lab partners."

I reached out my hand and Linda took it enthusiastically. "Glad to meet you, Kiersten. Josh showed me your picture in the yearbook. He was so hoping you'd be here."

I liked Linda and Josh. They hadn't given Tobin a second glance during the two minutes of meet and greet.

"Josh, Linda, this is Tobin Parks." I felt ridiculous introducing Tobin to everyone. It was like introducing Cher or Madonna or Kesha. Everyone knew who they were.

"You're one up on me, Josh," Tobin said, shaking his hand. "Kiersten never showed me her yearbook." She turned to me, her grin sending tingles up and down my body. "No more excuses, honey. I want to see it when we get home.

Because of the way Tobin's eyes glistened, the deep dimples in her cheeks, and the way she kissed me, even though her comment was designed for appearances only, turning dusty pages in a twenty-year-old book was the farthest thing on my mind when it came to how to spend the rest of the night.

We sat down between Josh and a guy I remembered from the band and his very pregnant wife. He looked starstruck, and she looked miserable, like she might pop that baby out any second.

We all made small talk about jobs, families, and teachers we had in common. Everyone at the table was polite, but I knew they were dying to talk to and about Tobin.

"Ladies and gentlemen," a voice said from the front of the room, immediately followed by shrill feedback from the microphone. "Oops, sorry," the speaker said. "Welcome to the twentieth reunion of Alhambra High School, class of…"

The room quieted as he introduced himself and other members of the reunion committee. Mercifully he was brief, and the servers started filing out of the side doors carrying trays of plates covered with silver lids. Forty-five minutes later he was back at the podium announcing who had traveled the farthest, had the most kids, and had died. The slide show began, and my anxiety kicked up from a five to an eight on a ten-point scale. Picture after picture faded in and out on the large screen in the front of the room. As each picture came into focus my former alumni greeted it with hoots and howls. I figured out that the pictures of those in attendance tonight stayed on the screen longer than those who had stayed home. I dreaded their reaction when it was my turn.

As with my entire high school and college years, luck was not on my side. I was well practiced in the art of showing no reaction to the cruelties of my peers, even though for the past twelve years I looked nothing like I had back then. However, I hadn't forgotten the skill. As soon as I realized my former self, all pimply, ugly, bad hair, big glasses, and braces could be on display, I prepared myself.

Dead silence filled the room the instant it was my turn to be immortalized from twenty years earlier. My stomach seized when I saw myself, and I was instantly transported back to that time. Loneliness and pain washed over me like a wet wool blanket. I felt both small and ginormous at the same time.

I wasn't sure if it was real or my imagination, but I heard a few snickers and a few gasps. I felt everyone looking at me so I simply smiled and shook my head as if to say, *Oh well, that was then, and this is now*.

I had worked hard, damn hard, to change my body and my attitude. My self-respect and self-confidence were much harder to change. Inside, where no one would see, I straightened my back and demanded my inner self-confidence to be stronger as a successful woman than it was as a child.

I wanted to look at Tobin, see her reaction, but I forced my eyes to remain on the old me. Finally, after what seemed like an eternity, the picture changed to the state-championship football game. The levity in the room slowly resumed, and I faked it as well as I had all those years ago.

With the slide show over, Tobin asked me to dance. Actually it was more of a dance-with-me than a would-you-like-to-dance? I probably would have said no so as not to draw attention to myself. My standard MO with this crowd.

When I hesitated she said "I'd like to dance with the most beautiful woman in the room."

"Don't patronize me, Tobin," I said sharply. "I don't need your approval or your validation. I have very tough skin, obviously callused from years of experience."

"Then dance with me," Tobin repeated.

"I'd rather not." I was suddenly nervous.

"Why not? Other people are."

"I don't care what other people are doing." Tobin frowned, and I knew I'd sounded a little abrupt.

"Are you afraid?"

"Afraid of what?" I asked stupidly. Of course I was. Afraid of people looking at me and seeing the fat girl with thick glasses trying so desperately to fit in. Afraid I'd make a fool of myself by tripping over my feet. Afraid of being too close to Tobin.

From the minute I'd opened my front door I had been completely aware of her. From the laces on her shiny shoes to the top of her wild black hair to the appreciative look in her eyes when she gave me the once-over, I'd been completely aware Tobin was my date.

The limo ride had been okay, the large backseat providing a comfortable yet acceptable amount of distance between us. I don't remember what we talked about, but conversation had flowed smoothly during the twenty-minute ride to the club. When we arrived Tobin exited the car first and extended her hand to help me out. I almost tripped when a shock of electricity shot through my palm, up my arm, down my middle, and landed right between my legs. Seeming to know my plight, Tobin just gripped my hand tighter and put her other arm around my waist to steady me. Thankfully she hadn't said anything. When she released me, my body reacted and I missed the warmth of her arm. She'd kept her hand at the small of my back as we walked up the steps into the lobby.

"Of what people might think?" Tobin asked, her voice still quiet.

"I stopped worrying about what people think years ago. I can't control that and I don't care."

"You like to be in control, don't you?"

I almost said yes but thought about it first. “Sometimes. When it makes sense, when I have to,” I answered, not sure if that was the whole truth or only partially so.

“Well, this is one of those times you can let go. Let’s dance.”

This time it wasn’t a question but more of a statement, punctuated by her standing up and holding out her hand, palm up. I didn’t have much choice but to accept.

Chapter Twenty-three

I waited for the sizzle I felt every time we touched. It had been a mild buzz of interest the first time, but tonight a much higher intensity kicked up to full power when Kiersten had opened her front door.

She was wearing a pale-blue dress that brought out the color of her eyes. Her hair was down, and all night I had fought the urge to run my hands through it. I loved long hair, and Kiersten's looked soft and thick, not stiff and sticky like so many others. She wore a little more makeup than she had the other times I'd seen her, the heavier hand bringing out the depth and contrast of her eyes.

The dress fit her perfectly, tight at the top, accentuating her breasts, fitted at the bodice, and flaring out just below her hips. She had on barely there hose and classic pumps with three-inch heels. She looked like the classy, sophisticated, successful woman she was. And I had no idea what I was doing here with her. I was completely out-classed.

It had been a lark when I asked her to take me as her date. I hadn't thought about it before I asked her. My mouth just opened and out it came. I'd gotten pretty good at inviting myself into a beautiful woman's arms, and I guess that's what I thought it would be in this case. Until I was standing on her doorstep I hadn't thought about it much at all.

As I stood there with my hand out, I could see Kiersten debating with herself about dancing with me. I very easily could have charmed her into it, but for some reason this needed to be her decision.

What was I doing here? Why had I gone out of my way to spend the evening with her? I had to cancel a couple of big promotional things, and Jake was furious. Too bad. He could get over it. I'd had my assistant Patty dig up everything she could on Kiersten, and it came as a complete surprise to see the amazing transformation. Other than the color of her eyes, Kiersten looked nothing like she had twenty years ago. What must she have had to do? How many hours in the gym and meals of fish and chicken and green leafy vegetables? Had she had some type of weight-loss surgery to kick-start her transformation? Did she eat like a bird now? She hadn't when we had dinner that one night. Did she keep a pair of fat pants in the front of her closet as a stark reminder to never go there again? Why was I so curious?

I could understand why she might feel unease in front of these people, but I gave her an extreme amount of credit for even being here. She was handling herself with class. She wasn't saying, "What do you think of me now, assholes?" She wasn't flaunting her success in their faces. She could buy and sell most of these people all day and not break a sweat. But she was humble, never bragging about JOLT or alluding to her eight-figure income.

I, however, was starting to feel like an idiot standing there with my hand out waiting for her to decide. It would be more than a little embarrassing if she said no. I wanted to feel her in my arms, hold her tight against me, inhale her scent that I had only tantalizingly sampled so far. I was looking for a chance to touch her hair, slide my leg between hers, and maybe kiss her again.

It was seduction 101, and even though I hadn't had to seduce anyone in years and might be a little rusty, I still remembered how. I said a silent thanks to some god somewhere when Kiersten finally placed her hand in mine and stood. My hand tingled and my stomach fluttered as I led her to the dance floor.

She moved easily into my arms, and I pulled her close. Her arm wrapped around my shoulders, her hand settled lightly between my shoulder blades. She smelled good and felt even better.

We moved around the floor, easily sidestepping the other couples around us. More than a few dozen eyes were on us, not only because we were the only two non-heterosexual couple at the event but because of who we were and that we were so obviously together. I was used to pretending to be something I wasn't, but this time I suddenly and inexplicably wanted it to be something else.

"You okay?" Kiersten asked when I missed a step. She pulled me closer to steady me.

I'm not sure what I wanted to say but didn't know how or what it even meant. Instead I said, "Yeah, sorry."

I couldn't remember the last time I'd danced like this. Dancing with the first lady of Spain last year had been fun but nothing more. I was in her country for a few shows, and she had invited me to the first-family residence. Just a few close friends, her personal secretary said when she connected with Jake. If eighty-four people were just a few close friends, throwing a garden party for all of them was probably as complicated as an elaborate state dinner. But I hadn't danced with a woman close like this, even under the guise of a date, in a long time—a very long time.

I never went to dances as a kid. I never wanted to, even if I'd had something decent to wear. No way was I going to subject myself to any more ridicule than I had to endure during mandatory school hours. That, and I was certain Debbie Stevens would have slapped my face for even suggesting she was queer, let alone let me kiss her.

"You're an excellent dancer," Kiersten said.

"Thanks." *And thank you for the private lessons, Val Shipley.* Val was one of the crew dancers on *Dancing With The Stars*. It would not be good to be thought of as having two left feet. Val had taught me more than a few dance steps during our time together.

The music was vaguely registering in the back of my brain, but Kiersten in my arms had all my attention.

I returned the compliment. "You as well."

"Forty lessons at the local Fred Astaire dance studio," she said sarcastically.

"What was the occasion?" I asked. I liked her sense of humor.

"Every young lady needs to know how to follow a gentleman around the floor with poise and grace."

"Let me guess," I said. "Your mother."

"Got it right on the first try."

"And did you?"

"Did I what?"

"Follow a gentleman around the dance floor with poise and grace." Kiersten laughed, and I liked the way her breasts felt moving against me.

"No."

"No?" I asked, hoping she'd elaborate.

"No," she said in that familiar final tone. I sure would like to hear her say yes with that same definitive confidence.

"Their loss. Something tells me your mother would not be too happy that all her expensive dance lessons were wasted on me."

When Kiersten leaned back so she could look directly into my eyes, her pelvis shifted closer to me. My body responded.

"She'd shit a brick," Kiersten said, completely deadpan.

I laughed and knew those few people who hadn't been watching us were now doing so.

"That's an interesting image," I managed to say.

Kiersten finally smiled—a big smile—and the world around me disappeared. Gone was the low hum of conversation, the clinking of cutlery, and the hiss of soda cans opening. Gone were the dozens of eyes watching our every move with cell-phone cameras at the ready.

The only thing that existed at that moment, that perfect moment, was Kiersten, eyes sparkling, head thrown back laughing, her nether regions pressed hard against mine. I managed not to step on her feet as we moved across the floor.

"When she finds out, she will have a conniption fit."

God damn, she was cute with her funny little sayings and infectious laugh. And she was hot in that dress with her hair around her shoulders, her body pressed against mine.

"I'll take that bet," I said.

"What?"

"I said I'll take that bet,"

"That's a guaranteed loser, Tobin." My heart skipped a few beats. It was the first time she'd addressed me by my name tonight, and it was an awesome sound.

"I'll bet you that your mother will not find out you took me to your class reunion."

Kiersten looked at me as if I were crazy. Who knows, maybe I was.

"Okay," she said hesitantly. "What are you betting?"

"A kiss."

"A kiss?"

"Yes, a kiss. If I win, you kiss me my way. If you win, you kiss me your way." I had no idea where that come from. My crotch started throbbing double-time when Kiersten's eyes dropped to my lips. She subconsciously licked hers. I stifled a groan.

"Where and when I want," I said. Might as well go for broke.

I watched as her breasts moved up and down faster as her breathing quickened. I felt her nipples pebble under her thin dress. This conversation had definitely shifted in my favor, and my instincts kicked in. I pulled her close, our bodies touching. I slid a leg between hers and moved seductively across the dance floor. I felt her body respond, and the throb in my crotch increased.

The sound of applause around us broke me out of my trance. Kiersten must have realized the music had stopped. She dropped her arms from around me and started to walk toward our table. I grabbed her hand and stopped her.

Well?" I asked, my voice much calmer than my pounding clit.

"All right," she said, her voice husky. "For how long?"

"How long do you have to kiss me?" I asked stupidly, but I was rewarded when she looked at my lips again.

"Ugh…No, how long before my mother knows?"

"Twenty-four hours." No clue where that number came from.

Kiersten concentrated and seemed to be calculating something in her head.

"You can't tell her."

"I won't," I said quickly, the mood shifting back to playful.

"And no one in your entourage can."

"I don't have an entourage. I have a crew, but she won't hear it from them."

"So how do we judge this?" she asked skeptically.

"I trust you." I gave her my best bad-girl look.

"Deal. Now take me home. It's late and my feet are killing me."

❖

What in the fuck was I thinking, taking her up on her silly bet? I wasn't thinking, that's what. Every time Tobin touched me or even looked at me, my Phi Beta Kappa brain turned into Phi Beta mush.

We were quiet on the ride back to my place. I had no idea what Tobin was thinking about, but I was calculating the flight time from Paris to Chicago. My parents were flying back from their annual trip tomorrow. Paris was seven hours ahead of us, and since it was almost midnight my mother wouldn't even be out of bed yet. After her standard dry toast and coffee, she'd be too busy trying to stuff all her shopping purchases into the spare suitcase she always took with her to Europe. Then they'd have to check in, the flight was almost nine hours long, then customs, a cab to their apartment, unpacking… They would just pass the twenty-four-hour mark before they had a chance to talk with anyone.

I'd have thought I would have felt smug when we walked in the door and everybody recognized Tobin. Or maybe when they realized how different I looked, or how successful I was, or that Tobin was my date for the evening. But I'd been too nervous to soak it all in. Now, away from the nosy eyes of people I hadn't seen in twenty years, the reality of the evening hit me. Little ole frumpy, dorky Kiersten Fellows had Tobin Parks as her date. What a coup, and I was the one everybody looked at in awe and envy instead of pity and disgust. So why was the idea of kissing Tobin more thrilling than that?

"I'll walk you up," Tobin said once the car stopped in front of my house.

"No need. I'll be fine," I said, more out of habit than anything else.

"Too bad." Tobin took my hand as she pulled me across the smooth leather seat toward the door. "If nothing else, I'm polite."

"You have excellent manners, and you're great with small talk. I hate trying to figure out what to say to people." I knew I was rambling, but all I could think about was if Tobin was going to kiss me good night. What would I do if she did? Let her? Turn my head at the last minute? I'd probably do something as mortifying as stick out my hand for a chaste handshake.

The accent lighting on the front walk grew brighter as we neared the front door. I stepped up on the porch and turned around. "Thank you," I said, facing her and fiddling with my keys. "I didn't think I'd have a good time, but I did."

"I did too." Tobin took my keys from my hand, unlocked the door, and stayed very close to me.

"Are you going to invite me in?" she asked just before kissing me on my cheek. Her breath was warm, and her lips on my skin were doing crazy things to my insides.

"I don't think that's a good idea," I somehow managed to get out.

"But we're not doing any business together."

Is this the time I tell Tobin I've never been with a woman? That other than a few clumsy gropings in a dark closet or at my front door I've never felt a woman's hands on me? That I've never had the thrill of hearing my name come from a woman's lips, my touch driving her wild with abandon, my fingers buried deep inside her? And how exactly would I make that confession? The longer I'm a virgin, the more difficult it is to admit. I'm a freak. No one is a virgin at thirty-six. She wouldn't believe me even if I was able to get the words past the lump in my throat and out of my mouth. My mouth that has never kissed the crook of an arm, nibbled on a neck, or traveled over hot, smooth skin. My tongue that has never licked sweat from the small of a smooth back, the inside of a leg, or flicked over a hard nipple. Lips that have never touched warm, wet heat, tasted want, driven a woman to the summit and held her there as she peaked.

And just how do I tell her? Do I tell her? I've faked and bullshitted my way through a lot of things in my life; this could just be one more. The humiliation I would feel if she turned me down or, God forbid, laughed at me would be unbearable. No way could I compare to the dozens, if not hundreds of women she'd been with.

I managed to step back just enough to break contact. My skin immediately cooled where her lips had been. "Good night."

Chapter Twenty-four

When I locked the front door, I noticed my hands were shaking. I had been a ball of nerves all week in anticipation of this evening. What was I going to wear? Who would I see? Would anyone recognize me? Want to talk to me? Be amazed at who I am today? Would Tobin like what I was wearing? Would she think I was pretty? Would she want to kiss me or kiss me good night? Would she dump me at the curb when she saw what I looked like twenty years ago? Why did she even ask me in the first place? Was this a pity date, something she could write in her biography or get press about? Was it a tax deduction, donating her time to a charitable cause? Based on her reported earnings, that would be a hell of a deduction even the IRS would question.

No wonder I was a basket case. I hadn't been able to concentrate, and my stomach had been in knots so that other than a few protein shakes, eating was out of the question.

Now that the reunion was over, I was crashing. The adrenaline rush of anticipation of the evening itself was over, my body was giving in to exhaustion. I knew I couldn't sleep so I dragged myself outside and tossed the ball to Rockette for a while, but not before grabbing a bottle of wine and a glass to take with me. The night was cool, the sky clear and full of bright, twinkling stars. The full moon reflected the pond behind my house.

I had bought the four acres as undeveloped land eight years ago. At the time it was seven miles from the nearest Quickie Mart and thirteen miles from the interstate. Now, a Dairy Queen, McDonald's, and Walmart were between me and I-79, along with a Home Depot and three Starbucks. Progress and capitalism at its finest.

I planted my own flowers, trimmed the trees that lined my driveway, and laid my back patio. Every Saturday morning from May through October, if I wasn't traveling I mowed my lawn from the seat of my John Deere Z540R Zero-Turn-Radius 60-inch deck mower, enjoying the fresh air. The only thing I didn't do was plow my driveway in the winter. I hired a service to do that since the distance from the street to my garage was over eighty yards

The smell of fresh-cut grass was still in the air even now, almost twelve hours later. I sat down on one of the lounge chairs, then kicked off my shoes, put my feet up, and laid my head back. Rockette's cold, wet nose nudged my hand.

"That's all for tonight, girl. I'm exhausted. I'm just going to unwind and go to bed." And try not to dream about the feeling of being in Tobin's arms. Or the scent of her cologne. Or the shape of her mouth. My eyelids drifted shut.

Tobin's lips were as soft as I remembered them to be. I'm certainly no expert when it comes to kissing, but if I had to judge, I'd say she had mastered it. The first kiss earlier in the evening was for show, but this one was for real.

She took her time exploring my lips, nipping and gently sucking on my bottom lip. Her kiss wasn't sloppy or messy. She didn't demand to be let in so I could have the pleasure of gagging on her tongue, like some others did. She just kept kissing me like she had all the time in the world. I opened my mouth first, needing more of her. Needing her to possess me, to possess her.

Tobin's hand ran up and down my back as our tongues alternatively dueled, then explored each other. My hands were in her hair, holding her close, urging her on the only way I knew how.

Her hands moved to my sides, then up to just below my breasts. She stopped there as if asking permission to go farther. How in the hell could she think at a time like this? It was all my brain could do to tell my legs not to buckle.

Her lips moved across my neck, and her warm breath caressed it. I still had my hands in her hair but let her go whenever she wanted. She must have read my mind or my body language because her hands slid up and cupped my breasts. I didn't even try to stifle a gasp of pleasure.

Tobin's lips came back to mine as she slowly moved my zipper, exposing my back to the cool air. When it was all the way down, her warm hands replaced the fabric, my skin heating under her touch.

"Your skin is so soft," she whispered against my lips.

I got busy pulling her jacket off her shoulders and letting it drop to the floor. She was rich. If it was ruined she could afford to buy a new one, or ten. Eager to touch her skin, I pulled at her shirt until it came free of her waistband, slid my hands under it, and touched her.

God, she felt good. Her skin was warm, and my fingers traced over solid, well-defined muscles. Tobin squirmed when I lightly ran my hand up and down her sides.

"I'm ticklish," she said, her lips on mine. I filed that fact away for future reference.

Tobin slid her hands up my back and across my shoulders, pulling my dress down my arms. It fell in a pile around my feet, and even though it was new and cost a small fortune, I didn't care.

"Beautiful," Tobin said, looking at me. I fought the urge to cover myself, more out of habit than shyness. The look on her face and in her eyes made those hundreds of hours at the gym, the thousands of miles of running, and the god-awful special meal plan all worthwhile. I knew she desired me, and that scared the hell out of me.

Was this the time to say, "Hey Tobin, want to hear something really bizarre? I bet you've never met a thirty-six-year-old virgin before." Or was "I've never done this before" more appropriate? Maybe I should just keep my mouth shut and pretend I knew what I was doing? Shouldn't be too hard. I have a bookcase full of lesbian romance books, one shelf full of erotica, and I've watched my share of porn. I knew what goes where. It's just I've never gone there and didn't know if I had the nerve to try. My body might not embarrass me so much anymore, but my actions would. I stopped thinking so much when Tobin ran her finger down my neck, across my collarbones, and down between by bare breasts.

My dress had a sewn-in bra so her travel was free of any unwanted clothing. When Tobin's eyes shifted to my breasts, my knees almost gave way.

She cupped my breasts, her thumb lightly tracing my erect nipple. Pleasure threatened to topple me, and I grabbed her shoulders to keep from falling.

"God, you are beautiful," she said before repeating the same maneuver on my other breast, that nipple screaming for attention. When her tongue flicked over the other nipple, I felt myself falling.

Tobin gathered me in her arms and laid me on the patio chair. She wrapped one arm around me and slid her thigh between mine while her mouth did delicious things to my breasts.

The pressure between my legs was building, and with every flick of her tongue across a nipple, I moved my hands against her.

OMG, if we kept this up I was going to come. Was that a bad thing? Wasn't that what I wanted? Then I wouldn't have to tell her anything. Sounded like a plan. Except when she lifted her head and said, "Can we take this somewhere else? Somewhere a little more comfortable?"

This was it. This was the time I needed to open my mouth and tell her. She had a right to know. Didn't she?

"Kiersten?" Tobin asked, concern replacing some of the desire in her voice. "You okay? This okay?"

It was sweet of her to ask. My body cooled when Tobin stepped back. I needed to say something, anything. The seconds ticked by, and I knew the next one she would step farther away and out the door. Is that what I wanted?

This was not a good idea. Mixing business with pleasure was a no-no in my book, even if I never had that chapter in school. But we weren't conducting any business together so it would be okay if we got down to business.

"Look, if you don't..." Tobin started to say, but I grabbed her hand and pulled her down the hall behind me.

Something wet on my hand jolted me out of my dream. It took several moments for me to realize where I was and that Rockette was sitting beside me, a guilty look on her face. My heart was pounding, as were other parts of my body, and my hands were shaking. The dream had seemed so real, and judging by my current state of arousal, my body thought so too. I gathered up my wine and my dog and went to bed.

Chapter Twenty-five

"You didn't invite her in?" Courtney asked, wiping the beer that had just spewed out of her mouth. It was the next day, and the after-church crowd hadn't yet swarmed liked bees for lunch at the Burger Barn. I had just told her how I had chickened out from dragging Tobin into my house and ravishing her in my foyer.

"Why not?"

I could barely get the words out. How do you tell your best friend that you've been lying to her for years? And why was I telling her now? I hoped she didn't hate me and jumped right in. "I've never done it before." I wasn't sure I said it loud enough for her to hear.

"Done what?" Courtney asked.

Damn. Why couldn't she read my mind? "I haven't…been with…I never…" I couldn't get the words out. I watched Courtney's expression change from confused to understanding to shock.

"You've never…?"

"Yes, Courtney. I've never," I finally said. "Don't make me repeat it." I was embarrassed enough that I was a thirty-six-year-old virgin without having to repeat it out loud again.

"I'm sorry, Kiersten. It's just that you caught me off guard. I never expected you to say that."

I hadn't planned on it either when Courtney had agreed to meet me tonight. She wanted to know every detail about my date with Tobin at the reunion.

"Wow, K. I don't know whether I should be in shock, in awe, or pissed off at you for not telling me sooner."

I wasn't sure which was winning either. "I'm sorry. I should have said something in the beginning, but you just assumed, and out of embarrassment I played along. Then it just got more and more awkward, and I guess it got to the point that I couldn't come clean. I was upset that I lied to you, even if it was a lie of omission."

"So how have you…you've never…I mean, you're gorgeous… and rich and…"

"I used to be fat," I blurted out. My timing was better this time because Courtney didn't have a mouth full of Corona. "I used to be fat, really fat," I said, emphasizing the word. "I was teased in school, called names, picked last for teams, the typical elementary-school behavior. High school was worse. I never had a boyfriend and started liking girls, which compounded everything. No self-esteem, no confidence, zero, zilch, nada," I added, just in case she didn't get it the first or second time. "January first of my senior year in college I went on a crash diet, went to the gym every day, and started running. Six months and over a hundred pounds later you saved my life in that shitty bar the first week of grad school." The entire time I was talking, I kept glancing around the room. Occasionally I was able to look at Courtney and found her watching me with intense concentration.

"The more time that passed, and the older I got, the more embarrassed I was. I've had a few fumbles, which usually ended up being humiliating experiences."

"Are you waiting to fall in love and get married?"

"What? No. It's not like that. I have no desire to get married. And end up like my parents? No, thank you."

"Then what are you waiting for? You date, meet a lot of women…"

As if it were that easy. "So when am I supposed to tell them I'm a virgin? On the first date, maybe the second or third? Never? Do I just go with it and not let them know at all? Don't you think they'll figure it out real quick?" These were the same questions I'd asked myself dozens and dozens of times over the years, especially after I met someone I was interested in.

"I see your point." Courtney nodded. "So what are you going to do?"

"Beats the hell out of me," I answered honestly. We were quiet for a few minutes.

"Have you thought of…maybe…using a…service?" she asked hesitantly.

"A what?" Was she suggesting I go to a prostitute?

"A service, you know. Where you don't have to ever see the woman again so you have no need to be embarrassed. Better yet, she can show you what to do." By the look on Courtney's face she thought it was a plausible idea.

"I wouldn't know the first place to look. It's not like I can Google it, and I'm pretty sure that regardless of the reason, it's still illegal."

"I can ask around," Courtney eagerly volunteered.

"No," I said quickly.

"No, really, K. Rachel will know who to call."

"I don't even want to know how Rachel would know," I said, picturing the short, stocky, fifty-year-old Target store manager.

"But I could help—"

"I don't need any help, thank you. And certainly not the type that could land me on the next episode of *Cops.* No," I said again when she started to say something else.

"Did you tell Tobin?"

"Are you crazy? If I hadn't told you, I'm certainly not going to tell anyone else—especially someone like Tobin."

"What do you mean, someone like Tobin."

"Come on, Courtney. You know her reputation. A girl in every city. She'd laugh so hard she'd pee her pants."

"But you wanted to sleep with her."

"Yes." There. I finally admitted I wanted to have sex with Tobin Parks. I'd thought about nothing but having sex with her. I'd stopped thinking about everybody else having sex, Tobin having my full attention. "So what do I do?" I finally asked.

"I have no fucking clue," she answered, deadly serious.

"What good are you then? You aren't holding up your end of the BFF contract." Now that some of the tension was released, I started to relax.

"And what part is that?"

"The part that gives me sound, sage advice on what to do."

"And if I did, what would I say?" She leaned back in the booth as if settling in for long words of wisdom.

"I have no fucking clue," I said. I barely got the words out before we were both laughing hysterically, tears streaming down our cheeks.

Chapter Twenty-six

Am I interrupting?"

The last thing I needed first thing this Monday morning was Tobin standing in my office doorway. I didn't win the bet with Tobin, and I'd heard an earful from my mother, who obviously pulled out the sibling reinforcements. Harrison and Marcus bent my ear, and my sister Meredith had regaled me with a list of STDs that I could catch by *dating* Tobin. She repeatedly emphasized, along with a graphic description, those that would not go away with a shot of penicillin. I told my mother to mind her own business, my brothers to mind their own goddamn business, and reminded my sister I was a grown-ass adult, not one of her fifteen-year-old patients.

"If I said yes, would you leave?" I asked Tobin, looking over the top of my reading glasses to see her standing in my doorway.

"No. I was just being polite."

"Then why bother to even ask?" My question was rhetorical, and I made a note to myself to make sure that if Bea ever left her desk, someone else was covering it. Like the times before, Tobin filled the room with her presence as she stepped through the open doorway, exuding an aura of something that made the room come alive. "What are you doing here? Don't you need to be on a bus going someplace?"

"I came to collect," she stated, coming into my office and closing the door behind her.

"How do you know you won?" I asked, bluffing. "Maybe I won."

"Either way it's good for me," Tobin said, hooking one leg across the edge of my desk and sitting half on, half off.

Her thigh was within touching distance, and I flushed remembering how it had felt pressed against me on the dance floor—and how I'd ridden it to orgasm in my dream.

"Well?" she asked when I wasn't forthcoming about the results.

I'd thought about lying, but other than doing so about my virginity, I wasn't a good liar and somehow she'd know.

"Three hours and seventeen minutes," I said, remembering the phone call at 4:10 yesterday morning. I hadn't even had a chance to say hello when my mother started.

"Kiersten, have you no self-respect? Have your father or I not taught you anything about appearances? About how something that looks innocent can haunt you for a lifetime? Did you not think of that? Did you not think of your family? Harrison is on Wall Street and Marcus is a senior partner in the firm. And Meredith's husband is a doctor," she added, as if that was the next best thing to God. Thank God, Maxwell is out of the country," she said with disgust.

"For God's sake, Mother. It's four o'clock in the morning," I choked out, not that she would care. Her job as a mother, purveyor of all things appropriate, was a twenty-four-seven job. One that she took very seriously.

"I don't care what time it is, young lady. You have some explaining to do."

I knew I was in trouble when the "young lady" came out. Thankfully it had been years since I'd heard it. I turned on the light beside my bed and squinted until my eyes adjusted. I sat up and tossed a pillow behind my back against the headboard. What I needed was a strong cup of hot coffee, but that would have to wait. I was talking to my mother, after all. No, actually she was lecturing me.

"Good morning, Mother. How was your trip?" That response was guaranteed to make her go even more nuts than she was. I wasn't disappointed.

"This isn't a social call, Kiersten." Her voice was almost shrill. "Imagine my shock when Brittney called to tell me you had

gone to your high school reunion with that...woman. Your reunion, for heaven's sake. Where everyone would see you!"

Why did it not surprise me that Brittney would be the one to spread the news like the bubonic plague? "That's what reunions are, Mother, a party where you go and see everyone you haven't seen in years—"

"And you go with her? That is how you wanted people to see you? On her *arm?" My mother sure did know how to accentuate her point.*

"Mother, it's the middle of the night. Can we talk about this in the morning, like ten?"

"We will talk about it now." Her words were clipped, and again, I felt like I was twelve.

"There's nothing to talk about, Mother. Yes, Tobin went with me to my reunion last night. We ate rubber chicken and mushy green beans, talked to a few people, and had a good time. That's it. No big deal. Nothing to talk about."

"You two were practically having sex on the dance floor."

That remark caught me off guard. "And Brittney would know that how?" I asked, not waiting for an answer. "There was nothing inappropriate about the evening, and that includes our time on the dance floor."

"You danced with a woman, that woman, in public!" My mother practically gasped the last few words.

"It's not the first time I've danced with a woman in public." Not that she needed to know it was in a dark, smoky bar and lots of alcohol was involved.

"How can you say that? Everyone knows us, and you own a respectable business. She is infamous for her...her..."

My mother was so angry she couldn't find the words to describe her complete disrespect for Tobin. "For her dozen-plus top-ten songs? Her sold-out concerts in every city around the world? The fact that she's met the US President, The Queen of England and her grandson William, and the Chancellor of Germany? Is that what you're referring to, Mother?" I was intentionally antagonizing her, but I refused to let her degrade Tobin.

"Kiersten—"

"We've had this discussion about Tobin, Mother. I am a grown woman, I am aware of the world around me, and I can and do make my own decisions. Now, I was out late last night and I'm tired. Good night, Mother."

"That bad, huh?" Tobin asked, as if reading my mind. "Do you want me to do something? I can talk to her—"

"No! Don't do anything. You'll just draw more attention to it." I thought about the line spoken by Queen Gertrude in *Hamlet*: "The lady doth protest too much…" or something like that.

"I have to do something," Tobin said. "It was a stupid idea."

I took several deep breaths. I had to pull it together. I was a master at façade. "No, please don't do anything," I said a little more calmly. "Just leave it alone. Tonight when you're seen with a new hot young thing, it'll blow over."

I heard Tobin take in a breath.

"I didn't mean that the way it sounded, but you have to admit you will."

"Are you calling me a player?" Tobin's tone was much cooler than before.

"Or whatever it's called, I don't know," I said, frustrated. "You have a different girl on your arm every night."

"And that makes me a player?"

"What would you call it?" I expected her to say something like lucky or some other sexually charged euphemism.

"Again, goes with the territory."

"Did you just say that?" I asked incredulously. "Are you that shallow? Or entitled?" I'd thought Tobin was an okay girl, but this change in attitude had my opinion changing right along with it.

"No, look, I'm sorry," Tobin said, exasperation in her voice. "That's not what I think, and it's certainly not who I am."

"Hard to imagine that," I added, rolling my eyes.

"Look," Tobin said forcefully. "That is not me. That's image, something the media consultants drummed up years ago."

"So you prostitute yourself for fame?" That was a bit harsh, but sometimes the truth hurts, and right now my head was killing me.

"No! Would you stop putting words in my mouth and just shut up for a minute so I can explain."

"Did you just tell me to shut up?"

"Yes, and if you don't, I'm going to say it again."

"And this is coming from the woman who wants JOLT, i.e. me, the one you just told to shut up, to sponsor your next tour?"

"What difference does it make? You've already said no."

My mouth snapped shut at that retort, and I hoped the sound wasn't loud enough for Tobin to hear.

"Look," Tobin said, her voice quieter. "Somehow this conversation got off track. I came over here because I—"

"What? Wanted to gloat?"

"Do you hate me that much?"

Her question caught me off guard. "I don't hate you. Whatever gave you that idea?"

"Well, at the risk of flinging more mud, you called me a player, then jumped right into accusing me of being a whore."

I grimaced because that's exactly what I did. I wasn't like this. I didn't judge people like that. But I had, and I realized how much it could hurt.

"I'm sorry. I don't know you well enough to even begin to say what kind of person you are."

"Then come with me."

"I beg your pardon?" Surely she couldn't mean what I thought she meant. Even in the middle of an ugly argument, my mind heads toward sex.

"On tour. Come with me for the rest of this tour."

"What?" What in the hell was she talking about?

"Come with me for the rest of this tour," she repeated a little slower, like that was all it would take for me to understand. "You're right, you don't know me. This would be the perfect opportunity for you to see for yourself how I live."

"And watch you have sex with Barbie and Skipper?" *God, Kiersten, enough with the sex stuff.*

"Who?"

"Never mind," I said, forgetting for a minute Tobin was way younger than me. "I can't do that."

"Why not?"

"Why not?" Was she really that clueless? "I run a multi-million-dollar company." There, that should clear things up.

"So."

Obviously I wasn't clear enough. "So? You have no idea what that entails," I said, looking around at the papers and folders on my desk, not to mention the unread emails that had come in during this ridiculous conversation.

"What? Meetings? Phone calls?" Tobin replied, as if it were that simple. "There's a thing called technology, Kiersten. You can do that stuff anywhere."

"It's not that simple," I argued ineffectively.

"Sure, it is. You do your thing during the day while I'm usually sleeping or we're driving from one show to the other. You can work in my coach."

"What?"

"You can work in my coach," she repeated, as if I hadn't heard her clearly. I had, but it wasn't making sense.

"We're rarely anywhere where we can't get some kind of signal. You can Skype or use Go To Assist or Web-X or whatever JOLT uses for remote meetings and conference calls."

If it were only that simple.

"Look, Kiersten. You don't believe me when I say I'm not my image, and I'm willing to prove it to you. No one comes into my coach, never has—*ever*. You can ask anyone on my crew. They won't lie to you. If I'm willing to let you move in for a month, then you'd better believe I'm serious. I'm willing to put my money where my mouth is, so to speak. Are you?"

"You can't be serious?" I asked, pretty sure I already knew the answer to the question. My mind was whirling with details, logistics, images, and flashbacks of my dreams.

"Dead serious. What are you risking, Kiersten?"

"What do you mean?"

"What are you risking?" she asked again. "Some inconvenience? I'm risking much more than that. I'm risking my reputation, not to mention my sanity being cooped up in a seventy-eight-foot coach for a month with you."

"The answer is still no."

"But—"

"But nothing, Tobin. You might not be used to people telling you no, but I did, and I haven't changed my mind."

"People tell me no all the time," she said impishly.

"Oh, please," I said, rolling my eyes. "Why do I find that difficult to believe?"

"I don't know, Kiersten. Why do you?"

"Because you're young, famous, rich, and sexy. No one says no to that."

"You think I'm sexy?"

God, did I ever, but I wasn't going to tell her that. "I read the papers. I've been to one of your concerts, seen your adoring fans falling all over themselves to get your attention."

"When?"

"When what?"

"When did you go to one of my shows?"

Shit, did I actually say that? "A few months ago. A friend of mine dragged me."

"What did you think?"

That you were hot, had a bedroom voice, and I couldn't take my eyes off you. "Don't change the subject," I said emphatically.

"All right, but give me one good reason why you can't come with me."

I named eight, and when she left I was even more exhausted and keyed up than when she walked in.

Chapter Twenty-seven

"So are you going to do it?" Courtney and I were sharing appetizers and half-price beers at Kline's, a pub not too far from her house. We were finishing our first basket of wings and our second beer.

"No." I should have said, "No way in hell am I going to spend four weeks in a motor home traveling all over the country with Tobin Parks."

"You need to loosen up, K. Don't look at me like that," she said. "You know you're wound pretty tight. When was the last time you did something just for the fun of it? And I don't mean mowing your forty acres," she added.

"It's not forty. It's four. And I happen to like mowing and puttering around the house. It's my relaxation."

"Fine. When was the last time you went out? And I don't mean with me," she said before I had a chance to.

"I went to Michelle's party," I said confidently.

"That was months ago." Courtney seemed exasperated. "Kiersten, all you do is work and, what did you call it, putter around the house."

"What's wrong with that? You do your thing for relaxation and what you enjoy in life, and I can't do the same?"

"Not when it's not good for you," Courtney stated.

I waited for the bartender to set down our beers and an order of fries before I asked, "And why is doing what I want to do and what makes me happy not good for me?"

"Are you? Happy, I mean?"

"Why do you keep asking me that?" I was starting to get a little perturbed.

"Because I'm not sure you are." She held her hand up to stop me from commenting. "Let me finish," she said. "I've watched you over the years, K, and you don't light up anymore. I mean, you do when you talk about JOLT and what's going on there, but when it comes to anything else, you're…well…flat."

"Flat?" *What the fuck is "flat"?*

"You go through the motions. Even when you come over and spend time with me and the kids, you're not the same. You're missing a big part of life, and I think it's finally catching up to you."

I didn't like where this was going, but I let her continue.

"Ms. Right is not going to knock on your front door unless it's the UPS lady, and you're never home. Bea doesn't let anyone into your office without an appointment made three weeks earlier."

I thought of the times Tobin had simply walked into my office.

"Kiersten, honey, I love you, and because I love you I'm telling you that you need to get out. Your life is too one-dimensional. And it certainly doesn't help with your other 'situation,'" she said, making air quotes.

I knew everything Courtney was telling me, but I just didn't want to think about it. Avoidance is sometimes a good thing, especially in this case. I wasn't a risk taker, at least in my personal life. I had learned painfully hard lessons when I stepped out and bared it all. I was laughed at, ridiculed, and bullied due to my size. The old saying about sticks and stones breaking your bones but words never hurting you is complete bullshit. No one ever laid a hand on me, but I was tormented and beaten all the same. I was always braced for rejection. I still was.

I'd learned to plan everything, from the time I got to school to avoid the crowds to the routes I took home. I thought things through and anticipated every contingency so it would lessen the chance I'd hear a giggle or a whispered comment. I was lonely but never made it appear that way. I convinced everyone, including myself, that I preferred to be alone. I rarely received an invitation to a birthday or slumber party, and never to swim at someone's house on a hot Saturday afternoon. I'd shrugged it off as nothing. I didn't care. I'd insulated myself from the pain of rejection, my emotional armor firmly in place.

After I lost all the weight I still maintained my distance. I didn't get close to anyone and didn't let them get close to me. The exception of course was sitting across from me in a smartly tailored Vera Wang suit with ketchup on her cheek. At times I loved Courtney and other times I hated her. She made me think and pushed me out of my comfort zone. However, she was not going to push me over the line on this one.

"What are you thinking?" Courtney asked.

"That I hate you." I tossed a French fry at her, which seemed to ease the tension at our table.

"JOLT is fine. I should know, I'm your accountant. You have a talented, competent staff. Let them do what they do best. Let them show you what they can do. Give them a chance to stretch their wings. You need to get away, you deserve it. Don't tell anyone where you're going. Just leave a number if they need to reach you. And make sure they know not to use it unless it's an absolute emergency. Better yet," she said, snapping her fingers and leaning forward on her stool, "give them my number. I'll screen the issue and call if I need you. And my God, K," she said seriously, "do not tell your mother."

Chapter Twenty-eight

I didn't know if I was supposed to knock or just walk in, so I took the safe route and chose the former. What in the fuck was I doing here? I had to be out of my mind to have even considered this invitation, let alone made arrangements to actually make it happen. I contemplated turning around and getting my ass out of here before it was too late, but when the door swung open I knew it was too late.

"Hey," Tobin said, greeting me with a smile that could stop traffic—or my heart. "I didn't think you'd actually come."

"Really?" I asked because it seemed the right thing to say. What else would I say? If you'd been one second longer answering the door I wouldn't be. Instead I remarked, "If I say I'm going to do something, I do. I keep my word." I tried not to sound too stuffy and righteous.

"And I for one am glad you do." She stepped back a step. "Come in."

I climbed the three steps into the coach and stopped just inside. "Oh my God, Tobin. This is beautiful." I'd been inside motor homes before, but not a custom coach for someone like her. I thought the outside was gorgeous with its custom-painted graphics that gleamed under the lights, power awnings, and stainless-steel trim, but the inside was spectacular.

To my right was a door separating the driver from the rest of the coach, with privacy shades over the front windshield. The dash panel was leather, illuminated in subtle blue lights with several screens containing images that I recognized as the exterior rear and both sides of the coach. To my left was the main room, with two plush chairs, a small table with a lamp between them, and a sofa with throw pillows and a lap blanket, making the area feel warm and cozy. A guitar leaned against the wall, papers and a book neatly stacked on a narrow table in front of the couch. The windows were covered with shades with a subtle accent and aisle lighting throughout the interior. Farther to the back was the kitchen area with a sink, stainless-steel refrigerator, granite countertop and tile backsplashes, a two-burner cooktop, dishwasher, and a small oven.

"Do you cook?" That was the only thing I could think of to say.

"No, not really, but I make a mean cup of coffee and can whip up a snack if I have to. Come in. Make yourself comfortable," Tobin said, stepping farther into the coach. "Can I get you anything?"

Was she as nervous as I was? "No, thanks. I'm fine for now." I looked around.

"Okay, then let me give you the grand tour. I'm kind of a tech geek, so bear with me," she said with a sheepish smile. My stomach dropped, reminding me of what a bad idea this was.

"She's nine feet wide and seventy-five feet long, has a Volvo D13 five-hundred horsepower engine, and stainless-steel chassis. She has four slide outs with roof-mounted power awnings, stainless-steel trim, and an auto leveling system. It has a color backup camera, side-mounted cameras, and docking lights. The main room here—it's called the salon, but I just call it the living room—has an XM/AM/FM/CD, Blu-Ray DVD, and satellite TV."

"Wow," I said, impressed. "Everything a girl could need."

"Wait, there's more. Through here," Tobin said, leading the way down a narrow hall, "is the bathroom. It has a hundred-and-eighty-eight-gallon fresh-water tank and one of those hot-water-on-demand units. I don't remember exactly what they're called," she admitted, "but I always have plenty of hot water."

"The bedroom is back here," she continued, taking a few more steps and opening a large six-paneled door. She hit the light switch, and soft lighting illuminated a queen-sized bed with lots of big, fluffy pillows. Thin nightstands flanked both sides of the bed, and a dresser lined one wall. I couldn't help but wonder how many women she'd had in this bed or if she got a new one at the start of every tour.

"Very nice," I said as we walked back into the living room. It appeared that she'd spared no expense on the design or furnishing of this home on six wheels. I saw only one problem: only one bed.

"Thanks, I like it," Tobin said, sounding more than a little proud.

"What's this?" I asked, picking up an old glass jar sitting prominently on a shelf. It had the word TIPS written in bold letters and taped to the side. Several crumpled dollar bills were inside.

"It's my first tip jar. It was on the edge of the stage at the first club I played at."

Understanding the significance, I counted the money inside. "Four dollars and seventy-five cents?"

"Yep." Tobin was watching me closely.

"How old were you?" I asked, remembering Tobin didn't answer that same question when she was interviewed on the morning show a few weeks ago.

"Fifteen."

"Fifteen? Were you even old enough to be in there?"

"No, but I clean up well," she said, making a joke out of what I thought of as a serious if not dangerous situation.

"And your parents agreed?" A flash of something angry and painful flashed across her face for an instant before she smiled and made another lighthearted answer.

"They didn't care," she said, her voice clipped before turning around and fiddling with something on another shelf.

"Well, you've come a long way, baby," I said teasingly, the tag line for the old Virginia Slims cigarettes coming to mind. My Aunt Georgia used to smoke them and regale me with stories of what she called women's liberation, explaining that the advertising campaign for the long, slim cigarette capitalized on the movement brilliantly. The look on Tobin's face reminded me yet again just how young she really was. I have jeans older than she is, I thought.

"Is something wrong?" Tobin asked.

"Where am I supposed to sleep?" I looked around. No way was I going to spend the next four weeks camped out on a hide-a-bed sofa.

"Oh, wow," Tobin said, looking somewhat embarrassed. "This is my coach. The one we'll be in is parked next door. It has two bedrooms."

I followed her out the door and into an equally impressive coach, and sure enough, there were two bedrooms, somewhat smaller than the one in Tobin's coach. I was both relieved and disappointed at the same time.

"You bought another one?"

"No, it's leased," she said matter-of-factly. "Just for this leg of the tour. This here," she opened a cabinet, "turns into a desk where you can work." She proceeded to show me the lights and plugs, and the hidden cubby holes to hold all my crap.

"Will this work for you?" she asked, almost sounding like a child eager to please. But then again…

"I guess I'll have to get used to it," I said, looking around the suddenly very small space.

"I can get something bigger."

"No," I said, meaning it. "This is fine. Actually it's very nice, though I've never traveled in something like this. Why do you call it a coach?"

"They're officially called motor coaches. No idea why, but I think it had something to do with stage coaches, then motorized coaches. We just call them coaches or, sometimes, rigs. Can I get you anything? I had the fridge stocked with water, Diet Coke, regular Coke, orange juice…"

"Water's fine, thanks." My throat had gone dry as reality sank in that I was actually going to spend the next four weeks in close proximity to Tobin Parks. Very close proximity.

We returned outside and walked around a few of the other coaches, and I introduced Kiersten to the members of my backup band. Russ, my drummer, was spread out on a lounge chair faceup, snoring softly.

"Hey Russ," I said, nudging his bare foot. He woke and shaded his eyes from the sun.

"Dude, this is Kiersten." Russ was the closest I had to a BFF, and he looked at Kiersten carefully. He, and the others members of the band and road crew, knew Kiersten would be traveling with us, but he gave her the once-over nonetheless.

"It's a pleasure to meet you, Russ," Kiersten said, extending her hand. She didn't seem to be disturbed or put off by Russ's frank appraisal.

Russ stood and shook her hand. "Likewise," he said, his Irish brogue evident even in only one word.

Kiersten tilted her head and frowned in concentration. "Scotland?"

"Most people say Ireland," Russ replied.

"Aberdeen?"

Russ raised both eyebrows appreciatively. "As a matter of fact, yes," he said, obviously impressed.

"Ever been?" His accent was strong.

"I spent a summer there when I was sixteen. Beautiful place and wonderful people." She smiled as if reliving a fond memory.

"Ever go to the Moon Fish Cafe?" Russ asked. This was more words than I'd ever heard him say to someone he'd just met.

"Yes. Best Yorkshire pudding I've ever had."

"That's my folks' place." He beamed proudly.

"Get out," Kiersten said. "Really?"

When Russ nodded, she said, "My God, it was fabulous. And the beer…" She waved her hand in front of her face, fanning herself. "Let's just say the last pint was as delicious as the six previous ones."

Russ whistled, impressed. So was I.

"I was young and dumb and stupid and on a dare," Kiersten replied. "But they certainly didn't taste as good coming out the same way they'd gone in." She made a sour face.

Russ laughed. Obviously Kiersten met with his approval, and I suddenly felt jealous for no apparent reason. Russ was my best bud and Kiersten was definitely a lesbian, so what was the problem?

"If you two are done with your trip around the world, we need to get going."

"You stop by anytime, Kiersten," Russ said. "Last time I was home, my mum sent me back with a few pints. I'd be happy to share with you. No need to be a roadie with the likes of that one," Russ said, pointing to me. "Jones and I have a lot more fun in our rig." Jones, standing behind Kiersten, readily concurred.

"I just might do that," Kiersten said. "Don't want to wear out my welcome." She cocked her thumb and pointed it at me.

"Nice guys," Kiersten commented as we walked toward the master trailer.

"We've been together a long time. They're harmless," I said, tossing my head in the direction we'd just left. "They meant what they said about roading with them. They don't ask just anyone to do that. They may look big and bad and scary, but both of them are sweethearts. You don't have anything to be afraid of with them except that they'll talk your ear off. Or beat you in gin rummy."

"I'll remember that." Kiersten chuckled.

Chapter Twenty-nine

So how do we do this?" I asked as Frank, Tobin's driver, pulled out of the parking lot a few hours later.

"We just sit back and enjoy the ride. We stop every few hours, more if we want."

"What do you do with all the free time?" The thought of nothing to do was terrifying, but I certainly didn't want Tobin to know that.

"Sleep, read, write."

"What do you write?"

"Songs."

"I didn't know that."

"There's a lot you don't know about me."

I was sure she was referencing the gossip that I did know. "I guess I'll have the chance to find out, won't I?"

"Anything you want," Tobin said, stretching out on the couch, her shoes off, feet on the cushion.

"Tell me about your family."

Something unpleasant crossed her face before she hid it. "I'd rather not."

Obviously still a sore spot. "What about your friends? Tell me about the people you picked." I watched as Tobin decided whether to tell me. I could see her weighing the pros and cons and the instant she decided.

"There's this guy, Mr. Justin, he says he's a retired CIA agent. But I think he's just full of bullshit. We have coffee together when

I'm in the neighborhood, watch any sport on his ginormous TV, and drink beer."

I noticed how her face lit up talking about the old man. Far different than when I asked about her family.

"Then there's Mrs. Foster. I think all she ever did was cook and clean because that's all I've ever seen her do. She has a boatload of grandkids, and her place is stuffed with pictures of all of them."

"How do you know them?"

"We met when I moved in next to Mr. Justin and across the street from Mrs. Foster."

"Where?"

"Hidden Acres Mobile Home Park."

"Hidden Acres? It sounds like a cemetery."

My heart skipped when Tobin laughed. "Almost. It's a senior-citizen park."

"You're forty years away from being a senior citizen."

"We have an understanding."

"An understanding?" I asked, curious.

"They take care of my little yard and my flowers while I'm gone, and I check up on them and make sure they have what they need."

"You have a yard?" I asked, more than a little surprised.

"You find that hard to believe?"

"Actually yes," I admitted sheepishly. "I guess I expected you to have some huge estate with eighteen bedrooms, twenty-two bathrooms, and an indoor pool. Either that or a penthouse apartment overlooking Central Park."

"Not hardly. I like my privacy."

That also surprised me. Tobin was so out there I expected that to continue into her personal life as well. I wanted to know more about this side of her. "How often do you see them?"

"When I'm not on tour. If we're close or I have a few days off, I try to swing by for a few days."

"I've never read anything about that," I said, giving away the fact that I've read everything available about her.

"That's because nobody knows. They wouldn't tell anyone," she said, her affection for the elderly couple evident. "And now you have to pinkie swear not to tell."

"Pinkie swear?"

"Yeah, you know." She sat up and scooted down the couch closer to me. She held out her right hand, pinkie bent. "We join pinkies," she said, taking my right hand and interlocking our fingers. "There. We're now bound for life sharing the secret."

My heart raced, and all of a sudden it was hard to breathe. The twinkle of humor in her eyes was replaced with something different, very different. And it wasn't funny. Tobin's eyes drifted to my mouth, and for more than a few moments I thought she was going to kiss me. While she was deciding, I was having difficulty breathing and felt more than a little light-headed. I was surprisingly disappointed when she released my hand and scooted back to the safe end of the couch.

"What do you do when you're not touring?" Didn't I already ask her that? Not even an hour into this ridiculous adventure, and I'd already lost my mind.

"Sleep, read, write," she repeated. "Play pinochle with Mr. Justin. You look surprised."

Surprised wasn't the word I'd use to describe how I was feeling. Aroused, confused were good for starters. "I guess I thought you would have been busy…"

"Throwing wild parties and orgies?"

My face heated from the image of Tobin naked at an orgy.

"I'm not that wild girl."

"No? Then who are all the girls in the pictures flooding the Internet?"

"It's just an image," Tobin said, and I felt her retreat from whatever personal connection we had.

"An image?"

"It sells tickets."

"I thought your music sold tickets," I commented.

A flash of something crossed her face, then disappeared. "Jake subscribes to the old adage that as long as your name is in the news…"

"And what do you subscribe to?"

"Whatever fills the venue," she said flippantly, almost rehearsed. I detected more than a little bravado in her statement but let it go.

"I really would think your music would fill the venue." Okay, I couldn't let it go.

Tobin didn't answer right away, and I waited for a flighty, superficial comeback. Instead, she just looked at me intently. It was as though she was trying to see through the layers and into my soul. I told myself not to break eye contact, and it was one of the hardest things I've ever done.

I had no problems holding my own across the negotiating table or the boardroom. One article passed around in a staff meeting claimed I had brass ovaries, which made me laugh, and my staff called me steely for weeks. I said what I meant and didn't dance around a topic. If I wanted something I asked for it and expected the same.

The longer Tobin looked at me, the more I wanted to fidget and look away. But I didn't. She wanted JOLT and I held all the cards. Then why did I feel like I was totally out of control?

"So tell me about you," she said, surprising me. "Other than you have a bitch for a sister-in-law."

"You don't know the half of it," I said, remembering the scene in my parents' living room the evening the "gal-pal" pictures hit the streets.

"We have all night," she replied.

I flashed on what I'd rather be doing with Tobin all night than talking about my family.

"Where did you go to school?" she asked.

A safe topic, I could do this. "Vassar for my undergrad and Stanford for my graduate work."

"Wow, beautiful and smart."

Surely she didn't think I was beautiful. I was ten years older than her, had lines on my face and saggy skin around my middle. One was a published fact, the other concealed with just a bit of foundation, and the third, no woman had seen. My reaction pissed me off. I had completely transformed myself from a laughingstock to a successful, self-made woman who had made something from nothing. But sometimes I had very little confidence in myself and how others saw me, and it made me more than a little angry.

"Did I say something wrong?" Tobin asked carefully.

"No, not at all." I was irritated I had been so obvious. I needed to work on that or it would be a long month.

"Do your parents still work?"

I proceeded to bore Tobin with my family tree and entertained her with stories of how utterly ridiculous and stuck-up Brittney could be. "I still can't believe my brother Harrison would marry someone like that."

"What about your friends?"

"I have a few," I said, not sure I wanted to delve this far into my personal life. Family was one thing because you were stuck with them, but friends were a personal choice and often said a lot about your own character.

"Have a BFF?"

The excitement on Tobin's face when she asked made my heart flutter again, and I started talking about Courtney. I gave Tobin the quick version of her profession, family, and how we met.

"Wow," Tobin said. "That could have ended very badly," she said, referring to the drug the guy had dropped in my beer.

"And that was years ago, before we heard so much about ruffies and Rohypnol. It's not like it is today. Women in bars are vigilant about keeping an eye on their drinks so they won't end up a terrible statistic, or worse."

Tobin nodded, then changed the subject to something lighter. "What do you do for fun?"

"I used to play rugby." Just saying the word shot phantom pain into my left ankle.

"Rugby?" Tobin said, clearly surprised. "As in bad-ass football-without-a-helmet rugby?"

"Yep, that's the one."

"Wow, I'm impressed. Beautiful and tough. You don't play now?"

"No. I broke my ankle. Figured that was a good warning note."

"So what do you do for fun now?"

"If I tell you, you'll laugh at me," I said, surprising myself. I rarely talked about myself and certainly not in a teasing way that begged for follow-up questions.

"I promise I won't. It'll be our little secret." Tobin crossed her heart, drawing my attention away from her tempting lips to her chest.

I suddenly wanted Tobin to know all my secrets. Correction—*learn* all my secrets.

"I mow my lawn."

The look of confusion on Tobin's face told me she didn't understand my answer. Nobody ever did.

"I mow my lawn," I repeated, starting to feel as ridiculous as I apparently sounded. "I love sitting on my lawn tractor, with the sun on my face and the smell of fresh-cut grass in the air. I can't really explain it other than to say it's relaxing and just something I absolutely love to do," I admitted. "My neighbors think I'm crazy," I added.

"Why is that?"

"Because everyone in the neighborhood has a yard service. Pickup trucks towing trailers with mowers, Weed Eaters, shovels, blowers, three kinds of rakes, and assorted other necessary tools pepper the streets every day. They pull up, four guys jump out and scamper around the yard, each with his own specific job, and before you know it they hop back in the truck and drive off. It seems like it's perfectly choreographed."

"But no truck pulls up in front of your driveway."

"Nope. If I had a dollar for everyone that gawked at me as they drove by, I'd have a bundle. Some don't even make eye contact." I chuckled. "It's as if it embarrasses them that I have to do my own yard. Like I can't afford a service. My God. We live in the same neighborhood. I can afford lawn service," I said, trying not to sound like I was flaunting my wealth.

"That's dumb. Don't they know who you are?"

"It doesn't matter who I am. I don't care either. I made it a point to get to know those on either side, in back of me, and across the street. Other than that, if they don't want to know who I am, that's their issue. I do have a snow-removal service in the winter though. But only during the week."

"Let me guess. You like to plow your own driveway," Tobin said, seeming pleased with herself that she'd figured it out.

"Absolutely, but I pay someone to do it. I leave pretty early in the mornings and get home late and need to be able to get into my garage. What about you? I'm sure you have dozens of stories of life on the road." I really did want to know, but as soon as the question was out of my mouth I wasn't so sure. I did not need to hear about all the women that had crossed her threshold.

Luckily Tobin only shared stories of some of the escapades of her crew. The more she talked, the more it became apparent that they were a tight-knit group and rightly so. They were together more than the members of any other profession I could think of right off the top of my head, and being in a different city every day wasn't conducive to having a wide circle of friends. When I glanced at my watch I was surprised to see it was as late as it was. I hadn't noticed the time fly by so fast.

"I guess I'll turn in," I said. I wasn't really tired, but the lull in the conversation was a little awkward. I felt uncomfortable being alone with Tobin and not sure what I was supposed to do next. She'd kept the conversation light and unthreatening, but a hint of sexual tension between us always lurked just below the surface. I didn't know if I wanted it uncovered.

"Sure," Tobin said, standing when I did.

My heart tripped again when her eyes went to my mouth. Was she going to kiss me good night? Make a move? And what would I do if she did?

"Do you need anything?"

It took me a moment to figure out she was talking about getting ready for bed. The longer she looked at me the more I was tempted to say something stupid and inane, like, are you going to tuck me in? "No, I'm fine," I answered, hoping the voice I heard actually said that and not the former. "Will we stop during the night?"

"Probably once. You don't have to get up or come out if you don't want to. You might even sleep through it."

"Probably." I chuckled. "I've been told nothing wakes me up. Good night."

Chapter Thirty

I felt an unfamiliar flash of jealousy of the women who had first-hand experience of how Kiersten slept. She was a beautiful, interesting woman with equally sophisticated women to pick from. There had to have been many lovers in her past and certainly many more in her future, and the green-eyed monster churned in my stomach.

The one and only time I felt like this was years ago. I'd met Carrie Chapman at a charity event, and we'd hit it off immediately, talking for most of the evening. Three days later we had dinner and, four days after that, at least six or seven orgasms between us. I was playing in an upscale club pretty regularly so I was in town more than out. We'd been seeing each other for several months, with Carrie coming to the club on Friday and Saturday nights. When I noticed a tall blonde paying a little too much attention to Carrie, I began to feel all the emotional crap of jealousy.

The first class I took on my way to my degree was English, and one of my assignments was to use Wikipedia to describe an emotion, so I chose jealousy. The online source stated that the word typically refers to the thoughts and feelings of insecurity, fear, concern, and anxiety over an anticipated loss or status of something of great personal value, particularly in reference to a human connection.

Okay, I get that with Carrie, all those years ago, but with Kiersten? And just by thinking of who might have shared her bed in the past? I am certainly not insecure or afraid. Nor do I have anxiety over the anticipated loss of something of great personal value. First, Kiersten and I barely know each other, so there's nothing between us of personal value to lose. Second, I can have just about any woman in my bed at any time, so it's not like I'm afraid of being alone. Third, I don't do human connection, so if I don't do it I can't be afraid of losing it. There, that was a logical, if not a redundant way of rationalizing my situation. So why hadn't I convinced myself?

I wasn't really tired, and no way would I fall asleep with Kiersten in the bed right across the hall from me, so I fired up my laptop and signed in to class. Might as well get some homework done instead of sitting here brooding over the women in Kiersten's life.

I was three courses away from my degree in business and was determined to finish. I had managed to keep my enrollment in the program a secret from the prying media, and everyone else for that matter. I was proud of what I'd accomplished. As an offspring of trailer trash I was never expected to amount to anything. Not that anyone cared one way or the other, but it was just a given. I was as much a product of the cycle as I was an integral cog taking my place at the appointed time. But I had gotten away by sheer will, talent, and more than a few lucky breaks.

As much as I tried, macroeconomics just didn't hold my attention for long tonight. I wasn't a good reader and often had to read things at least twice, but my mind kept wandering from the words on the screen to the woman down the short hall.

Why was I so interested in Kiersten? I rarely asked anyone about their personal life. It's not that I didn't care. It's just that I don't usually care that much. I knew a lot about my band, Jake, and a few stagehands, but that was only because they mentioned something in a conversation. And I certainly didn't want to have to answer any questions about mine. But our conversation tonight didn't scare me, only fed my curiosity of everything about Kiersten.

She was bright, intelligent, interesting, and way too serious. I get that she has devoted the last twelve years to getting JOLT off the ground, but other than her friend Courtney, it didn't appear she had anything else. She worked, and from what she'd said so far, her social life revolved around JOLT-related events. I wondered where she went on vacation, what books she read, her favorite movies, and her to-die-for dessert.

I'd only been in the foyer of her house the night of her reunion, and even that small space felt warm and inviting. There were wood floors, soft lighting, and a lot of color, at least in the areas I could see. I wondered if she decorated it herself or hired a professional. I guessed she did it herself, but then again, if she was an outdoors person, maybe the interior didn't interest her. I'd have to ask her about that. I wanted to ask her about a lot of things.

I pictured her on her lawn mower with a floppy hat and a tall tumbler of iced tea in the cup holder, driving back and forth making perfect, neat rows in the green grass. I have never mowed a lawn in my life. Not much opportunity for grass to grow in a cement-slab trailer park. Weeds certainly found their way into any crack or crevice, and even without any water, they grew like, well, weeds. At the beginning of one summer I measured one at the back of our trailer. I wanted to see just how tall it could get, and every day I charted its growth inch by inch in a worn spiral notebook I'd snagged out of a neighbor's trash pile. I stopped tracking it when it extended past the top of my head; I was five feet six inches at the time.

I got a bottle of beer from the refrigerator and touched my keyboard, waking my laptop. I still had three questions to answer from this week's assignment and the thirty-eight pages of Chapter Seventeen to read for next week. My study time was limited because of the secrecy around what I was doing, so I needed to get it done. Twenty minutes later, my mind still on Kiersten, I gave up.

CHAPTER THIRTY-ONE

I heard Kiersten moving around in the kitchen area, cracked open an eyelid, and glanced at the clock on the side table. I was surprised to see that I'd slept a few hours. The last thing I remembered was tossing and turning, images of Kiersten feeding my fantasies.

I tossed the covers back, got out of bed, and pulled a robe over my naked body. I ran my hands through my hair and rubbed my eyes, making sure there was no disgusting sleep-gunk residue. Doing as much as I could without running water in the bedroom, I opened the door.

I squinted, the bright light from the kitchen blinding me for a minute. When my eyes adjusted I saw Kiersten sitting at the kitchen table, her back to me.

"Do I smell coffee?" I croaked. It had been years since I'd been up this early, and I wasn't sure I was even awake.

"I hope I didn't wake you," she said, turning in the chair.

Her hair was disheveled, and the dark circles under her eyes signaled that she too hadn't slept much. "No, not at all," I lied. "I smelled the coffee. No one ever makes me coffee in the morning." I shuffled to the cabinet and pulled a cup from the shelf above the pot. I drank my coffee black, and by the lack of any evidence to the contrary, Kiersten did as well. I took a sip, cautious of the steam billowing from the cup.

"Mmm. Delicious," I said. It was so good I almost purred. "I don't know if it's because you made it or you added something special to it, but this is better than delicious." I took another sip, the hot liquid sliding down my throat. "May I join you?" I asked, indicating the chair to her right.

Kiersten used her toe to push the chair away from the table a few inches in invitation. "Nice color," I said, lifting my chin to indicate the cobalt-blue polish on her toes. "Sexy."

Kiersten scoffed. "You really do need coffee," she said, tucking her feet under her chair.

She was sexy, with her hair up in a loose ponytail, her face scrubbed clean of any makeup, and that sleepy, just-waked-up look. She appeared soft and vulnerable, and it suddenly hit me that it had been years since I'd had a woman in my kitchen first thing in the morning. Or any time of the day for that matter. Other than work, the only thing I did with women is fuck. We never had a conversation, never talked about movies or the plight of the poor. Very few words were ever spoken that weren't along the lines of "Oh yeah," or "right there," or "harder." That realization was unsettling.

"How long have you been up?" I asked. This was a situation I'd never experienced. I never did morning-afters and never had anyone travel with me, so coffee chit-chat was foreign to me.

"About half a cup," she answered, using the amount of coffee consumed as a time reference.

"Did you sleep?"

"Not too much," she replied honestly. "It takes me a couple of nights before I get used to sleeping somewhere other than my own bed."

A wave of heat coursed through me with images of nights in her bed, and I coughed as my coffee took a detour to my stomach. My throat burned and my eyes watered as I leapt to the sink, filling an empty glass with water. Kiersten was beside me in an instant.

"Are you okay?" she asked, her hand on my back.

When I could speak again I said, "Just went down the wrong pipe." I coughed a few more times before I was sure I wasn't going to choke to death. "I'm fine, really," I said, trying to convince both Kiersten and myself. I settled back in the chair. Kiersten refilled her cup and returned to her place as well.

"Hungry?" she asked. "I saw some eggs in the fridge and muffin mix in the pantry." She blushed. "Sorry. I wasn't snooping. I was looking for the coffee."

"No, no problem." I waved her statement away. "Mi casa, su casa," I assured her. I glanced at the clock on the microwave. "We usually stop for breakfast about now. Gives everybody a chance to get out and have a good meal. Let me check with Frank and see how much longer. If you're starving I'm sure we can scrounge up something."

"No. I'll be fine. What's on the agenda for today?" Kiersten asked.

"When we get to Madison we'll pull in under the stadium and park. The convoy trucks should already be there unloading the gear and equipment. It'll take them most of the day to set everything up, and when everything is ready I do the sound check," I said, explaining hours of technical activity in less than fifty words.

"What does that entail?"

Kiersten crossed her legs, and I caught more than a glimpse of bare leg before it disappeared under the table. I was glad I didn't have my cup at my mouth or I might not have gotten out of that choking fit alive. I dragged my eyes away from the spot where I'd last seen her legs.

"We get miked up and play a few songs as I move around. We're checking to make sure there's no feedback or dead space anywhere on the stage. If we have a new song we'll use the time to try it out a few times, see how it sounds. And I need to know where the blocking areas are so I don't step in front of the video camera. No one wants to see my ass," I added, getting out of my chair to top off my cup.

I felt Kiersten looking at my ass as I walked by her and tried not to trip over the small green rug on the floor between the sink and the stove. When I turned around I caught her eyes quickly moving from my butt to the dark liquid in her cup. Her face was flushed. *Interesting*.

If this had been any other woman I'd take her up on the invitation she was extending. When a woman looked the way Kiersten was looking at me, I had no doubt what she wanted. But I don't think Kiersten knew what she was doing.

I returned to the table and sat down with one leg under my butt. When I hooked my elbow around the back of the chair my robe slipped open, and Kiersten's eyes shot to my almost-bare chest. A self-respecting woman would delicately pull it back together and probably secure the belt a little tighter. Since I'd enjoyed the expression on Kiersten's face more than resecuring my modesty, what did that make me? I had self-respect, but I was also a hot-blooded twenty-five-year-old lesbian who had a beautiful woman staring at her chest. It would be more unbelievable for me to cover myself than to do nothing.

My breathing became shallow, and my nipples hardened at the raw desire I saw in her eyes. Kiersten had to have noticed because I had nothing between my two stiff peaks and the silk fabric. My stomach started to tingle and my girly parts grew warm.

I was aroused just by a look, albeit a long, sustained look. It usually took me a long time to feel like this, and sometimes when I was with a woman I never did, particularly lately. I explained it away by saying I was tired, stressed, and road weary. It sounded good at the time.

I had to work hard at not squirming under Kiersten's stare. I was hot all over, and the cool air on my skin felt refreshing. I wanted to take her in my arms and make love to her until I couldn't breathe anymore. I wanted to hear my name whispered from her lips in passion, feel her heart beat next to mine, hear her scream out loud when she came. But I didn't move for fear I would break the connection between us and Kiersten would look away. So I stayed perfectly still, except for the racing of my pulse.

Kiersten stood and Frank hit the brakes hard. She stumbled and fell into my lap. She was straddling me, her lips mere inches from mine. Subconsciously preparing for a kiss, I licked mine, and the white-hot heat from her eyes that were a moment before on my breasts now focused on my mouth. My hands were on her hips, and her quick breathing matched mine. Heat radiated off her, and the only thing that existed was the sensation of her in my arms. I slid my hands up her back and pulled her to me. It didn't take much effort, and in a long, agonizing instant our lips were touching.

Jolts of pleasure shot through my body like nothing I'd ever experienced before. My senses jumped to life, my nerve endings drinking in every sensation. From the pressure of her warm lips to the feel of her body against mine, my body was humming with desire. Kiersten Fellows was kissing me. Me. When she could have her pick of rich, sophisticated women, she was kissing me.

Kiersten's kisses were hesitant at first, and I didn't push for more. Intuitively I knew that she needed to be the taker here, not the other way around. I kept my hands still until her tongue parted my lips and demanded entry. Quickly, feverishly she explored my mouth. She wrapped her arms around my neck and kissed me harder. My clit started to throb, and my hands wandered up and down her smooth back. I slid one of them under her T-shirt and touched hot, soft skin.

I think I moaned, but I couldn't be sure, and frankly I didn't care. It didn't matter who was doing what to whom, and it was pretty damn obvious we were both enjoying what was going on. I shifted in the chair and Kiersten pulled away, a look I could only describe as shock and horror on her face. Apparently realizing where she was, she practically jumped off my lap and took several steps back. Her hands were over her mouth as if stifling a scream, her eyes wide. I started to say something but didn't know what. I'd never been in this position before, and it was definitely not where I ever wanted to be again.

"I…I'm sorry." Kiersten was still breathing quickly, and I tried not to focus on her chest.

"Kiersten," I said. She stepped back farther and turned her back to me.

"I shouldn't have done that."

I didn't know if she was trying to convince herself or me.

I stood, surprised my legs were as weak as they were. But then again the kiss was pretty powerful. I stepped toward her, but when she turned around, her words stopped me.

"That will never happen again." She emphasized every word, like it was the eleventh commandment.

I could only watch as she disappeared into her room.

Chapter Thirty-two

"Come with me," I commanded, taking Kiersten's hand and pulling her off the couch and out the door. It had been another hour after the kiss before we stopped for breakfast, and somehow we'd managed to avoid each other until then. When she was in the shower I was up front with Frank trying not to think about her in the shower. When it was my turn, she was in her room getting dressed. The cold water did little to ease the pressure in my clit that that one hot kiss had ignited.

Kiersten sat with Russ and Jones at the table behind me and the rest of our band. I tried to pay attention to the conversation at my table, but my ears picked up the sound of Kiersten's voice behind me. It sounded tight, her laugh forced.

After breakfast she accepted Russ's invitation to ride with them, and I spent the next three hours alone, trying to figure out what had happened. I replayed the entire conversation between us, stopping to daydream about the good parts. I admit the kiss completely surprised me. There was a definite attraction between us, but I hadn't expected it to explode like it had.

Maybe I was out of practice. After all, I rarely engaged in foreplay and never had to seduce anyone. I didn't keep track of time, but my sexual encounters probably lasted less than thirty minutes, and most of the time even less than that. The phrase "wham, bam, thank you ma'am" came to mind. There was nothing wrong with that, and it was always enough for me, but I could have kissed Kiersten for hours.

And that was another mind-blower. I didn't kiss. I licked and sucked every inch of a woman's body, but I never kissed her. To me, kissing was more intimate than sucking a clit or burying fingers deep inside warm, tight wetness. My reaction to Kiersten's kiss and the instant before she kissed me was completely foreign. But I wanted to experience it again. And that scared the shit out of me.

"Where are we going?"

I pushed the door to the coach shut and tugged on her hand. "We need to get you a pass."

"For what?"

"You don't want to be stuck in the coach twenty-four seven, do you? It's a pass, so you can go wherever you want. If you don't have one, you'll be stopped by security. They'll probably think you're a groupie and toss you out on your cute little ass." That was the most we had spoken since we parked in the underground staging area of the arena twenty minutes earlier.

"Do you have many of those?" Kiersten asked, pulling her hand out of mine. I figured she'd want to forget this morning ever happened. I wasn't there yet.

"You'd be surprised what people will do to get backstage," I said, shaking my head as I remembered some of the stupid and dangerous things I'd seen.

"What are they looking for? What do they want?"

"Mostly to get a photo or a piece of the equipment, or something from the band. A special souvenir or something they can sell for big bucks on eBay."

"People actually do that?" Kiersten asked, clearly surprised.

"All the time. I could spend hours talking about the things fans do that are funny, sad, and downright scary. But I'll save that for another time."

I opened the door of a plain-white eighteen-wheel cargo container. The master trailer, as it was known, was the nucleus of the Tobin Parks tour. Inside was one half of everything we used at every stop. The other half was in an identical trailer parked to the right. We'd learned the hard way not to put all of our eggs in one basket, as the saying goes, when one of the rigs swerved to miss a deer in the road and turned over, spilling hundreds of thousands of dollars of equipment in the median of the north-and south-bound lanes of I 85. Since then we separated the gear just to be safe.

"Hey, Barb," I said, stepping inside the cool, windowless box. "This is Kiersten. She needs an all-access pass." Barb was the Jill of all trades on the tour. She fetched coffee and doughnuts, always had a spare guitar string or pick, and knew the location of every truck-stop diner within fifty miles of wherever we were. She had a cure for everything and an answer before you even asked the question. She never told her age, but I guessed her to be in her mid-sixties, and she stood well over six feet tall.

"Got it right here, Tobin." Barb opened the drawer of her metal desk and pulled out a brightly colored card about the size of a piece of paper folded in half.

"Just need to get a pic, and in two minutes she'll be good to go."

Barb motioned Kiersten to the wall behind her and pulled out her phone. Two clicks and one lamination later, the all-access pass for the Tobin Parks tour hung prominently around Kiersten's neck.

"Thanks, Barb. You're a gem."

"You say that to all the cute girls," she quipped back.

"Naw," I said, getting up on my tiptoes and giving her a kiss on the cheek. "I tell them they're hot. You're much better. You're a gem."

"Yeah, yeah. Get out of here and go make some money. I'm due for a raise." Her voice drifted away as we walked down the steps.

"She's interesting," Kiersten said, looking at her pass.

"She was the starting center for Texas Tech women's basketball for four years until she broke her leg her senior year."

"How long has she been with you?"

"Ever since I could afford her."

"Sounds to me like she needs a raise," Kiersten teased.

"She says that every year."

"And?"

"And every year she gets one. And an end-of-tour bonus and a Christmas card."

"I see why she stays with you," Kiersten said, smiling.

"Yep, it's the Christmas card. Best retention tool in the market. Come on," I said, taking her by the elbow and walking toward the stadium. "Let me give you the ten-cent tour."

"I thought it was the nickel tour."

"Inflation has hit everywhere," I replied. "It's getting harder and harder to keep up." Kiersten laughed and my pulse raced, my heart stuttered, and I tripped over my feet.

Kiersten had a good sense of humor and was very easy to be around. She had a way that made people comfortable around her—at least the people I knew. And mine were as jaded as they came.

Kiersten asked questions as I showed her around. We met up with Reggie and took the opportunity to mark my spots and block out tonight's show. Reggie explained where the lights were and the direction of the spotlights and a few other important tidbits of information. Twenty minutes later we were at the mess tent ready for lunch.

After lunch was a series of radio interviews taped for stops later in the tour. I did two television interviews for the local stations, and at two thirty I was done until the sound check at six. Barb came over right as the last camera was packed up.

"Frank's ready whenever you are."

"What's next?" Kiersten asked.

I debated on telling her and thought three or four times about taking her along. I was going to have to let her in if I wanted JOLT sponsorship.

"Grab your purse or bag or whatever you need. I have to run an errand."

"Where are we going?"

"It's a surprise." She looked at me skeptically. "It's perfectly safe. Trust me."

Frank held the door and pushed the seat forward so Kiersten could crawl into the backseat of my 2012 Jeep Wrangler. I got a great view of her ass in her tight jeans when she did and tried not to drool on my new Nikes. We towed the Jeep behind my coach so I could get out on my own if the time and place allowed. I used it almost every stop if I had a chance. On those days when we pulled into town on the day of the show there really was no way. But today was a good day.

I'd been stopping at various nursing homes for an hour or so every year since I was on tour. The first time was a complete publicity stunt and photo op, but when I saw the power of music transforming the faces of the residents I made it a point to do it as often as I could. Except without a camera or any pre-notice. The facility director knew I was coming but was sworn to secrecy so as not to cause a mob and upset the residents. "I had no idea," Kiersten said from the backseat. I'd let her in on our destination a few minutes after we left the stadium.

"You're not supposed to," I said. "That's the whole point."

Chapter Thirty-three

I was still shaking my head in disbelief when we pulled into the parking lot of the Rosedale Care Center. I'd been nervous as hell the entire ride, praying Tobin didn't bring up our kiss in front of Frank. I'd have been embarrassed and even more mortified if she pressed me why I'd bolted the way I did. Somehow I knew I wasn't going to get off the hook.

I had to have been out of my mind when I kissed her.

Frank slid out of the driver's seat and had Tobin's guitar out of the back before I got my feet on the ground.

Tobin thanked him and took the scuffed black case from him. "Shall we?" she asked indicating the front door.

A man who couldn't have been a day younger than ninety was sitting in a chair to the left of the door, a straw stuck out of the top of his multicolored adult sippy cup. His shirt was freshly ironed and the crease in his khakis razor sharp. His brown slippers looked well worn.

"Afternoon," the old man greeted us, tipping his straw hat politely.

"Yes, it is," Tobin replied. "Good afternoon to you as well. Are you a resident here?"

"Yep. Too ornery for any other place," he said jokingly. I doubted that was true.

"I'm Tobin Parks." Tobin stepped closer, extending her hand in greeting.

"Hollis Albert," the man said. "And this young lady is my missus, Phyllis." He motioned to the elderly woman to his right. She wore a paisley blue-print dress and stark-white tennis shoes. Her hands were folded neatly in her lap. She wasn't much younger but her eyes were flat, where Mr. Albert's were full of life.

"It's a pleasure to meet you, Mr. Albert, Mrs. Albert." Tobin addressed the unmoving woman.

"She doesn't talk much," Mr. Albert explained.

"Do y'all like music?" Tobin asked.

Mr. Albert's face lit up. "We used to go dancing every Saturday night when we were dating," he said, a flash of nostalgia filling his lined face.

"Well, sir, why don't you and your lovely missus come inside with us. Your director has been so kind as to invite me over to sing a few songs. Who knows? Maybe you'll have the urge to get up and take your wife for a spin again."

The old man smiled and looked from Tobin to me. "She your missus?" He addressed the question to Tobin but was looking at me.

My mouth dropped open. I certainly never expected that question to come out of his toothless mouth. Tobin laughed. I really liked her laugh.

"No. I'm afraid we're just friends." Tobin recoiled. "This is Kiersten Fellows."

"Don't you want to marry her?" he asked me seriously.

"Well, Mr. Albert, she hasn't asked me yet." I was joking, but my stomach bounced around at the thought.

"Why not?" he asked Tobin. "She's a looker." He winked at Tobin, which made her laugh.

My stomach tickled again.

"Yes, sir, she is," Tobin said. "But we don't know each other well enough to be thinking about marriage. Besides, I'm not the marrying type."

My heart hesitated then resumed beating.

"Why not? Everybody's the marrying type. You just haven't met the woman of your dreams yet," Mr. Albert said, like that was all there was to it. I liked him. If only life were that simple.

"That's going to be pretty hard, Mr. Albert. You took the prettiest woman off the market years ago," Tobin said, smiling and looking at Phyllis. She stepped back. "I'm going inside to see Mrs. Gough and get set up. Better hurry. The good seats fill up fast."

We walked past Mr. Albert and his wife, and the automatic doors opened with a whoosh. Another set of automatic doors didn't open until the first ones closed, and I wondered out loud why that was.

"It's a common safety measure in facilities like this. It's what they do so residents can't wander off. Usually you need a code to get out the first set, then a different one to operate the outer doors."

"How do you know that?"

"I've been inside a lot of these kinds of places. They're all pretty much the same. Some are obviously much better or worse than others..."

She didn't need to finish the sentence. I'd heard horror stories of facilities that were little more than storage places for the elderly.

A rail-thin woman in her mid-fifties, with dyed red hair and way too much lip liner, greeted us and introduced herself as Joanne Gough, the manager of Rosedale, and said everything was set up for Tobin's mini concert. At least a dozen residents were sitting in wheelchairs placed around the perimeter of the room, some grouped together, and their occupants were chatting away. Others were alone, while some had their chins on their chests napping. More than a few looked at us with curiosity. Tobin gave a simple hello to everyone she made eye contact with.

We probably did look a little different than the average person coming through the front doors. At least Tobin did. With her spiky black hair, her bright-red tank top, black biker boots, and the way she filled out her hip-hugging jeans, she definitely did turn a head or two. Even mine. She had a tattoo of a phoenix bird on the inside of her left arm and a feather on the right. I wondered if she had any others that the general public didn't see.

We followed Mrs. Gough across the lobby, past the reception desk, and into a large carpeted room just off the main hall.

"This is our PT room," she said, explaining the stationary bike in the corner adjacent to a treadmill and four colored beach balls of different sizes sitting neatly in a rack by the window. It didn't have all the mats and machines like the physical-therapy clinic I went to after I broke my ankle, but I suspected they didn't need much more than a few items for these patients.

"I thought the acoustics would be better for you in here than the dining room. That's all tile, you know," she said, as if we knew her residents might spill.

"This is perfect, Mrs. Gough. Thank you."

"I'll go round up everyone. I know they'll be thrilled you're here." She scurried out of the room in search of Tobin's audience.

Tobin laid the guitar case on a low, padded exercise table and snapped open the three latches. She lifted the acoustic guitar out and pushed the case out of the way. She sat and began strumming a few chords, tightening or loosening a few strings as she did.

"Do any of these people have any idea who you are?"

Tobin looked at me for a few moments before answering. "Some of the staff maybe. But it doesn't matter. I'm not here to get anything, and frankly if I get a few smiles or a foot or two tapping along to the beat, I'm happy."

"Why do you do it?"

"Because they need it and I can give it to them." She strummed a few more chords, her fingers moving expertly over the strings. She hummed quietly as a few residents began to shuffle in.

For the next hour I sat stunned at the beautiful, melodic sounds emanating from Tobin and her guitar. No backup singers singing harmony, no drums pounding out a sensuous beat, nothing to distract from the pure, strong sound of her voice. This was a Tobin I'd never seen, or even knew existed for that matter. She'd said it was a secret, one that my research staff hadn't uncovered. This was something JOLT could stand behind.

Tobin played a mixture of what could be classified as golden oldies, and I struggled to remember some of the words. Tobin sang favorites from Bing Crosby, Nat King Cole, Duke Ellington, and the Andrews Sisters. She took requests and knew every single song that was asked for. Several of the residents did, in fact, tap their foot, and more than a few smiles filled old, craggy faces. I saw Mr. Albert walking toward me.

"Would you care to dance?" he asked politely, holding out his hand, palm up.

"What would Mrs. Albert think?" I asked seriously. I'd kept an eye on the cute couple but saw no sign of recognition from his wife even when he held her hand. My heart hurt for him.

"She wouldn't mind," he answered, sounding a little sad. "She knows how much I like to dance, and since she can't, she'd want me to have fun."

How could I refuse? I put my hand in his and he moved it to the crook of his elbow, like any respectable gentleman would. I walked beside him to the front of the room, my arm actually supporting him. He stopped and I stepped into his arms.

Other than at the reunion it had been a few years since I'd danced, and many more since I'd danced backward. However, it wasn't too difficult, as Mr. Albert was barely able to do more than shuffle his feet. He held me at a respectable distance, his hand barely touching my lower back.

"You're a wonderful dancer, Mr. Albert," I said honestly. My compliment was returned with a beautiful smile from this kind, elderly man. "How long have you and your wife been married?"

"Seventy-two years this June," he answered proudly, including information on their eight children, thirty-two grandchildren, and seventeen great-grandchildren. His eyes glowed as he talked about his family, and I wondered if I would ever have the same.

"The lady singer. What's her name again?"

"Tobin." I liked the sound of it coming off my lips.

He frowned and shook his head. "Never heard a girl called that before. Never mind," he said, changing the subject. "If she won't ask you to marry her, then you need to ask her."

I chuckled at his continued insistence that Tobin and I get married. "Mr. Albert, we barely know each other."

"Phyllis and I knew each other for six weeks before we tied the knot. Look how long it's worked for us."

"Mr. Albert, I have to say that I'm very surprised at how liberal you are about…"

"Homosexuality? I may be old and sometimes forget where my teeth are, but people are people. It doesn't matter who they sleep with. It's none of my business."

"I appreciate that, Mr. Albert." A little smattering of applause stopped me from saying more. Mr. Albert dropped his hands and bent at the waist.

"Thank you, miss. It's been a long time since I've danced, and it was a pleasure to share the occasion with you. Please thank the other lady for coming. It's not often we have something as enjoyable as this has been. Now I'd better get back to my wife. She's not the jealous type, but I don't want to push my luck. My back can't handle the couch anymore." He chuckled and winked at me as I walked him back to his chair, stunned when his wife reached for his hand.

I glanced up and saw Frank standing in the doorway. I looked at my watch and was surprised at how long we'd been here. Tobin had less than an hour to get back for the sound check.

Tobin must have seen Frank as well, because she told her audience that she'd take one more request before she had to leave. An elderly man in a faded army jacket raised his hand politely and asked for a song I'd never heard of. However, Tobin had, and five minutes later she was shaking the hand of everyone in the room. She stayed a few minutes longer for punch and cookies, and I watched her interact with these strangers.

For someone so young she was completely at ease with these elderly people. She didn't patronize them or talk to them like they were children, which in some cases I wasn't so sure. She held hands with some of the women and flirted with some of the old men. She didn't skimp on touching an arm or a pair of arthritic, mangled folded hands sitting quietly in a lap. She adjusted one woman's blanket that slid off her knees and wiped the crumbs off the cheek of another. She was completely at ease here and obviously did this often. She signed a few autographs for the staff and the cast on the leg of a forty-something-year-old man, who proudly stated he was finally going home tomorrow.

"I now get why you do this," I said as we exited the building. We were walking right into the afternoon setting sun, and I squinted and reached for my sunglasses.

"They're always so appreciative. It doesn't take much to put a smile on their faces, unlike the rest of the crazy world. They don't want anything from me, and because of that I give them everything I have."

I thought about that and many other things on the return ride to the stadium. The few hours I'd spent with Tobin told me more about her than all the articles I'd perused. I was good at reading people, really good, and I hadn't detected anything other than pure, selfless pleasure from Tobin all afternoon.

As we rounded the corner, the crowds around the building were heavier than when we left. There was an excitement in the air that wasn't there earlier either, and I remembered what it felt like to go to a concert on a warm summer night.

Frank pulled up to the door, and Tobin got out of the front seat. I took her offered hand and climbed out of the small, cramped backseat. "Remind me to call shotgun next time," I said, teasing.

"Frank and I are always alone on these visits," she said quietly. The guard at the door nodded at us and quickly opened it.

"Why is that?"

Tobin didn't answer for a few moments, our shoes clicking on the tile floor the only sound. "Because it's not about me, or anyone else that would come along. It's about giving these wonderful people something to smile about, someone to take their hand and tell them they're special, that someone remembers them. I'm afraid if I took anyone with me, it would interfere with that."

"Then why did you take me?"

We walked a few more yards, and I wasn't sure Tobin was going to answer. Finally she said simply, "Because I knew you were different. Because I knew you'd get it," she added.

We stared at each other for several minutes, neither of us breaking eye contact. The sexual tension that had been brewing between us and had flared this morning was even more electric. At least it was for me. Watching Tobin play for those wonderful people just for the sheer joy of it was powerfully moving. She strummed the guitar strings like she was touching a frail bird. The words to songs I didn't recognize seemed to have a special meaning to her. I especially liked the way her eyes lit up when someone asked for a song and she could give it to them. This was a side of Tobin I hadn't seen, and from what she'd said, it was reserved for these select few.

"Thank you for inviting me," I said, a bit choked up.

"Mr. Albert was a hoot, wasn't he? I saw the way he looked at you. He may be old, but he certainly isn't dead yet."

"No, he certainly isn't." I laughed. We walked a few more steps before I added, "He said that I should ask you to marry me." The idea made me just as warm as when he suggested it.

"Did he? Hmm. Maybe he has something there."

"You assume I'd want to marry you," I teased her.

"What's not to love? I'm cute, funny, and rich."

"No, you're hot, sweet, and filthy rich." I took at least three or four more steps before I realized Tobin wasn't beside me anymore. I turned around. She had the strangest expression on her face. "What?"

"You think I'm hot?"

"I also think you're sweet. What's your point?" It made me nervous that she focused on the "hot" descriptor. "That's not news, Tobin."

"It is that you think I am," she said, closing the distance between us.

"You should be focusing on the sweet part."

"Instead of what?"

"Sleeping with anyone in a skirt." I bumped my shoulder against hers, signaling I was still teasing her.

"I do not."

"You do too."

"I do not."

I laughed because we sounded like squabbling siblings. "For a songwriter you really have a way with words." I was enjoying this verbal banter. Tobin did have a good sense of humor and a quick wit.

"Okay, let me rephrase my rebuttal. There have been many, many women in skirts that I have not had carnal knowledge of."

I laughed and stopped and turned to look at her. "Carnal knowledge? Good God. Now you sound like a Victorian romance novel."

"I don't sleep with every woman. I do have some scruples."

"Uh-huh," I mumbled. "By the way, since you're so experienced in all things sex…"

"I would say thank you for the compliment, but somehow I don't think it was meant as one."

I glanced at Tobin to make sure we were still having a light conversation and I hadn't upset her. "Why does everyone call it sleeping together? I don't know about you, but when I go to sleep, it's nothing like sex. Am I missing something?" I was, but I just needed to ask the question.

"Maybe, because right afterward, you just want to curl up and fall asleep, you know. At least if you do it right," she added, this time bumping my shoulder with hers.

I didn't reply because I didn't know.

"Why are you so interested in my sex life?"

Because I want to be your sex life, I thought. Instead, I said, "Because you want my company to sponsor you. And your very public sex life affects your image. Ergo, it affects me."

"Dang, and I just thought you wanted to have sex with me," Tobin said as she started walking again.

I stumbled over probably nothing. *Oh, fuck, did I say what I was thinking out loud?* "Just professional curiosity," I said, trying to regain my composure. All this talk about sex combined with seeing Tobin lose herself in her music and her close proximity had made my sex start throbbing—again.

Chapter Thirty-four

I could get used to a traveling partner, I admitted to myself one night. If that partner was Kiersten. I admit I didn't know what I was thinking when I invited her along. I'd never had a roomie in my personal life and certainly not in a fifty-foot, self-contained home on wheels. I should have been crawling the walls or at least trying to sneak into her bed in the middle of the night, but I wasn't and I hadn't. Okay, I'd thought about it more than a few dozen times, but I hadn't done anything about it. That was another thing that was unusual. I hadn't had sex in two weeks, which, when I was on tour, just did not happen. I'd had opportunities, plenty, as a matter of fact, but no one seemed to interest me. Actually, the thought of mindless sex with a complete stranger didn't appeal to me at all, and that scared the shit out of me.

Mindless sex had been all I wanted, all I was capable of giving, and all I needed. I was in no position to have any kind of steady girlfriend, even if I wanted one. I was on the road more than I was at home, which made it hard to try to build and maintain a relationship. It's not that I was unhappy, far from it. I loved my life, the excitement of a new town every day, a new crowd screaming my name. It was a rush, plain and simple. After going full speed for days leading up to a show, then the sheer euphoria of the crowd that had come to see me, my body was like a shaken champagne bottle. I needed a release, and sex was the popping of the cork, so to speak.

I suppose some shrink would probably say that because I'd had such a shitty childhood with neither of my parents giving a damn about me, the tens of thousands of screaming fans were my substitute. They would go on to conclude that since I'd had no normal affection as a child, I mistook sex for emotional connection. Well, they would be wrong. At least the part about sex as an emotional connection. I enjoyed sex. It felt good leading up to it, during, and after. When it involved two consenting adults, then why not? It was like skiing or tennis or any other recreational activity. Sex was something my body needed, like food or water, and when I found something I liked, like pizza or beer, I imbibed. Nothing more complicated than that. But all that changed when Kiersten came on board.

We'd been on the road for six days and had quickly fallen into a comfortable routine. We'd pull into town, and, time permitting, I'd play a few songs at one of the facilities Jake had arranged for me. Kiersten had replaced Frank as my driver and was much prettier to look at and smelled better as well. She was a good pilot/navigator, and we got lost only once. After making a few calls we were quickly on the road again, laughing at our stupidity for confusing Blankenship Avenue with Blankenshire Avenue. We both kept pretending the kiss never happened, but I caught her looking at me more than once.

Kiersten would disappear into the coach or wander around on her own during the sound check and pre-concert interviews. Several times during a show I'd catch a glimpse of her stage right or sometimes sitting in the first row. I found myself looking for her all the time and couldn't quite settle into the set until I had. It wasn't like I was looking for her approval of the show. Far from it. The decibels of the crowd told me all I needed to know. I just needed to know where she was, whether it was to make sure she was safe from the strangers wandering around backstage or to make sure she was enjoying herself. I know it wasn't my job to entertain her or keep her happy, but I found myself trying to nonetheless.

Tonight was no exception. It was a warm summer night in Biloxi, and the beer was cold and inexpensive. The first four or five rows were filled with scantily clad women and more cleavage displayed than should be allowed. I, however, wasn't complaining.

Neither was Jones, my bass player drifting to the front of the stage far more often than ever before.

The after-show interviews were tedious, and I fought the urge to tell everyone to just get the hell out. I was keyed up and had a bad case of the jitters. I needed some fresh air. Finally, everyone was occupied with the free booze and food, and I managed to slip out unnoticed.

I was a dozen steps down the hall when I heard my name yelled from behind me.

"Tobin, phone call." It was Howard, one of my road crew. "He's pretty insistent," he said, holding my phone out toward me.

"Great show tonight," the voice said into my ear. It was familiar, but the noise coming from the room I'd just left made it difficult to hear clearly.

"Who is this?" I asked, impatient to be in the next room.

"You don't recognize my voice? I'm hurt." The voice was gruff and a little garbled, like he was holding the phone too close to his mouth.

"Look, I don't have time for this shit. Who is this?"

"Carol, this is your brother Jimmy."

When I heard my birth name my heart stopped, and I knew before the caller went any further I was not going to like whoever it was. I should have immediately hung up, but for some perverse reason I didn't.

"What do you want?" I asked sharply. I didn't even bother to ask where he got my number. I'd had it changed after the call from Mommie Dearest, but, amazingly, my family members, who couldn't hold a job or their alcohol, somehow always managed to get my unlisted number.

"What's the matter, Carol? On your way to a hot date?" Jimmy laughed the sleazy way he did when he was talking about my liking girls. It didn't take much to imagine what he was doing with the hand that wasn't holding the phone.

"Two seconds and I'm hanging up." I needed my head examined for giving him that many.

"My new truck hasn't arrived." This time his voice was tinged with anger. The hand must not be working.

"That's because it's not coming. At least not from me." I hadn't even considered it.

"Mama told you—"

"And I told her she wasn't getting another cent from me." I kept my voice calm but low. "That goes for you and every other member of your useless family. Do not call me again." I dropped the phone to the floor and stomped on it with my boot. I spun on my heel, crushing it even more, and bent over and picked up the chip, tucking it into my pocket. I turned toward the door that separated me from mindless escape. I needed this. I really needed this now. I stepped forward.

Chapter Thirty-five

"How's life on the road?"

"Not what I expected it to be." The coach lurched and I stumbled onto the couch. I quickly buckled the seatbelt with one hand, holding my phone to my ear with the other. Peering out the tinted window I saw nothing but absolute blackness.

The clink of a glass made me picture Courtney filling it with her favorite beverage. I knew I was right when she said, "Let me get a glass of wine and you can start from the beginning."

Tobin's bedroom door was closed so I moved as far away as I could and kept my voice low. She'd been uncharacteristically quiet when she came in tonight. She'd barely looked at me and mumbled something, then disappeared into her room. I'd developed a blistering headache during the show, so I didn't hang around for the after-concert activities and certainly wasn't going to push a conversation where one wasn't wanted.

"Okay, the kids are in bed, Tom's watching a game in the other room, I have a full glass, and my feet are up. I'm good to go." I heard her loud sigh all the way through the line. "So, spill."

I didn't know where to start. Should I give her the play-by-play replay of everything that had happened since I stepped foot in this mobile house on wheels? Should I just hit the highlights? Tell her about the venues and the concerts? About how I practically threw myself at Tobin? How she kissed like there was no tomorrow? How good she tasted? How soft her lips were? How fast my heart beat, and how the kiss took my breath away. How I wanted her so bad I forgot everything, including my own name? How sanity came crashing down around me and I scampered away like a frightened child? How humiliated I was by retreating the way I did? How I've done nothing but relive the kiss? How many times I've wanted to ask her to kiss me again? How many times I've started toward her, then turned away? How my skin tingles when she's near and aches when she's not? How I'm aware of everything about her? How her eyes light up when she's excited and get dark when she looks at me? How empty my arms felt when I stepped away? I couldn't decide what to tell Courtney so I told her everything.

"Wow, K, I had no idea."

I couldn't help but laugh. "Neither did I." What an understatement.

"What are you going to do?"

"Not let it happen again!"

"Why not?"

"Why not? Because she's Tobin Parks." That sounded as stupid as my previous comment, and Courtney confirmed my view.

"So? She's single and obviously attracted to you."

"She's Tobin Parks." I tried again to make my point. "She's had dozens of women, maybe even hundreds. There's no way in hell I'm going to embarrass myself by having sex with her. No, wait," I said, "*try* to have sex with her. She'd see right through me and laugh me out of her bed."

"That's ridiculous." Courtney scoffed at my hypothesis.

"That's reality, Courtney." My head was starting to pound again.

"Kiersten, you don't give yourself enough credit."

"Oh, I give myself plenty of credit, Courtney, in areas where I deserve it, and there are plenty. But having sex with Tobin Parks isn't one of them. I'm not going to be a notch on her guitar neck and certainly not a funny story she can tell at a party. And she's ten years younger than I am," I added for emphasis.

That didn't sway her into my way of thinking. "Cougar is in."

"Shut up, Courtney," I said, not as angry as the words implied. "I am not going to have sex with someone who has no idea who was the president eight years before our current jackass."

"But if you don't make a move, or let her, how are you ever going to—"

"With somebody else." I was beginning to regret telling her I was a virgin.

"Who?'

"I don't know who, but I know who it won't be. Now, can we talk about something else?" It took several more attempts before I was able to shift the topic from Tobin, who was in bed fifteen feet from me, to safer subjects.

❖

I silently closed the door. I'd been lying in bed staring at the ceiling. After the phone call from Jimmy I needed a distraction. Sex was my go-to entertainment, but no one had caught my eye in quite some time. I kept comparing everyone to Kiersten, and they all came up short. Instead of a much-needed orgasm, I had six beers with my band and had come back and fell into bed. Somehow I needed to erase the memory of Kiersten's kiss from my mind. I could have my choice of women that were more than eager to do the job, but it would be Kiersten's voice I heard in my ear, Kiersten's hands in my hair, Kiersten who trembled under my touch.

I had no reason to feel guilty for thinking about another woman. Kiersten and I were nothing but maybe business associates. We shared the coach but that was all. It wasn't like we were gobbling each other up every spare minute. The kiss was a fluke, and I kept telling myself that. One of these hours, I'd start believing it.

I knew Kiersten was on the phone but couldn't hear what was being said. I didn't want to interrupt but had to pee. I held it for as long as I could, but eventually I couldn't hold it any longer. I was hoping to be able to sneak in and out of the bathroom without Kiersten knowing, but when I heard my name and the word sex together, I stepped back inside. I did, however, shamelessly leave the door open a crack.

I got the impression she was talking to her BFF. Or at least I thought it was her. I didn't have a best friend, but they usually talked about sex and boyfriends and girlfriends with each other, didn't they? From what I could tell it sounded like the BFF was trying to convince Kiersten to sleep with me. Kiersten wasn't having it. Dang. Too bad.

I'd had more than a few fantasies of Ms. Kiersten Fellows. One involved a tub, lots of bubbles, and water all over the floor. The other was a rocking Ferris wheel seat, and another was right here in this bed.

The lights were low, and we'd walked in here together. There was no groping or tearing off clothes or heated kisses as we fell onto the bed. We were two adults who had every intention of getting naked together. We knew what was going to happen, and that's what made it hot. We would have no excuses of getting caught up in the heat of the moment, or swept away in desire, or any of the other excuses people used to explain their coupling. When you calmly walk into a room knowing exactly what's going to happen—it doesn't get any sexier than that.

In my imagination, Kiersten was assertive, knew what she liked, and wasn't afraid to ask for it. She was a thoughtful yet demanding lover and expected the same from me. She rode me, rubbed me, and paid particular attention to my most sensitive parts. Her technique was exquisite, her tongue talented, and her orgasms powerful. When I heard her laugh I opened the door quietly and just as silently closed the bathroom door behind me.

CHAPTER THIRTY-SIX

The next few days mirrored the ones before. Same set, different cities. Same white lines on the road, different exits. With the exception of the kiss, of course.

Kiersten kept a respectable emotional and physical distance between us, we kept on safe topics, and both of us pretended what had happened a week ago didn't rock our world. At least I think it rocked hers. I know it did mine.

I couldn't have set it up better if I'd tried. Talk about a beautiful woman falling in your lap. Lucky me. However, when she'd leaned in and kissed me, I'd been completely surprised. The tension between us was there, but I thought it was because I wanted JOLT and Kiersten was the one I needed to convince. I was on my best behavior, which really wasn't that difficult. I wanted this bad enough that it wasn't a sacrifice to get it. But Kiersten's lips on mine changed all that. Kiersten's *responsive* lips on mine. Kiersten sucking my tongue completely sent this to a different level.

I played out the scene in my head more than once, each time ending in a slightly different way. What was the same, however, was that Kiersten didn't pull away and certainly didn't say that it would never happen again. As a matter of fact, she sought me out and even fucked me behind the stage. She was hot, insatiable, and I completely lost my mind. But it was only a dream, a fantasy that would go nowhere.

"It's what?" I heard Jake practically snarl into his phone. "So what are we supposed to do, float in?" Jake had been my manager for years, and I knew his moods. Whoever was on the other end of the line was not conveying good news. "How long will it be?" We'd stopped at a rest area, and he was pacing back and forth in front of two of the coaches as he listened. His shoulders dropped a little more each time he passed us. He ended the call and turned and walked in our direction.

Kiersten and I were sitting on a bench under a huge tree. We'd stopped twenty minutes earlier, giving the drivers a rest break and a chance to stretch their legs. I'd suggested a walk and Kiersten quickly agreed. We'd stopped under the shade to enjoy the cool breeze.

"What's up?" I asked as Jake came close. I wasn't sure I wanted to know the answer to my question.

"The whole place is flooded," he said succinctly. I appreciated brevity, but even this was a little too brief because I didn't understand what he was referring to.

"You need to be a little more specific, Jake. Start from the beginning."

"Lake Charles, our next gig. They've had twenty-three inches of rain in the last two days, and the whole town is under water."

"The entire town?" Kiersten asked.

"Well, maybe not the whole town, but the parts we have to get to are. The civic center has three feet of muddy bayou water in it, and God only knows what else is swimming and crawling in there." He shuddered to make his point. "New Orleans is pretty much the same."

"What does that mean?" Kiersten asked, looking between Jake and me for the answer.

"It means we have a few days off," I said. I wasn't sure if I was disappointed not to have the four sell-out shows or grateful for some additional downtime. I think it was the latter.

"Yeah, even if the venues were dry, the entire area is knee deep in alligators. People wouldn't be able to get to the show even if they wanted to."

"So what happens? Do they get a refund or do you reschedule?"

"Both," I said first. Jake handled the business side of things, but I still kept an eye on what was going on, and that included insurance. "We have an insurance policy, kind of like trip insurance," I said, using a common analogy. "If for some reason the show is canceled due to the inability for us to perform, like in this case, the venue has insurance to either refund the ticket price or arrange to honor the tickets at a later date."

Kiersten nodded. "What do we do?"

"Since our next show is six days out in Orlando, we drive to the nearest airport and everyone goes home for a few days. The guys will take the busses and the equipment rigs and head there, then take a few days off," I explained, already looking forward to drinking coffee and catching up with Mr. Justin and listening to the latest stories from Mrs. Foster about her grandchildren.

"Since you don't have anything else to do, why don't you come home with me?"

Kiersten looked at me as if I were crazy. Considering the words that had just come out of my mouth, she was probably right. "I mean, you were going to be on the road with us anyway," I added, taking a preemptive strike at her declining my offer. Thank goodness Jake was out of earshot, or he would have had something to say about my invitation. He'd had plenty to say about Kiersten tagging along.

I've never invited anyone to my home. It was where I could be me, not who everybody expected me to be. I was selfish about this little piece of my privacy. I thought for a moment that maybe I'd invited Kiersten as a subconscious ploy to get the JOLT sponsorship. Funny, since I hadn't thought about it since Kiersten kissed me.

"Come on, Kiersten. It'll be all right. My house is bigger than the coach and has real grass in the front, fresh flowers, plenty of hot, running water, a full-size tub, and a real toilet."

Kiersten chuckled at that last one, obviously remembering how she'd needed instructions on how to flush the RV toilet.

"What will your neighbors think?" she asked, obviously unsure what my answer would be.

"They'll be shocked. But what they'll really care about is that you don't smoke, litter, or play your music too loud. Oh, and that you park in your assigned space."

The expression on Kiersten's face loosened a bit, and then she broke into a smile. "Well, I guess I'm fortunate that I don't have a car then."

❖

Five hours later we were pulling into the parking spot assigned to me. Kiersten teasingly gave me the third degree, making sure the space next to my house did, in fact, belong to me.

The car door had barely closed when Mr. Justin stepped onto his front porch. "You can't park…Tobin?" He frowned and looked at me closely.

"Yes, it's me, Mr. Justin," I replied, stepping around the car and moving closer to him. His eyesight wasn't the best, and he refused to wear his glasses. "Makes me look like an old man," he'd say.

"Whose car is that?"

It was a relevant question, if a bit rude. He was used to my green Jeep in my space, and I could understand how a blue Chevy could throw him off. "It's a rental, Mr. Justin. We flew in this morning."

He stepped off his porch and I gave him a hug. "How are you, old man?" He called me "young lady," and I called him "old man." It was our thing, with no disrespect on either side.

"Getting older and crabbier, but every day I'm on the sunny side is a good day. Who's your friend?"

"Oh, jeez, sorry." I turned toward Kiersten, who was still standing by the passenger door. "Mr. Justin, this is Kiersten Fellows. Kiersten, my neighbor, Mr. Justin." I supposed I didn't need to add the neighbor qualifier, but I did nonetheless.

Kiersten came around the rear of the car and extended her hand. "Pleased to meet you, Mr. Justin. Tobin's told me all about you."

Mr. Justin gave Kiersten the once-over but not in a sleazy or sexual way. It was his way of checking her out to make sure she wasn't going to hurt me. "Yes, ma'am, it's a pleasure to meet you. However, Tobin hasn't ever said a word about you," he said, scowling at me.

"It's not like that, Mr. Justin. Kiersten is roading with me for a few weeks, and our shows were cancelled due to the flooding in Louisiana, so I invited her to crash with me before our next one in Orlando."

I wasn't sure if he believed me. The old coot could be quite skeptical and could figure out if you were lying to him before you even got the words out of your mouth.

"Is that a problem, Mr. Justin?" Kiersten asked.

"No, not at all. Tobin here has the right to invite anyone she wants to her place. As long as you don't smoke, drop your trash, or park where you're not supposed to, we'll get along fine."

Kiersten and I exchanged knowing glances before taking our bags inside.

Chapter Thirty-seven

Tobin's house wasn't large; it was small, like a mini mobile home. I guessed it to be about forty feet long and maybe fifteen feet wide. Gray vinyl siding with a darker shade for the shutters flanked each white-framed window. A large composite deck extended off the front door, complete with a barbeque protected by a thick black cover and a patio table with four chairs. Pots full of colorful flowers lined the deck, and a hummingbird feeder hung from a branch in a nearby tree. Tobin pulled a set of keys from her pocket and unlocked the front door.

"Come on in." Tobin reached inside and flicked on a light. She held the door open for me, and I stepped inside.

The air was still, and Tobin apologized for the dank smell as she pushed several buttons beside the door. A ceiling fan silently started rotating, and the shades automatically rose, letting light into the dark room.

"Make yourself at home. I'll put your bag in the bedroom."

My pulse raced when I looked around again and didn't see another bedroom. Did she expect us to sleep together? She hadn't in the coach. Had something changed and I missed it? I practically jumped when her voice came from behind me.

"I'll take the couch," she said. "I don't have a guest room because I never have any guests."

I raised my eyebrows. "Really?" I found it hard to believe that she didn't have friends that would come over and jam or do whatever musicians do on their day off.

"No one knows about this place," she said, suddenly serious. "Well, Jake and Frank, but that's it," she added. "Would you like something to drink?" She opened the fridge and pulled out a bottle of water and offered me one. I took it and moved to the rack of CDs in the front of the room.

"Quite an eclectic taste," I commented, picking up the greatest hits of Aretha Franklin. It was between ABBA and rap artist Drake.

"I like variety," Tobin stated, looking directly at me.

Heat flushed through me, and I had no doubt it was written all over my face. I found it hard to breathe, and my nipples hardened painfully. Tobin must have sensed a shift because her eyes traveled slowly across my face, down my neck, and settled on my breasts: the ones with the rock-hard nipples poking out of my T-shirt. My knees almost buckled when she licked her lips.

The room was suddenly too small, and I was very aware that Tobin and I were completely alone. No one would bother us for at least five days. No interviews, rehearsals, or sound checks. No photo ops, rest stops, or schedule to keep. Nothing and no one for five full days. Whatever would we find to do?

"I'm very aware of your love of variety." There was more than a little sarcasm in my voice. It was my standard defense when I was uncomfortable, and I was definitely uncomfortable.

"Are you going to hold that against me forever?" Tobin stopped looking at my chest and sat down in one of the recliners.

"Sorry." I mumbled an apology. "I guess I'm just tired." Tobin looked at me again, and I could tell she was trying to determine if I was telling the truth or feeding her a line of bullshit. I think it was a little of both.

"Your place is really nice," I said, changing to a safe topic. "What do they call this?" I waved my hand around the room.

"It's called a park model. Smaller than a typical manufactured home but with all the same features. It works for me."

I finally felt like my legs could function properly and walked the few steps to sit down on the couch. The fabric was something incredibly soft, and the two cushions were plump and firm. "What do you do when you come here?"

Tobin kicked up the footrest on the recliner and crossed her ankles. "Absolutely nothing." She waited a few moments before continuing. "Well, not quite nothing," she said, chuckling. "The first day or so, all I do is sleep. Then when I feel human again, I have coffee and get beat in pinochle by Mr. Justin, and I join Mrs. Foster across the street for afternoon tea and cookies. I putter around the yard, take walks, and binge-watch Netflix. Sometimes I pick up a guitar and work on a few things, but only if the urge strikes me."

"You sang some songs at the nursing facility I'd never heard before."

"Just a few little things I'd written. They're a very forgiving crowd," she added with a touch of self-deprecation.

"They were very good." Very good couldn't even describe what I thought of them. The lyrics told a story, the guitar adding the mood. Some were funny, some sad, and others were often touching. "Why don't you play them in your show?"

Tobin shook her head firmly. "They aren't show quality," she said simply.

"What does that mean?"

"That means they wouldn't fit anywhere in the set. The songs are put in a certain order to set the mood or get the crowd pumped. Always open big and close even bigger." She took another drink and set her now-empty bottle on a coaster on the table.

"Then make a new set." Like I knew anything about what I was talking about.

"No. It's not that easy."

"Why not? It's your show." Sounded simple enough to me.

Tobin didn't answer right away. She had a faraway look in her eyes, like she was envisioning something no one else could see.

Finally she answered me. "They aren't for public consumption. They're just some things I threw together when I was killing time."

I looked at Tobin, thinking. First she said they wouldn't fit in a set, then that they weren't for public consumption. Which was it? I decided to let it go. It wasn't any of my business what songs she played.

"What are you working on now?" I asked, hoping to hear more. Tobin's voice was strong and melodic. I pulled my leg up under me and turned so I could face her.

"Nothing special. Just something I've been messing around with."

"Can I hear it?"

Tobin looked at me for so long I was getting nervous and was about to recant my request, when she reached over and picked up her guitar.

She played a few chords and then sang one of the most beautiful ballads I'd ever heard. Her voice was strong, and every word reached into my soul. It was as if it was the first time I'd ever heard music. The song told a story of two people who fell in love, experienced heartbreak, then found each other again years later. It was poignant, tender, and moving—absolutely not what I'd expected.

"That was beautiful." My voice was thick with emotion. "You should sing it in your show."

"No," she said, sounding a little harsh. "It's just for me, not anyone else." She seemed less emotional this time.

"Why? It's beautiful."

"It's not a Tobin Parks song."

I was confused. "Didn't you say you wrote it?" Tobin nodded. "Then why is it not one of your songs?"

"It is. I said it wasn't a Tobin Parks song."

"I'm sorry. I'm not getting this."

"You've seen my shows. Sultry ballads of lost love are not what people want to hear. It's not what I sing."

"Why not?"

"I have…" She looked from me to her guitar and back again. "An image, and that song doesn't fit it."

I thought for a moment about her explanation. Yes, her songs were all edgy, some much more so than others, but to not share that song was almost sinful. Kind of like having an original van Gogh painting and hanging it on the wall in your bathroom.

"But—"

"No, Kiersten. The song is mine and it stays mine. It doesn't go anywhere."

"Do you think your fans won't like it?" Before she had a chance to answer I added, "Or you?"

"Fans are fickle," she said, standing and moving the guitar to behind the chair. She took another bottle of water from the fridge, and I nodded when she offered me one.

Our fingers touched when I took the bottle from her, the lightning heat shooting up my arm and landing in the pit of my stomach. Tobin felt it too because she didn't move. Our eyes locked and I didn't breathe. Everything except Tobin and this moment drifted away. I'd read about this phenomenon in books and magazines but never experienced it. Until now. Tobin was the only thing I could focus on, and I watched the muscles in her jaw clench. Was she in pain? Wanted to say something but stopped herself? Wanted to do something but stopped herself?

I don't know how long we stayed that way, but the buzzing of my phone broke the mesmerizing moment. Go figure. I was seriously thinking about stripping and jumping into her arms. So much for that idea. By the time the irritating buzzing stopped, the moment had passed.

"Well, I thought it was beautiful."

"Thanks." Tobin picked up her bottle and headed toward the small kitchen. "Hungry?"

I pondered her question for a moment, and then my empty stomach answered for me. Tobin laughed and my pulse skittered.

"I'll take that as a yes." She opened a few cabinets and the refrigerator door again. "I need to restock a few things tomorrow, but I think I have some gumbo in here." Tobin's freezer was on the bottom, and I had a bird's-eye view of her ass as she bent over the drawer. Her jeans pulled tighter across her butt when she reached into the back of the large compartment. She pulled out a gallon-size Ziploc bag and held it over her head like a prize. "I knew I had some. I can get some rice going and thaw this out in no time."

I didn't need to answer. Tobin was already setting two stainless-steel pots on the stove.

Forty minutes later I pushed my empty bowl away. "I can't eat another thing." I'd had two servings of the steaming, spicy soup, which was delicious. Chunks of chicken and sausage were surrounded by green onions, celery, and a variety of other delicious smelling and very tasty ingredients.

She'd opened a bottle of wine, and after dinner and an hour on the patio, nothing was left in the bottle. I was relaxed and had a nice little buzz going on. The sky was clear, and thousands of stars were sharing the quiet evening with us.

"I love your place. How did you ever get here?"

"I was in a helicopter going from the airport to the arena and just happened to glance down as we were flying over." Tobin looked up as if she was remembering the scene. "My life was crazy at that time, and when I saw it, well, it sounds corny, but I just felt at peace. From the air it's this little enclave sequestered from everything else. The houses were lined up in neat little rows, spaced perfectly apart. Everything was neat and tidy and orderly. I've never had neat and tidy and orderly in my life."

"What did you have?" I asked quietly. The tone of Tobin's voice warned me that she was sharing something she probably didn't tell many people.

"Chaos. White trailer-trash chaos. When I was little I swore I'd never live in a trailer again, that I'd rather be homeless than set foot in one again. And look at me now. I travel across the country in one on wheels, and here I am," she opened her arms to encompass everything around us, "living in another one."

This was the first I'd heard anything about Tobin's life before she hit it big. There were countless articles on her but nothing before she was discovered in a nightclub in Harrisburg, and she refused to answer any questions about her past. It surprised me that in this day and age anything could be kept a secret. Especially if you were as famous as she was. Someone was always sniffing around looking for dirt no one else had uncovered.

"What about your parents?" I asked and was immediately rewarded with a scowl and Tobin's sharp tongue.

"My family, if any, is off limits. Don't ever ask me again." Her voice was hard and unforgiving. "You'll find clean towels in the bathroom. Lock up when you come in. I'm going to bed." And with that any conversation was definitely over.

I was up early the next morning and opened the bedroom door quietly. I didn't want to disturb Tobin. When I'd come in last night she was asleep on the couch, her head on a flat pillow, a blanket casually thrown over her legs. Her shirt was off, and she was wearing a white wife-beater undershirt. Her arms were long and muscular but not very tan. That verified her statement in my office that she didn't get out much. A three-inch tattoo of a red guitar was on her left bicep, the accompanying notes drifting upward from it. The outline of her nipples was evident under the thin material, and I swallowed hard. She was so young and completely off-limits, and I needed to keep reminding myself of that as I tried to fall asleep.

I cracked open the door and saw that the lights were on over the kitchen table. Maybe she was up and had made the coffee. I hoped so because I certainly needed it. I'd gotten no more than four or five steps when I saw her, this time sitting in a chair, bent over the table. I gasped, thinking the worst, and hustled to her. I was just about to call either her name or 9-1-1 when I realized she was sleeping. She was still wearing the wife-beater, and this time I could see she had on a pair of Calvin Klein boxer briefs. I don't know why I was surprised to see her sitting there in her kitchen in her underwear. It was her house, after all.

Her arms were folded under her head, and I noticed a large opened book, paper, and a pencil on the table around her. I careened my head to read the words on the page, and it took a few moments for me to realize I was looking at a textbook. The subject was the only class I'd gotten lower than an A in. Physics. And I was pretty damn glad I passed with a low C.

What was Tobin doing reading a physics textbook? I picked up the tablet, careful not to wake her. I skimmed the contents of a few pages, and the best I could figure out she was writing some kind of a report on Stephen Hawking. Her handwriting was neat and small, her punctuation and sentence grammar flawless. Being a snoop, I touched the trackpad of her computer. The screen jumped to life, and I looked at Tobin to see if the bright light woke her. She was still sleeping, and God, she looked cute.

The screen was locked, requiring a password, and even if I could figure it out that would be a huge breach of privacy. I looked around at the clutter and didn't see any other information that would answer my question. I decided to leave it be—for now.

A long strand of hair fell over her forehead, and I had an overwhelming need to touch it. I reached out, careful not to wake her—shit, careful not to get caught was more appropriate—and touched it. It was soft, and I quickly pulled my hand away before I did something really stupid that I would get caught at.

I grabbed a well-worn book off one of the shelves and sat in a large, overstuffed chair. I wasn't normally interested in biographies, but I was curious about what Tobin found interesting about Eleanor Roosevelt. Enough light was coming in from the window shades I cracked so I could see, so I opened the cover and started reading.

I felt eyes on me before I turned my head to see Tobin staring at me. She was looking at me intently, and I felt almost naked. I had to clear my throat to find my voice. "Good morning."

She sat up, giving me a glimpse of bare skin through the arm hole of her shirt. 'I didn't wake you, did I?"

"No," she said simply. Her morning voice was scratchy and sexy. I needed an ice-cold glass of water to quench my parched throat, or a cold shower to quench other things.

"You looked uncomfortable, but I didn't want to wake you," I said, indicating the table.

"Thanks. I guess I fell asleep." She started gathering up her books and papers.

"Physics?" I asked, like that question would answer all the questions I'd built up sitting here across the small room from her.

She blushed, then continued stacking the papers on top of the book. "Yes, and it's killing me."

I smiled, relieved she wasn't angry that I'd looked at her stuff. "It killed me too. Got a C, barely. And then only because I think my teacher had a crush on me."

"This is an online class. Nobody sees anybody. Anonymity is the way to go," she added, pointing at her laptop.

I took a leap of faith she'd talk about it. She might still be upset about the parent question last night. "What are you studying?"

"Business. I've completed all my other prerequisites and all my core classes, but I saved this one for last. Why does anyone need to know these things? Do we ever use the theory of relativity in our everyday lives? Those that do can learn it. Why do I have to learn it to run my business?"

I chuckled. "I asked the same question." Fifteen years ago, I thought but didn't add. "I think it's one of those rites-of-passage things. You know, like an initiation into adulthood or something." Tobin smiled and my heart skipped.

She looked so goddamn cute and hot sitting there in her underwear, with her mussed hair and sleepy face. I grabbed the arms of the chair I was sitting in to keep from standing up and going to her. I didn't have the guts and certainly wouldn't know what to do if I did.

"How long have you been up?" she asked, scooting her chair back and coming to sit on the couch in front of me. She curled her legs up under her, which gave me a lot of bare flesh to try not to stare at. I failed.

"Two chapters." I held up the book I'd forgotten was in my hand. I had no idea if it was one, two, or eight, or even if I'd read anything. My eyes had kept drifting to Tobin asleep at the table, her face calm and smooth. She had absolutely no lines on her face, which again reminded me just how young she was.

"I'm sorry about last night, how I snapped at you when you asked about my parents."

"It's okay," I said quickly. "It's none of my business."

"No. It's just that I don't talk about it. They're not worth the words or the air it would take, so I just don't."

That simple statement spoke volumes about her childhood and her family. The hurt was back in her eyes, and I changed the subject. "What are we going to do today?"

❖

Not what I want to do, that's for sure. "I promised Mrs. Foster I'd fix her bathroom faucet next time I was home. It drips," I said. Wow, what a stark contrast in activities—have sex with Kiersten all day or fixing a leaky faucet. I must be losing it, I thought.

What I hadn't lost was my appreciation of a beautiful woman. I was in between sleep and being awake when I felt Kiersten beside me. I could wake up and didn't want to. The scent of her, the heat coming off her body, and just the nearness of her were intoxicating. When I'd opened my eyes I was looking directly at her, and a warmth coursed through me.

She was framed in the morning sunlight, her legs crossed at the knee, a book clutched in her hands. She was completely focused on what she was reading, and I simply enjoyed the view. My neck was killing me, and I was just about to move when she looked my way.

Her face was flushed, either from what she was reading or because I was looking at her. It was probably the former, but my ego wished it were the latter.

"I can't believe you're going to fix a faucet," Kiersten said, laughing.

My stomach flip-flopped, and my clit throbbed when she laughed. "Why not? I know how. And if I run into any trouble I just YouTube it."

"I don't know. Maybe because you're Tobin Parks." Her tone made the statement sound like "duh."

"You're right. I am Tobin Parks, neighbor across the street from a sweet little old lady who needs her faucet fixed. And when I'm done, Mr. Justin invited us over for lunch."

We'd been pretty much inseparable that day and the two days after that. We watched old movies, laughed at reruns of *I Love Lucy*, and I tried real hard not to cry at the end of *Ghost*. Mrs. Foster fed us, and Mr. Justin filled our afternoons with stories of his days in the CIA. Kiersten was completely enthralled by them, and I was completely enthralled by her.

She was older than the women I'm normally attracted to. She had a sophistication about her, a sense of confidence that only came with being completely comfortable inside her skin. And did she have beautiful skin. I couldn't see much, but what I did see was tan and firm. More than once I caught her running around the block, and she visited the weight room in the clubhouse once a day.

I was coming in when she was coming out of the bathroom, and I froze right where I was. The green towel did little to cover more than her girl parts, and I reminded myself to get smaller towels next time. Beads of water glistened on her neck and shoulders, and I desperately wanted to lick them off. I wanted to lick other things I couldn't see as well. She was barefoot, her hair up in a towel. She was the sexiest thing I'd ever seen.

Our eyes locked, and I couldn't move even if I wanted to. And did I want to. I wanted to walk to her, peeling my clothes off along the way. I wanted to kiss her red lips, the curve of her jaw, and the back of her knee. I wanted to use my hands and fingers and mouth to discover what made her giggle and what made her sigh with pleasure. I wanted our skin to touch, our bodies to move in the rhythm they were designed for. I wanted to bury myself deep inside her and hear her call my name. And judging by the look on her face and the way her breathing quickened, she wanted the same.

"Sorry," I said, turning around and stepping back outside. *Sorry*! According to the way Kiersten was looking at me, I'd just blown the chance of a lifetime. What an idiot. I never miss an opportunity, NEVER.

I dropped down into one of the chairs on the deck. I leaned back, my head resting on the top of the chair. I was completely off my rocker. I had to be. I had a half-naked woman in my house, and I'd stammered and run away like a schoolgirl. She was willing, and I was out of my mind with lust, so why was I sitting out here watching the birds shit on the car?

Maybe I was just out of practice. Yeah, that was it, just out of practice. That was stupid. It hadn't been that long, so no way was that it. I didn't need to work at having a woman. It just came naturally. I'm sure the women came to me because of who I am, but I didn't care. It worked for me, wink, wink, nod, nod. But Kiersten was different.

I admit that in the beginning I was charming and flirty, but I think that was just habit—or a preservation thing. I didn't know any different, and I certainly had never met anyone like her, but then again, when I think about my life for the past few years, it was no wonder.

I admit I'd do her in a heartbeat, but I really enjoyed talking with her. I didn't mind that she'd seen me with my face literally buried in my physics book. That surprised me because I was very careful to not let it slip or give any indication that I was getting my degree. I didn't see judgment or pity in her eyes. In fact, I think I saw admiration, but I wasn't sure.

She had a great sense of humor and introduced me to Humphrey Bogart, Clark Gable, and Joan Crawford. I admit *Mommie Dearest* hit a little too close to home, and I was glad when it was over. She picked up pinochle pretty quick and almost beat Mr. Justin. I've never beat Mr. Justin!

After dinner we'd sit on the deck and talk about nothing or everything or nothing at all. It was comfortable being around Kiersten, and my hands itched to touch her every time she was near. It was a long five days and a short five days at the same time. When it was time to head to the airport to join the band in Orlando, I was tempted to say to hell with it all and stay right where I was. That scared the bejesus out of me.

Chapter Thirty-eight

"Tobin, have you seen my pass?" I had turned over every scrap of paper on the table and opened every drawer in the coach. It was close to time for the sound check, and I wanted to touch base with Joanne Tyler, one of Tobin's road crew. We'd talked for a few hours the other night about financial planning, and I wanted to follow up to see if she'd made any headway in aligning her personal finances.

We'd been back on the road for four days, and our relationship had changed. Well, we don't really have a relationship, but after spending a few days away from the craziness of the tour and being "normal" people, we'd become more comfortable around each other.

"Did you look in the Jeep?"

"Yes, but it's not there. I took it off before we left." Earlier in the day we'd gone to a group home occupied by eight surly teenagers ranging from thirteen to seventeen. After a few minutes of trying to make conversation and a few songs, their truculent attitude had shifted to that of typical fans of their age group. Soon she had them singing along and even got two of the boys to get up and dance.

"What's it like being a dyke?" one of the boys asked. Several others looked at him as if he'd just disclosed nuclear secrets.

"What's it like being straight?" Tobin asked back.

The kid sitting next to the questioner jabbed him in the side with his elbow. "She got you there, bonehead."

Tobin silenced the jostling boys with a look. “It was a legitimate question,” she said, giving the kid one of her dazzling smiles. He might not have thought so, but I certainly did. “I mean it’s just me. It’s no different than being straight.” That got a laugh from everybody.

“When did you know you were queer?” another boy asked.

“We prefer lesbian, not queer, and you need to be careful who you call a dyke. That offends some girls. They may take it as an insulting slur, because most of the time when it’s used, it is.”

Tobin answered a dozen more questions, but they were all about her tour and the bands she’d played with and what life on the road was like. She was engaging and didn’t talk down to these kids or treat them any different than she would have if they were just sitting around a rec center, not a home for seriously troubled kids.

“Here it is,” Tobin said, coming out of the bathroom. “It was on the counter.”

“I probably put it there to keep it from getting wet when I washed my hands.” After three weeks with Tobin I was suffering from complete inattention to anything that wasn’t the sexy woman herself.

She stepped closer, stopping a few feet in front of me and uncoiling the lanyard attached to a laminated colorful card. I caught a glance of the large green B as she moved even closer and raised the cord over my head. She settled it around my neck, like a medal. Her face was inches from mine. Her hands slid under my hair and lifted it, allowing the rope to lie against my skin. I detected a hint of cinnamon gum, but there was no mistaking the look of desire in her eyes.

My heart started pounding and I was suddenly giddy all over. My pulse raced, and the room started to tilt when her eyes drifted down to my lips. She was going to kiss me. Yep, no doubt about it as her mouth crept forward, filling the space between our lips.

Tobin’s hands were still in my hair, and she pulled me to her. When our lips met, a current shot through me all the way down to my toes. Her lips were as soft as I remembered them, her kiss as gentle and probing as when she’d first kissed me at the reunion. This time, however, there weren't dozens of eyes watching us; we were alone. All alone. In her coach. With a big couch behind me and a bigger bed down the short hall. Privacy all around us.

All these things and more bounced through my brain as Tobin opened her lips against mine. As she deepened the kiss, instinct kicked in and I wrapped my arms around her neck, my turn to pull her closer. Tobin ran her hands through my hair and her tongue down the side of my neck. My head fell back, giving her full access to whatever she wanted. And whatever she wanted, I wanted.

"God, you feel good," Tobin said as our bodies pressed together.

I was having a hard time standing upright and leaned into her for support. Tobin pushed me backward until the backs of my knees hit the couch. She guided me down to the wide cushion, with her following.

She kissed me again, this time long and so thoroughly I felt faint. I dragged my lips from hers and gulped in several deep breaths. My head started to clear until I felt her hand slide under my T-shirt. I concentrated on everything, wanting to savor this moment. But when her palm circled my breast I couldn't remember my own name. And when she expertly unhooked the front clasp I didn't care.

My body arched into her touch. Words like *wanton* and *eagerly* and *shamelessly* came to mind to describe the way I was responding to her. When her finger grazed my nipple I couldn't hold back a moan of desire.

My hands found their way under her shirt, and the feel of soft, warm skin made me sigh with pleasure. Tobin released my breast and reached behind her to grab my exploring hand and lift it above my head. My right arm was pinned under her so I was at a disadvantage. If that's the way she wanted to play it, I'd let her. All the better if she wanted to be in charge. What did I know anyway? I figured when my time came I would simply do to her what she was doing to me.

I kept telling myself to just relax and enjoy this. My body wasn't having a problem, so my mind should just go for it as well. So what if I was with Tobin Parks, female Lothario? Wait, what?

"What did you say?"

"Your skin tastes so good."

Those few words jerked me out of my sexual haze and back to my senses. I'd heard those exact same words from the two babes in the elevator in Boston. I was just another woman for her. I wasn't stupid enough to have to be in love to make love, but I had enough self-respect to not be another notch on her guitar strap.

"Get off me." I freed both hands and pushed against her chest.

I pushed harder when she didn't stop. "I said get…off…me," with a final push knocking Tobin off the couch and onto the floor. I scrambled up and stood on shaking legs.

"What the fuck?" Tobin asked, obviously bewildered by the rapid change of events.

"I said get off me."

"That's not what your body was saying." Tobin stood up, and I thought she was going to try to convince me of such.

"I'm not one of your girly groupies." My face burned with humiliation. I was no better than that, practically throwing myself at her, allowing myself to be swept up in the moment.

"You seemed to be enjoying yourself," she said, looking at my still-erect nipples. "We were just having a little fun, that's all."

"Well, I'm not interested in having 'fun' with you."

She looked at me, disbelieving.

"If you think that just because you have to be on your best behavior that means you can get your fill with me, you can think again, and this arrangement," I waved my hands around the interior of the coach, "will be over."

CHAPTER THIRTY-NINE

Don't pull that righteous-indignation shit on me, Kiersten," I said, tucking in my shirt. "Don't lie to me and don't lie to yourself. You were all over me and you know it. You wanted it just as much as I did." I knew I'd hit the mark when her face blanched, then flushed bright red. "But don't worry about it," I said, my defenses falling firmly back in place.

Somehow the instant I kissed Kiersten I wanted it all. I wanted her sighing my name, wanted to feel her respond to me, not Tobin Parks, the superstar. I wanted to take my time and explore every inch of her, not just her breasts and pussy. I wanted to learn what made her tremble, find where she was ticklish, and make her lose control. I wanted her to touch me, and nobody touched me.

A knock on the door startled me. "Tobin?" Jake's voice was muffled coming from the other side of the door. "Sound check is ready."

"I'll be right there," I answered before turning back to Kiersten. I grabbed my hat and slammed the door behind me.

"You okay?" Jake asked warily. He'd seen my fits of anger, and he, as well as everyone on the crew, knew to stay out of the way. But this time I was mad at myself for letting my desire for a beautiful woman override my defenses.

I half-listened to Jake as we walked the fifty yards to the stage. I went through the standard sound check by routine, completely distracted by what had happened with Kiersten.

I hadn't felt what I felt with her in a long, long time, maybe even years. Maybe even never. But Kiersten was different. From the first moment I met her it just felt different. Maybe it was because she was unlike any woman I'd ever met. Sure, she was older than me, but so what? It's not like she could be my mother or something creepy like that.

So why did I treat her like all the others? Habit? Self-preservation?

"Tobin! Tobin!"

Jake's voice penetrated my musings.

"Are you sure you're okay?" he asked, climbing the few steps to join me on the stage.

"Sure, why?"

"You've been distracted since you came out of your coach. I had to call your name four times before you heard me."

I realized why he was confused. I was always totally on when it came to anything to do with my music, even something as routine as the sound check. "Yeah, sure," I replied, trying to get my head back where it belonged—onstage. This was my job, and I was due to clock in in three hours.

Four-and-a-half hours later it was over. At least the part when I was truly myself—playing my music. It didn't matter if I was in front of tens of thousands of people or sitting alone on a park bench; music made me whole. It filled all the empty spaces and made me feel alive. The stress, craziness, and ugliness of the world floated away on the chords of my guitar. I didn't need words to sing, just the escape of the music.

But tonight the show had felt flat. You couldn't tell by the screaming fans, the thunderous applause, or the two encores they insisted on. The show went off exactly like it had been choreographed. I had no special effects, and other than a giant screen behind me for occasional videos, it was just me and my band. Some artists had lights, smoke, and a variety of other crowd-pleasing elements to their shows, but that wasn't me. My music was my show, not the razzle-dazzle that often accompanied others.

Tonight I'd sung the same songs as I had the previous dozens of nights, said the same lines between songs, got the same reaction to the same jokes. But instead of being thrilled by the fact that these people were here to see me, it just felt like what it was: well-rehearsed. Too rehearsed. And act two of the play was about to begin.

I was hustled through the backstage crowd's congratulations and accolades coming from those who had wished me well ninety minutes ago. Jake handed me a water bottle, and I downed the twenty ounces without stopping. He handed me another, and I repeated the action just as quickly. He exchanged the empty for a travel mug of warm tea with honey and four sugars. The water was for my dehydrated body, the tea for my voice. It was a routine I followed religiously after every show. I'd learned the hard way that an IV could easily take care of my body, but my vocal chords were much more sensitive and very particular about what they needed to recover.

Kiersten's eyes were on me as I worked my way through the obligatory meet-and-greet and photo ops. I knew when she was anywhere near the stage during the show. She hadn't been standing off to the side or in front of the stage, at least not the eighteen times I'd looked tonight. Her pass enabled her to have access to anything and go anywhere she wanted during the tour. But tonight she'd been conspicuously absent, and it was probably because of the fiasco of the kiss.

Chapter Forty

I was hustling to get back to the coach before anyone saw me, especially Tobin. I had intended to not go to her show tonight, my nerves too frazzled from the earlier kiss, but I couldn't stay away. I needed to see her. Such a simple yet complicated need. I know, it made no sense but I was having serious trouble with restraint when it came to Tobin.

I had pushed her away when she whispered the same words to me that Bimbo One and Two had giggled that she'd said to them. It hit me in the gut that I was nobody special, and I do mean "no body" special. She probably used the same canned phrases and empty endearments on all the women. I did not want to be one of her women. So why in the hell did I slink around to see her show?

I heard raised voices, one of which was Tobin's, coming from around the corner. I hurried to get away but stopped when I heard her say, "What in the fuck are you doing here?"

"You won't return my calls." It was a woman's voice, and so far this did not sound good.

"Because I told you not to call me."

"Well, that's too bad, Miss Famous Music Star." The voice was older, or at least it sounded older, but maybe I was imagining it.

"Go home," Tobin said firmly. "I've given you enough."

"You haven't even begun to pay me back for how you've treated me," the woman said. She was definitely not happy.

"I am not giving you another cent, Irene. I'm no longer your personal ATM machine. Now you can get your pathetic ass back on the bus or however the hell you got here, and get the fuck out of here."

I didn't wait around to hear the rest, nor did I want to be caught eavesdropping on what was obviously a private conversation. I hurried back the way I came, turning the opposite corner from where Tobin was with the mystery woman.

My mind was racing as fast as my heart. Who was Irene, and what did she have on Tobin that she was paying her? Was it to keep quiet? About what? It obviously wasn't a love child or anything sordid like that. Was it drugs? Something she had done in her past that she didn't want to get out? Something that could ruin her? Something that could blow back on to JOLT if we were her sponsor?

I was frozen to that spot thinking all this and didn't hear Tobin until she rounded the corner and ran into me. I stumbled back a few steps, and she reached out and grabbed my arms. Even though I didn't want her to touch me, I was glad I hadn't landed on my ass in front of her. That would have been completely humiliating.

"Kiersten, are you okay?" Tobin asked, her face full of concern. Still holding my arms, she stepped back and looked me over. My body obviously didn't get the memo that I was supposed to be angry at her and not go all aflutter and tingly when I was near her. That made me angrier—at myself.

"Kiersten?"

No, but I certainly needed to have my head examined, I thought. "No, I'm fine."

"What are you doing out here? I thought you were inside the coach."

I shrugged out of her grasp, which admittedly was harder than I expected. Her touch was warm and the calluses on her fingers sensuously rough on my skin. "I was just getting some fresh air," I lied.

"Out here? This late?"

Okay, so I'm not that good of a liar. I chose offense instead of defense. I looked around. "Where's Jake? You never go anywhere without him." Especially on concert night.

"I had to…ugh…talk to someone," she finally replied, but not before looking over her shoulder. She wasn't that good of a liar either.

"And Jake doesn't know about this…ugh…someone," I said angrily.

"He doesn't run my life," Tobin snapped, surprising me and herself, I think. "He runs my business, not my life." She was calmer this time when she said it. I think she was trying to convince herself of that fact.

I didn't have anything else to say about this entire scene. I wanted to know what was going on, but it was none of my business, and I sure as hell didn't want to get involved.

"I'll leave you to it then." I turned around and started to retrace my steps back to the coach

"I'll walk with you," Tobin said, hurrying to catch up with me.

"No need. I can find my way. And besides…" I held up my tour pass. "I have an all-access pass, remember?"

Chapter Forty-one

"Courtney, I'm not going to tell her. Stop trying to convince me."

I didn't mean to eavesdrop, but I couldn't help it. When I came in later that evening and didn't see Kiersten, I assumed she was in her room. I was a few feet away when I heard her side of the conversation. Several moments passed before Kiersten asked, "And when do you suggest I tell her? Before, during, or after?"

I could hear only one side of the conversation, so before or after what? I should do the honorable thing and step back and give Kiersten the privacy she obviously thought she had.

"Well, let's see, Courtney, I could say, Tobin, there's something I need to tell you. That would be a mood killer. She'd probably think I have some contagious STD. Or maybe when it's really getting hot and heavy, I blurt it out? And the best one could be after, as we're lying in the afterglow I say something like that wasn't as scary as I thought it would be. None of those is going to happen, Courtney."

There was another lull in Kiersten's side of the conversation. What in the hell were they talking about? One-sided conversations are just that, one-sided, and this one made absolutely no sense without hearing the other.

"Did you tell?" Kiersten asked. "I didn't think so."

I don't know who was more surprised when Kiersten stepped out of her room, she or I? Her face suddenly went from flushed to very pale. I stood there knowing I had been caught without an escape route.

"Courtney, I've got to go. I'll call you later."

Kiersten stabbed at her phone to end the call. "I didn't hear you come in," she said unnecessarily. If she had, she would have hung up the phone much earlier.

"What aren't you going to tell me?".

Panic replaced the shock on her face. "Nothing."

"If it's nothing, why do you look like you want to run?"

"Because you startled me," Kiersten explained. "That's all."

"What aren't you telling me?" I asked again. Somehow I knew it was something important.

"It's not important."

"Which is it, Kiersten? Nothing or not important?" She tried to step past me but I didn't move. Fortunately the hall was only wide enough for one.

"Both. Now would you please let me by."

"Not until you tell me."

"You eavesdropped on a private conversation. It's none of your business," she said defiantly.

"When it comes to me, it is my business."

"You have an ego the size of this bus," Kiersten shot back. "What makes you think I was talking about you? I could have been talking about anyone."

"I heard my name and saw the look on your face, Kiersten. It had guilt written all over it."

"It did not."

"It did." Our conversation sounded like we were both six years old.

"In that case, I'll tell you what I told Courtney. I'm not going to tell you. Now if you'd please let me by, I'd like to take a shower and go to bed."

I searched Kiersten's face for any sign of what she was keeping from me. It had to be something big for her to have this kind of reaction. She couldn't look me in the eye, and she kept fidgeting. I took a step nearer, closing the distance between us. That got her attention. She finally looked at me. I stepped closer, and fear replaced defiance in her eyes. What on earth could she be afraid of? I pushed my advantage and moved even nearer.

Our breasts were almost touching. I could see the dark flecks of blue in her eyes, feel her warm, sweet breath on my face, feel the heat coming off her body. Her hair smelled like lilac, and her lips glistened. The pulse in her neck beat wildly, and she was breathing fast. I leaned in closer, my lips lightly brushing her ear.

I sensed her leaning into me. It was probably instinct but I didn't care. I knew I could have her with just one more move. But I didn't want her by seduction. I wanted her to come to me. Big difference.

When I knew I had her full attention I said, "You don't need to be afraid of me. But I will find out. I can wait," I whispered, my lips grazing her ear. Before I was tempted to do more and before she had a chance to reply, I stepped around her and went into my room and closed the door behind me.

❖

"Fuck," I said, then repeated it a few more times. It was the only word I could use to describe what had just happened. I pulled myself together and stumbled to my bed, where I sat down, trying to catch my breath. "Fuck." My vocabulary consisted of the most descriptive word I could think of.

This day was completely messed up, from the kiss this morning to the conversation I'd overheard to this. I guess karma really is a bitch.

I tossed and turned for what felt like forever. I looked at the clock for the umpteenth time and saw that not even twenty minutes had passed. Shit. I'd never get any sleep at this rate. I couldn't get Kiersten's conversation out of my mind. I knew she was talking with Courtney, but what had they been talking about? They were best friends, and what could it be that BFFs talked about that could get heated?

I'd seen right through her smoke screen of maybe it was somebody else she was talking about. The look on her face told me otherwise. I replayed what I'd heard in my head and tried to connect it to what I knew. There was the part about when she would tell me. There was a before, during, or after. After what? The before was scary when she said something about an STD. The entire world knew an STD was a sexually transmitted disease. The during was, what were her words, when it was really getting hot and heavy and the afterglow? What the fuck was afterglow?

Suddenly every organ in my body seemed to stop. I couldn't breathe, couldn't think, and I was sure my heart had stopped beating. It couldn't be. Could it? No way. Not someone as beautiful as Kiersten. Not someone as charming and witty as her. Not someone who lit up a room when she walked in and took all the air with her when she left. Not someone with a smile that could light the dark and a laugh that could echo in any auditorium. But it had to be. All the signs pointed to it.

I got out of bed, pulled on my robe, and went across the narrow hall. I raised my hand to knock but stopped. We all had our secrets, and if this was Kiersten's, who was I to pry into it? I was certainly the poster child of *don't ask because I'm not ever going to tell*, so why would I expect anything different from her? If it was what I thought it was, Kiersten was right. It was none of my business. But I wanted it to be my business. I tapped lightly on the door twice and opened it.

"Kiersten?" She didn't acknowledge that she'd heard me. Maybe she was asleep. I moved into the room and called her name again. Her back was to me, and the quick, uneven cadence of her breathing gave her deception away. She was not sleeping.

"Have you ever been with a woman?" I'd thought and rehearsed what I was going to say, and that was not it. What a bonehead I was. I knew she heard me because her breathing stopped for a moment, then was even faster.

"Get out." Her voice was muffled but her command clear.

Without answering the question she had answered it. It was my turn for my heart to race. I'd never been in this situation before. I didn't know what to say, but I was with it enough not to say something stupid like "Why and how" and the dozens of other questions I wanted to ask. But she was right. This was none of my business. Yet when she kissed me it was my business. When she pushed me away she made it none of my business. When she had her hands up my shirt it was my business. My head started to spin. I'd been getting conflicting message from her practically from the day we met. Definitely for the last two weeks. I might not yet be a college graduate, but I wasn't stupid either.

"Kiersten." I reached out to touch her arm. She jerked away from me like my touch was searing, and not in a good way.

"I said get out."

Chapter Forty-two

"Tobin! Tobin!"

I roused myself out of a deep sleep to someone banging on the door.

"Tobin!"

"All right, all right," I grumbled, dragging myself out of bed. I hadn't slept much the night before and was paying for it now. I grabbed my robe and opened my bedroom door.

Kiersten had come out of her room as well and was standing in the hall. She stopped, her eyes grazing quickly over me. Then I realized I hadn't put the robe on yet and was standing there in what God gave me.

I had an uncharacteristic urge to cover myself and fought it. I wasn't modest, but the way Kiersten was looking at me made me feel a little shy. This made absolutely no sense, and I pulled the robe over me and cinched the belt. I sidestepped her and unlocked and opened the door.

"For Christ's sake, Tobin, what did you do?" Jake said, barely separating his words. He stepped inside and pulled the door closed behind him.

"You woke me from a sound sleep, Jake. What are you talking about?" I heard Kiersten pour coffee. I'd made the pot and set the timer before I went to bed last night.

"Irene. She's given HSO a fucking tell-all interview."

All sleep flew out of my body when I heard Irene's name. There were millions of Irenes in the world, but I knew Jake was talking about mine.

"When?"

"It's online this morning. And, shit, you have the interview with Bibbie Williams this afternoon. For sure she's going to ask you about it." Jake rubbed his hands through his hair and paced in the small room.

"Who's Bibbie Williams," Kiersten asked, a puzzled look on her face.

"Just the hottest news-magazine reporter," Jake answered. "We have a no-holds-barred interview scheduled for this afternoon at Fulshine College."

"I'll handle it," I found myself saying calmly.

"What?" Jake asked, clearly confused.

"I said I'll handle it." Instead of melting into a puddle or going ballistic like Jake, I was absolutely calm. Okay, maybe not absolutely calm, but much more so than I would have expected. I really didn't think Irene would ever have the nerve to follow through on her threat.

"Who's Irene?" Kiersten asked, coming up behind me and offered Jake a cup of coffee. He refused the offer.

When I didn't answer right away, Kiersten looked at me, then Jake, then back at me. "I'll leave you two alone." She turned to go back to her room.

"My mother." Jake was as shocked at my admission as I was. I never spoke about my family. Not in interviews or with anyone. This was the first time I'd said her name to anyone other than Jake in ten years. I'm sure the look on my face told Kiersten that as well.

"What did she say?" Kiersten asked the question I was afraid to.

I nodded when Jake looked at me. He answered for me. "Everything."

CHAPTER FORTY-THREE

"Tobin, this morning Irene Brown, a woman claiming to be your mother, gave an interview with HSO news magazine. She claims that you've paid her and your brother and sister for years to stay out of sight. She claims you view them as an embarrassment to you. They've never been invited to one of your concerts, and you haven't spoken to them in over ten years. She said they are on a fixed income and live in a rundown trailer and have no means of transportation."

This was it. The moment I'd been dreading for years. The moment I'd be paralyzed with fear would happen. HSO was a trash online magazine with more slander lawsuits than readers. But scandal sells, and this was big news. The fact that this interview was being held in the student union of one of the country's largest private educational institutions added to the sizzle.

"Is there a question in all that?" I couldn't afford to antagonize Ms. Bibbie Williams, but that was a statement, not a question. She was more than a little surprised but recovered quickly.

"Is it true?"

"Yes."

I could tell by the expression on her face that my answer was not what she expected.

She quickly regrouped. "So she is your mother?"

"Yes."

"And you paid her…"

"To stay out of my life, yes," I answered honestly.

"Is your family an embarrassment?"

"Yes."

"Okay," Bibbie said as she formulated her next question. Obviously she'd prepped for complete denial from me. "They live on a fixed income?"

I wasn't sure if that was a question or a statement. I treated it as if it were the former. "I don't know. Until a few weeks ago I sent them a monthly check. I don't know what else they do to earn a living."

"And they have no transportation."

"I don't know. That's what they claim." Again, I answered honestly. I didn't know anything other than what they told me. Bibbie called me on it.

"You don't know how your own family is doing?"

"No, I don't."

"Why?"

"Because they wanted nothing to do with me when I was growing up other than to be their maid, cook, and punching bag. I left when I was fifteen, and even though they knew where I was, they never came to bring me back home. When they did finally come sniffing around, I paid them to stay out of my life." There. The dirty laundry of my life was out in the open, and it felt great. A weight that I didn't know was crushing me was suddenly lifted.

"Don't you feel ashamed?"

"Of what?"

"Your actions. After all, they're your family."

She made it sound so simple, and it was anything but. "No, not at all, Bibbie. I believe that family is who you choose to surround yourself with, not your bloodline. Where were they when I was singing in a piece-of-shit bar when I was fourteen? Where were they when I had to walk home alone from that piece-of-shit bar? Where were they when I didn't go to school, have any friends, or ever go to a birthday party because there was no money to buy some cheap present? Where were they when I did go to school and had to wear dirty clothes because my mother and father drank and smoked the last dollar we had. Where were they when I was running down the hall escaping from the creep that was one of the many boyfriends my sister brought home? Where were they to support my dreams, to give me encouragement or pick me up when I stumbled?" I took a breath to calm myself. This is more information about my family than I had disclosed in my entire life.

"Nowhere. That's where they were, and that's where they can stay. I don't know them, don't want to know them, and don't care to ever know them. Judge me if you want, but that's the way it is, and to answer your question, no. I'm not ashamed of my actions. Not at all."

You could have heard a pin drop in the auditorium. The interview was live, and hundreds were in the audience, so there was little chance it would be edited. The swear words would be bleeped, but the rest was what it was. The reporting on this interview would pick out some key sound bites, but in my opinion, my entire statement was one big sound bite.

"So what now?"

"Nothing," I said. "There is no more. No more money from me and no more threats from them. The world knows, so they have nothing to threaten me with."

"Let's switch gears to your sex life." Bibbie was known for her bluntness and had often been referred to as the female Howard Stern.

"What about it?" I asked, grateful for the change in subject but not sure I wanted it to be this one.

"You've been quoted as saying that sex is simply a natural bodily function. That it's an emotionless act."

"I said I believe it's as natural as any other bodily need, like hunger or sleep. I never said it was an emotionless act." I hate it when I'm misquoted.

"So when you have sex, you are emotionally involved?"

"If it's done right, yes." I couldn't see them, but I heard the audience snicker. I knew what she was driving at so I beat her to the finish line. "What I feel during sex is no different than what I feel when I'm enjoying a good meal or listening to wonderful music or watching a great movie. There is emotion in all of those things, sex included."

"But you've admitted to sleeping with many women. I think you said," she put on her reading glasses and checked her notes, "and I quote, more than I can remember."

"I didn't sleep with any of them. I had sex."

"Isn't that quibbling over the word?"

"Maybe," I admitted. "But in my mind there is a difference. Sleeping together implies falling asleep in each other's arms and waking up together. That I do not do."

"Why not?"

"Well, first of all I'm on the road three hundred days a year, and second, I don't think I'm wired that way."

"What do you mean?"

"I mean intimacy. I just don't feel that close to people and haven't yet with a woman. So, when the mood hits, I strike, so to speak." The crowd did a little more than giggle over that one.

Bibbie had a few more questions, and then the interview was over. She thanked me for my honesty, and when she hugged me she whispered in my ear, "You've got guts, young lady. I admire you."

The ride back to my coach was quiet. Jake didn't say much, and I was all talked out. What else was there to say? The pundits, gossips, and news hounds would have plenty to keep their ratings up for days. Good for them. Whatever I can do to help stimulate the economy was fine by me.

Reporters were waiting for me when Jake turned the corner to enter the secured parking area. They mobbed the car like ants converging on a sugar cube. Lights flashed, microphones and cell phones were pushed up against the car, waiting for a response to the dozens of questions they shouted at me.

"How old were you when you moved out?"

"What was the name of the bar?"

"Who was the guy that chased you down the hall?"

"Did he catch you?"

"When did you drop out of school?"

And those were just the ones I could understand. Others were simply a jumbled bunch of words, everyone talking over each other and making no sense. I'm sure those questions were very similar.

I got out of the car, held my head high, and walked toward the door to my coach. I didn't make eye contact with anyone, and I certainly didn't answer any questions. I'd told my story and had nothing more to say.

The raucous noise quickly retreated into mumbles when I closed the well-insulated door behind me. I leaned back against it and exhaled. I was exhausted. Completely exhausted. The last four hours had drained the life out of me. I told Jake I was going to bed and to inform the paparazzi I would not be making any more comments about my family. I knew better than to think they'd believe me and pack up and go home, but I didn't care.

"Good night, Brewster!" The crowd roared, wanting another encore. I wasn't up for it so I waved and walked off the stage. I went through the after-show motions almost on autopilot. Jake hovered beside me, stepping in whenever a question came up about the statements I'd made on the Bibbie Williams Show this afternoon. After about the fourth time I told him to take a hike, that I could manage on my own. Kiersten, however, was always near without being over-protective. All I needed to do was turn my head slightly, and I saw her milling around the beverage table or the snack tray. She was talking with several of the roadies but seemed to have had one ear tuned to my conversation.

Every time I looked for her she was there, often with a slight smile or nod. I felt safer with her than with Jake all over me like a blanket in summer. Kiersten had a calm, confident way about her that, lately, extended to me. I'd noticed I was a different person when I was with her. I no longer played the part of Tobin Parks around her.

She hadn't said anything about the interview, but then again she really didn't have an opportunity, and I hadn't had a chance to pin her down about the conversation I'd overheard. I guess we both had things we didn't want flown from the nearest flagpole.

It was quiet in the coach when I finally went inside. The stark difference in the noise level, let alone the energy level, always surprised me. One minute I was rich and famous, and everyone wanted a piece of me. The next I was just a twenty-five-year-old woman alone.

Being alone doesn't bother me. It was my time. Time to regroup, pull myself together, and disappear into music. My music. But tonight when I came in, the coach just felt empty. I knew immediately Kiersten wasn't there. The last time I saw her she was in the corner of the room, her phone in one hand, the other over her ear trying to hear above the noise. She did not look happy. A wave of claustrophobia had come over me, and I'd just had to get out of the commotion, pressure, and demands on me, so I left word with one of the roadies I was going back to my coach.

I toed off my boots and unbuttoned my shirt. A flashback of Kiersten touching my collar just before I stepped onstage tonight took my breath away. She had called me back, and when I turned to her she'd reached up and adjusted my shirt collar. Her fingers had grazed the back of my neck, and her breath was like a caress on my face. I'd searched her dark eyes, looking for a message. Did she want me as much as I wanted her? Did she feel the same connection and energy I felt when we were together? Did she feel the same emptiness when we were apart? She'd kissed me on the cheek. "Play a new song."

My nipples tightened as I remembered the touch of her fingers, the way her eyes burned, and the way her lips felt on my skin. God, I had it bad for this woman.

I showered and put on a pair of jeans, leaving my feet bare. As soon as Kiersten got here we were going to hit the road. We had one more show before the end of this tour. Three more days until she left.

The door opened behind me, and my pulse raced when Kiersten walked in. There was nothing special about the way she looked. She was as gorgeous as ever. There was nothing special about what she was wearing, other than the fact that I'd had to convince her to wear the Tobin Parks T-shirt. But when she walked into the room or was anywhere near me, my body came alive.

"Hey," she said, closing the door behind her.

"Hey, yourself."

"I looked for you. Didn't know you'd already left."

She'd looked for me. That made me feel all warm inside. "I left word with one of the roadies. I just needed to get away."

She sat on the other end of the couch, a respectable distance from me. "Are you okay?"

"Yeah. I'm fine." She looked at me skeptically. "Okay. I'm a little tired." I've never admitted I'm anything other than perfect.

"You've had a busy twenty-four hours."

I laughed but it wasn't funny. "That's one way to put it."

"Do you want to talk about it?"

"Only the part about last night." I saw her blanch and knew she immediately regretted her question. "Only if you want to." It just felt right to add that.

I watched as Kiersten debated whether she wanted to go there, wherever *there* was. A muscle in her jaw tightened, and after a moment she lifted her gaze to mine.

"No," she said quietly but firmly.

Shit, now what? No, she didn't want to talk about it or no to my question. I looked at her, mentally imploring her to elaborate. I didn't know how far to push.

"The answer to your question last night. No. I've never been with a woman."

I was stunned. Even though I'd approached the possibility last night, I hadn't expected her admission. How could that be? She was elegant and sophisticated in her business attire, chic, classy, and beautiful in her party dress. She was breathtakingly beautiful when she laughed and incredibly hot when she was angry. She was charming, funny, smart, and whimsical. She made me think, defend my actions, see the other side, and…my God…she'd made me grow up.

A jolt of awareness shot through me. I was a different person since Kiersten came into my life. I was no longer the playgirl. No longer the girl who didn't have a care in the world other than my next lay. My life was empty. The women, parties, interviews, fans flocking around me were only there to fill time. God, what a mess I was. I wanted to get off this merry-go-round.

"You're probably asking yourself how can that be? No one is a virgin at thirty-six."

"I'm certainly not one to judge, Kiersten. Your life is your business."

"I was severely overweight until I graduated from college," she said. "As a result I had no confidence and certainly never had a boyfriend or a girlfriend once I figured that one out." She scowled. "As time went by it was harder and harder to do anything about it."

She stood, walked to the fridge, and took out two bottles of water. She came back and handed me one. "Courtney suggested I use a service."

I choked on my mouthful of water, hoping it didn't come out my nose. Talk about a mood killer. "A service? Like a…" I didn't want to say the word for fear I'd gotten it wrong. "Someone who… well…you know."

I could see she was embarrassed, but she continued.

"I can't do that. I mean, I'm not saving myself until marriage or anything like that, but the idea of paying someone…I guess it just sounded too clinical."

I nodded, encouraging her to keep talking.

"That's what you overheard. Courtney was trying to convince me to tell you."

"Why would you tell me?" When she didn't answer, I said, "Kiersten? Why would you tell me?" I thought I knew the answer, but no way was I going to jump to any conclusions here.

"We'd had this debate whether someone who was a virgin should tell the person they're with before, during, or after."

My heart beat a little faster. "Before during or after what?"

"Having sex with them."

"And Courtney's view was…" I asked, prompting her.

"Tell you before," Kiersten said, not looking at me.

Me? Did she say tell me? Not only was my heart beating, but my clit was keeping the same fast beat. “And what was your position?”

“That no way in hell was I going to embarrass myself by telling Tobin Parks I was a virgin.” Her words came out in a rush.

“Why not?” She didn’t answer. I rose and walked over to her. “Why not?” I asked softly.

“Because Tobin Parks would laugh at me. Tobin Parks, who can have any woman she wants, who has had more women at her age than I will have in ten lifetimes, would laugh at me. And that would kill me.”

My heart swelled with something very unfamiliar. This woman. *This woman who has everything wants to give me something so beautiful.*

“Kiersten, look at me,” I said, my voice gentle. “Kiersten, look at me,” I said again, a little more forcefully. It took her a moment, and before she did I saw her inhale deeply, setting up her defenses for whatever I would say. Her eyes were filled with doubt but steely resolve.

“Do you want me to kiss you?” She nodded. “Do you want to kiss me?”

“Yes.”

“Do you want me to touch you?” Again, same answer. “Do you want to touch me?”

Her answer this time came out in a whisper. “Yes.”

My knees almost buckled. I’d felt passion and desire before, even lust, but never a yearning to possess. What once was just sex, a simple, uncomplicated bodily function, was now something much, much more. I needed to please Kiersten like I’d never needed to before. I wanted to do it for her, not for me.

“This has nothing to do with JOLT,” I said. “You need to know that.” I didn’t want Kiersten to think that the way to get the sponsorship of my tour was through her undies.

“I don’t care.”

Her words shocked me. I didn’t want her to think less of me. I wanted to be better than that for her, for me. “I do. This is not about JOLT," I repeated. I looked deep into her eyes for several long moments until I was positive she believed me.

"You know what?" I asked playfully.

"What?" Kiersten asked.

"You owe me, and this seems like the perfect time to collect."

"I owe you what?" Her look of apprehension turned to confusion.

"A kiss."

Her eyebrows shot up. "A kiss?"

"That's right. We bet that your mother would hear about your date to your reunion in less than twenty-four hours. You owe me a kiss." I saw her start to relax.

"And I always honor my bets," she said, surprising me.

"Then kiss me." This time my voice was little more than a whisper. "Right here," I added, pointing to my right cheek. I inhaled when Kiersten lowered her head and brushed her lips on my cheek. "And right here," I said, pointing to the other one. She repeated the kiss, and I pointed to the edge of my mouth. "And here." This time the other side of my mouth.

"That was more than one kiss." Kiersten was teasing me, raising her head and looking at my mouth.

"And right here." I pointed to the center of my lips. Kiersten stared at the place I indicated, and I wasn't sure I was even breathing anymore. The pounding in my chest was so loud I couldn't hear my own thoughts. This kiss would forever change my life and surely change hers. A heartbeat later she lowered her head and kissed me.

Chapter Forty-four

My body exploded in sensation. Tobin's lips were as soft and electric as I remembered them to be. My pulse raced, my heart hammered, and I couldn't breathe. It was like no other kiss before. It was hot and wet and demanding. My tongue went into her mouth, and my arms slid around her neck. I pressed my body to hers. I couldn't get close enough to her. I finally broke the kiss, breathless and gasping for air.

"Kiss me here," Tobin said, pointing to the edge of her strong jaw. "And here, and here, and here."

I followed her commands one by one and kissed every place she indicated. Her hands were in my hair, holding me close, and I was thrilled that I was exciting her.

"Keep kissing me and take off my shirt."

Again I did as I was told, and somewhere around the third or fourth button her demands turned to requests. She was telling me what to do, what she wanted, not *telling* me what to do. I pushed her shirt off her shoulders and trailed my fingers over her hot skin. She shivered under my touch, and my confidence soared.

"Touch my breasts."

Tentatively I reached out, my hands trembling slightly. I cupped each one, which fit perfectly in my palm.

"Pinch my nipples." Her voice was hoarse.

Her breasts were full and heavy in my hand and seemed to swell as I touched them. I slid my fingers over her nipples, and she moaned into my mouth. I dropped my head and kissed her neck as my fingers found and pinched the tight peaks.

"Oh, God, I like that," Tobin said in more of a sigh than a statement.

"Lick them," she said after a few minutes. Her fingers were digging into my waist, and I bent my head farther.

My tongue lightly slid over one nipple, then the other, and she sagged against me.

"Oh, God, that feels good."

I could say the exact same thing if I could manage to say anything at all. But I couldn't.

"Suck them, hard."

Oh, God, this was everything I'd thought it would be and more. She tasted like strawberries and woman as I took one breast, then the other into my mouth. They were small and fit perfectly into my palm and even better in my mouth.

"Harder," Tobin croaked, and I happily gave her what she wanted. I sucked a tight nipple into my mouth. A moment later she grabbed my face with both hands and pulled me up into another searing kiss. I rocked my hips into her.

"Put your thigh between mine."

I did, and the image of our dance at my reunion flashed into my mind. It had been slow and sensuous, nothing like this red-hot heat between us now.

"Unsnap my pants," Tobin said between kisses. "Slide down the zipper."

She hadn't got the word out before I had it all the way down. My fingers itched and tingled to get inside. Fortunately I didn't need to wait long.

"Slide your hand into my pants. Slowly," she added. "Feel everything, imagine what this feels like for me. Make me want it. Desperately."

I didn't know if she was talking about me or her. The anticipation was driving me crazy, the need to feel her warm wetness on my fingers driving me forward. *I* was desperate to touch her.

"Touch me, now."

Three simple words. Not the three that most people wanted to hear, but they were the most powerful and needy I had ever heard.

I moved my hand farther south, holding my breath for the instant my dreams became reality. It was my turn to moan in pleasure when I felt soft, hot, wet flesh. Tobin wrapped her arms around my neck and fell back against the wall.

I moved with her, pinning her back to the hard surface. My mouth was on her breasts licking, sucking, and biting while I caressed and stroked her sex with my fingers. I felt the rigid nub of her clitoris grow harder, and she was rocking against my hand. I felt powerful and completely female with the ability to give this woman such pleasure.

"Oh, God, Kiersten, just like that," Tobin cried out, her voice muffled by her hands wrapped around my head holding me in place.

Her sex grew in my palm, dripping with excitement, heat filling my soul. I opened my eyes and looked down at my hand in her pants. The scene wasn't crude or sordid but the hottest thing I've ever seen. Tobin stiffened, and I increased the pressure and speed of my fingers on her clit. Her body was telling me what to do now, and I wouldn't disappoint her.

"Ugh…ugh…ugh" Tobin moaned as she came in my arms. Her sex spasmed, and I came right after she did.

❖

I caught my breath before my head cleared. It might have been the other way around, but it really didn't matter. Sometime during our little tryst my pants had fallen to the floor, but Kiersten's hand was still on me. I'd had orgasms with the women I'd been with, but never this powerful, and never had I allowed any of them to touch me. My legs started shaking, threatening to topple us both.

"Kiersten," I said, running my hands through her silky hair. She was still breathing fast, her face buried in my neck. "I need to sit down. Better yet, I need to lie down."

She lifted her head but didn't look at me. I kissed her gently before speaking. "You killed me, but if I don't lie down, we'll both end up on the floor. Not that that's a bad idea, but the bed is much softer, don't you think?"

Kiersten stepped away from me. The cool air hit my damp skin, and my body immediately rebelled at missing Kiersten's heat. I pulled up my jeans and snapped them. I thought about just tossing them to the side but didn't want to embarrass Kiersten by running around with my bare ass hanging out. I watched as Kiersten's thoughts were clearly visible on her face. She was in the process of making a decision.

I hoped it was the right one. With firm determination she took my hand and led me down the hall.

Chapter Forty-five

I had no idea where my courage was coming from; all I knew was that I needed to feel Tobin's hands on me, her mouth on my skin, the whispered sound of my name. I stopped just inside my bedroom and hesitated. What in the fuck was I doing? Had I lost my mind? I uncharacteristically pushed the questions out of my mind and turned to face her.

She was holding her pants up, and heat flooded me remembering the sensation of her warm center in my hand. Desire and raw need were in her eyes. but I also saw patience and self-restraint. It was clearly my show. I was calling the plays and I was in charge. I felt something funny inside my stomach but couldn't describe it. That she would turn over control to me was breathtakingly empowering and arousing. I admit I didn't know what I was supposed to do, but when something feels right, do we really *not know* what to do? I don't know if it was instinct or knowledge I gained from the hundreds of lesbian novels I read or my porno collection, but I knew exactly what to do.

Tobin watched as I unbuttoned my shirt. As each button slid through the hole exposing more of the blue lace underneath, Tobin's eyes darkened with hunger. When the last one was freed I slid my shirt off my shoulders and let it drop to the floor. Whether it was the cool air or Tobin licking her lips, my nipples hardened. My shallow breathing enhanced the pounding that started at my nipples and ended between my legs.

Tobin's obvious pleasure over my breasts gave me more courage, and I unbuckled my belt. The sound of the zipper sliding caught her attention, and I sucked in a breath as my pants fell soundlessly down my legs. I stepped out of them. Slowly I pulled the left, then right bra straps off my shoulder. Tobin's eyes followed every move. Reaching behind me, I released the hooks and tossed the blue lace to the growing pile on the floor. I linked my thumbs under the slim waistband of my panties, and they too joined the pile.

When I lost all my weight I treated myself to expensive panties and bras because I finally, finally felt sexy. Tobin was the first person to see me in them, and she was the first woman to see me out of them. I had worked hard to transform my body, and my efforts had changed me as well. I was confident, emotionally strong and self-assured. When I was a teenager I never thought I'd be in this position—open and exposed. Subject to complete and total scrutiny. A familiar stab of shame and humiliation threatened to knock me down. I could not let that happen. I would not let that happen. I had come too far and I was not going back. I pushed away years of habit and shame and stood in front of Tobin completely naked, physically and emotionally bare.

The two steps I took toward Tobin pulled her out of her trance, and she looked at me. Fire burned in her eyes, frightening and empowering at the same time. Whatever I had unleashed, I was capable of handling. This was my moment, my life, and I was taking control.

Tobin gasped when I skimmed my hands over her bare skin. It was soft and heated, and I knew she was as aroused as I was. Her breasts were small and firm, she was only twenty-five after all. I pushed back a negative thought about mine that were ten years of gravity and hundreds of miles of running older. Her arms were a darker shade than the skin I revealed, and I was tempted to make a teasing comment. Something about her needing to get some sun, but I couldn't find the words to get past my very, very dry mouth. My hands were steady when I reached for her pants. Pushing her hand away, I took hold of the waist of her pants and tugged. I didn't let them drop to the floor, instead kneeling and slowly pulling them down.

Her legs were muscular and smooth, and I felt them tremble under my hands. I filled my lungs with the scent of her arousal, the knowledge that I was affecting a woman like Tobin Parks a powerful aphrodisiac.

"Look at me, Kiersten." Tobin's voice broke the silence, thick with need.

I leaned back on my heels, taking advantage of the glorious landscape as my eyes traveled up Tobin's perfect body. Her stomach was flat and muscular, her breasts were full, nipples hard and begging for my attention. She was breathing rapidly and swallowed several times. Finally, our eyes met, and the pure, raw, hunger looking back at me took my breath away.

"As erotic as this image is, I can't stay standing much longer. Please let me take you to bed."

Her voice was soft, almost pleading its command, her need crystal clear. My knees were weak, and when I lifted my hand, Tobin took it and gently pulled me to my feet. It was my turn to gasp when our breasts touched, shooting flames of desire through me.

Tobin released my hand and turned on the small light beside the bed, a warm glow flowing over the bed.

"I want to see you."

Her voice was husky and dispelled any remaining nervousness I had. I reached out and pulled her lips to mine. The kiss started gently but quickly turned, Tobin eagerly exploring my mouth and tongue with a thoroughness that threatened to bring me to orgasm. Her lips were on my neck, sucking on a spot I had no idea was so sensitive. Her hot, wet mouth moved quickly down my chest, and she hesitated just above my right breast. Hot breath caressed my nipple an instant before she closed her mouth around it.

My knees started to buckle, and Tobin slid her hard thigh between mine to keep me steady. She teased my nipple, sucking then biting it with just enough force to make me see stars behind my eyelids—very good stars. I pulled her head closer, wanting more, needing more. Her hands expertly traveled over my bare back and down to caress my ass. She lifted me slightly, giving my clit more direct contact with her strong thigh, and I exploded against her.

We fell onto the bed and Tobin covered my mouth with hers and I breathed her air in as if it were my own. The feel of her body on mine was exquisite, nowhere near how I imagined it would be. We fit together perfectly, the combination of hard arousal and soft flesh merging together like notes in a song. Her long legs intertwined with mine. Skilled hands roamed, then were replaced with lips and teeth as she expertly navigated her way around my body.

I was consumed by sensation. Every nerve was alive, every sense on high alert as my body responded like God had designed it to. I stiffened for an instant when Tobin's wandering hand brushed against my clit. I hadn't been able to keep track of where it was and it surprised me. Tobin lifted her head from my breast and looked at me, a question on her face. I couldn't speak so, instead, willingly spread my legs, giving her the access we both desired.

Tobin's eyes burned hot as her fingers slowly explored virgin territory. I couldn't look away, the connection between us so strong. I should have been shy or embarrassed or some other ridiculous virginal behavior, but I was frozen in this moment. Tobin slid a finger inside, then back out, then deeper, judging my response. I was wet beyond anything I had ever experienced, the smooth rhythmic action driving my passion higher and higher. Tobin flicked my clit with her thumb on each outward stroke, and I thought I was going to come out of my skin with pleasure. My legs moved over the bed, my hips lifting to meet each stroke.

Tobin dipped her head and traced my bikini line with her tongue. Her hot breath on my wetness gave me an instant chill, and I shuddered. When her mouth finally settled on me, I grabbed the sheets to keep myself from flying off the bed as my orgasm ripped through me.

Wave after wave of pleasure rocked through Kiersten, and I felt every spasm. I wanted this woman like I had never wanted anyone before. I fought the urge to crawl up her body, take her in my arms, and never let her go. Kiersten was unlike any woman I had ever known. Suddenly she pulled away and rolled onto her side, effectively shutting me out. I moved up behind her, our bodies close. She stiffened.

"Hey," I said gently, touching her arm. "Are you okay?" I didn't really know what to say, and that certainly sounded lame. When she didn't answer I tried again. "There's nothing to be embarrassed about." She still wouldn't acknowledge me.

I put my hand on her shoulder and rolled her onto her back. I took it as a good sign that she didn't fight me. With my finger under her chin I tipped her head up. "Kiersten, look at me. Kiersten, please," I practically begged when she didn't. Finally she looked at me, then glanced away.

"You are so beautiful. It was everything it was supposed to be. Kiersten, please look at me." Finally she did.

Kiersten studied me for several moments. I don't know what she was searching for, but I smiled and caressed her cheek. "Really, it was amazing. You are amazing." It was the truth, not some made-up line to get me out of here or get me more.

When was the last time I'd said something like that and really meant it? When was the last time I forgot who I was and completely lost control? Tenderness replaced calloused indifference. Warmth refilled areas that had always felt sterile. Wanting her to stay replaced the need to flee. The hunger for more replaced the usual sense of finality.

"What are you thinking?" I asked. The longer Kiersten didn't answer my question, the more nervous I grew. Should I say something else? If so, what? Jesus, I could make a song out of nothing but a word or two, but I had no idea what to say to this wonderful, beautiful woman.

"I can't believe I just did that."

"You say that like it's not a good thing."

"It's not."

That wasn't the answer I expected, and it was like a blow to the stomach. Suddenly I was having a hard time catching my breath.

My heart was pounding, but not for the reason it was a few minutes ago. Was it just a few minutes ago that I asked her, no, begged her to put her hand down my pants. FUCK!

"I swore I wouldn't do that. That I wouldn't let myself fall under the Tobin Parks spell. Wouldn't make a fool of myself over you."

My throat was so tight I wasn't sure I could speak, and if I did, I didn't want her to know how much her words had affected me. *This* was why I didn't get involved. *This* was why I had nothing more than sex. *This* was why I didn't get close to anyone. It hurts. It. Fucking. Hurts. And a long time ago I swore I'd never let myself get hurt again.

"Well, we all do things we don't mean to do now and then." Somehow I managed to sound pretty normal, like she'd eaten a piece of pie that wasn't on her diet, not had sex for the first time. "You're not superwoman." Obviously neither was I.

"I've never—"

"Well, you have now." I think she flinched at my insensitive words.

"I've never crossed the line," she said. "The line between business and pleasure, right and wrong."

"Oh, for God's sake, Kiersten," I said angrily, getting up and reaching for my clothes, my shield. I pulled my pants on. I didn't want to have this conversation buck naked. "It was just sex. I know it was a big deal for you, but it happened. Only two people in the entire world know, and I don't kiss and tell. And I certainly don't fuck and tell."

This time I did see her cringe, and I felt like a complete shit. I was angry and hurt, and lashing out was my go-to defense mechanism. It could have been worse. I could have been insultingly sarcastic.

"How dare you," Kiersten replied, rising from the bed and looking around frantically for her clothes. She pulled on a robe instead. She stopped so close to me I saw the sparks in her eyes. "Insult me like that. That," she pointed to the bed where it had all occurred, "was not a fuck, and you know it. And if you think I'm going to fall apart because I lost my head or fall all over you because you were the first, you can think again. I said I'd give you one month, and in three days that time is up. I'll be going home and back to work, and my original decision about sponsoring you stands. Not because of that," again she pointed to the scene of the crime, "but because I don't want to. Now get out of my room."

Chapter Forty-six

I must have been out of my fucking mind. *Jesus Christ, Kiersten. What were you thinking?* I know what I wasn't thinking. I wasn't thinking of the public embarrassment and humiliation I would suffer if word got out. That I would never forget the feel of her skin, the taste of her mouth, the warmth and readiness of her sex. Never forget the tremor of desire or hear her gasp of pleasure. I wasn't thinking that I would fall crazy, stupid, head-over-heels for a twenty-five-year-old singer.

I slammed the door behind Tobin and eased myself down onto the floor, my back against the closed bedroom door. Dropping my forehead to my knees, I wrapped my arms around my legs. Flashes of Tobin filled my brain. The sound of her voice commanding me to kiss her, suck her nipples, and touch her filled my body with white-hot desire—again. The power she had over me was frightening. The complete breakdown of my defenses was terrifying. The sensation of Tobin losing control in my arms was beyond anything I ever could have imagined.

Being with Tobin, those few hot minutes, released something inside me that I didn't know I was capable of. I had the ability to experience complete, total abandonment of everything except of the sound of Tobin's voice and the feel of her skin, the way she reacted to my touch, her surrender. I had absolutely lost my fucking mind. And once I got over how foreign, how alien that feeling was, I wanted to go there again. But I couldn't. Not with her.

I was zipping my suitcase when Tobin knocked on the bedroom door. It was just before eight, and since I hadn't slept the night before, I was up, showered, dressed, and ready to go.

"Kiersten, may I come in?"

I opened the door and turned back to my suitcase without inviting her in.

"Can we talk about—"

"There's nothing to talk about. It happened, it was nice, but it's not going to happen again."

"Nice? It was nice?"

"Okay, it was better than nice, but there will not be a repeat."

"Why not? And don't give me that business-and-pleasure bullshit. I told you it had nothing to do with JOLT. What happened between us was between you and me, and it meant something to me. Something special. Not just because you gave me something beautiful and precious, but because you trusted me enough to give it to me. You are so very different from any other woman I've known. I want to—"

"It's not going to happen again," I repeated.

"Why?"

"Because it just won't." If I couldn't explain it to myself, I certainly couldn't explain it to her.

"That's a chicken-shit excuse."

"Well, it's the only one I have," I said angrily. I was frustrated, tired, and completely confused. I wanted her again but this time to spend hours exploring every inch of her body. I wanted to find every freckle and childhood scar, discover her sensitive areas, the ones that made her tremble and took my breath away. I wanted to drive her crazy with desire for me and take her over the edge.

"You're a very smart woman, Kiersten. Think again."

I whirled to face her, and when I did she was closer than I thought. Heat radiated off her, and my mouth went dry remembering heat in other places. Her eyes burned, but this time with anger, not desire. She was tense from this confrontation, and not because she was moments away from orgasm. My eyes went to her mouth, and for a moment I thought I was actually going to kiss her. That would certainly send a mixed message.

"Where are you going?" she asked, looking over my shoulder to where my suitcase lay on the bed ready to be snatched up as soon as we stopped for gas.

"Home."

"Home? That's it, you're leaving?" When I didn't reply she continued. "You're not even going to give me the courtesy of talking about what happened between us." It was a statement, not a question.

"There's nothing to talk about," I replied stubbornly.

"Then I obviously taught you everything I know about sex because this is exactly what I've done for years. Suck 'em, fuck 'em, and duck 'em." She practically snarled the words.

The crack of my palm on her face reverberated in the small room. My hand stung, but probably not nearly as much as the red spot on Tobin's cheek did. "How dare you imply I'm anything like you."

"Then stop acting like me," she shot back. "Stay and talk to me."

I had to admit I was tempted, but I'd been over this entire conversation with myself all night. The honking of a car horn saved me from myself. My cab had arrived.

❖

Three weeks later, Courtney was reading me the riot act—again. "You need to snap your ass out of it, Kiersten. I mean it. You need to get over her, get on with it, or go back and get her, because you're making me and everyone around you fucking miserable."

"Jeez, Courtney, why don't you tell me how you really feel? Go ahead, don't beat around the bush. Don't pull any punches. I'm a big girl. I can take it." We were sitting in my living room with our feet up on the coffee table and seven empty beer cans between us. She'd given me so much shit since I returned from Tobin's tour, I hadn't even tried to find her favorite wine at the liquor store this afternoon.

"Then pull up your big girl panties and get to it." Her voice was a little louder than normal, signaling me she would either spend the night or need a ride home later.

I admit I had been a bit of a workaholic bitch lately. The day after I got home I showed up in my office and started tackling the pile of work on my desk. My staff had done a good job of taking care of the day-to-day things, but I still had a shitload of things to do. Because I came home early, no one was expecting me, and they scampered around like ants when I stepped off the elevator.

I'd been at the office by six thirty every morning at the latest and often didn't leave until after nine or ten at night. The only thing that got me out before then was if I had a dinner meeting or some other obligatory business event to attend. Weekends were much the same. As a result I was churning out work faster than my staff could take it in. They were running on empty and tempers were short. Courtney had been in a few days working with our accountants, and she noticed the shift in the mood in the office as well. She'd called me on it twice before.

"My panties are fine," I said defiantly. They weren't, but I'd clammed up again even with Courtney. I didn't even want to think about my family. They too had plenty to say about my adventure, and I didn't want to hear it. Rockette, however, gave me unconditional love every minute I was home. She'd loved staying with Courtney's family and had basked in the attention from her boys.

"Did Tobin get into them?" Courtney asked for at least the fifth time.

"Why do you keep asking me that?"

"Because one of these days you'll drop your defenses and tell me." Courtney was still sore that I hadn't confided in her what had happened.

"Yes."

Courtney sat up so fast the contents of her beer spilled on the floor. "What?"

"You heard me, obviously," I added, wiping up the spill with a napkin.

"How was it? Does she look as good naked as she does in clothes? Was she any good or just all show? Did you tell her? Was it good for you? Where did you do it? In that little trailer of hers? Tell me *everything*."

I took another swallow as Courtney rattled off her questions in rapid fire. She looked at me expectantly.

"Unbelievable, definitely, yes, yes, in her coach. There. I told you everything."

Courtney looked at me and cocked her head. I saw her rethinking her questions and my answers, putting together the pieces. "Good," she said hesitantly, "but you haven't told me everything. You've told me nothing. Spill, girlfriend."

Two beers later she knew the entire chain of events. She sat back on the couch looking a bit stunned. "And you left?"

"The next morning, yes." Pain shot through me like it was today.

Courtney tossed a pillow at me, bringing me back to the present. "So what are you going to do now?" she asked.

"Go on with my life. Chalk it up to an experience I'll never forget and, like you said, move on."

"You are so full of shit, K. You can't tell me that wasn't a turning point in your life."

"I never said it wasn't."

"Then why aren't you doing anything about it?"

"And just what am I supposed to do, Courtney? Follow her like some groupie from town to town? Live on the crumbs of attention I'd get? Play second fiddle? Sloppy seconds? My God. She can have any woman she wants."

"And she wanted you."

"No, Courtney. She wanted my body." I recalled Tobin's interview with Bibbie when she stated she wasn't wired for intimacy; she didn't feel close to people, and when the mood for sex hit, she struck. "And I wanted hers, so we both got what we wanted. End of story." One of these days I might admit I got more than I bargained for. Much, much more.

Chapter Forty-seven

I was more than a little nervous. Scared shitless was more like it. Jake had hastily arranged this mini-tour, and it was opening night. It had been a month after our last gig. Four weeks and three days since Kiersten left. But I was the only one counting. I hadn't heard from her, but then again I didn't expect to. Kiersten had made it very clear she didn't want to see me.

I peeked out the curtains on the side of the stage. Jake had told me earlier that every seat was sold. There were only twenty-six hundred seats, but I was more nervous than I was when I played in Yankee Stadium. The theater was in the round, meaning the stage rotated in a circle throughout the show, giving me a three-hundred-sixty-degree view of everyone in their seats. I'd never played in a venue like this. The acoustics were said to be perfect, with limited real-estate for much else on the stage other than the performer. And in this case it was me. Just me. Just me and my red guitar. I heard my name called and stepped out onto the stage.

My phone rang and I ignored it. A few seconds later the familiar ding notified me I had a voice mail. A few minutes later it rang again, this time with no accompanying ding. I answered it the third time.

"Kiersten, turn on Phoenix City Limits, channel eighty-three."

It was Courtney, and she sounded like she was hyperventilating.

"What?"

"Channel eighty-three, turn it on. Now!"

"Okay, okay," I said, looking for the remote. I hadn't had the TV on for several days, preferring to work in silence. Rockette didn't mind either. "What am I looking for?"

"Just watch it."

I found the remote and hit the bright green On button. Then I went back to reading the report on my lap while the black screen slowly came to life. My heart stopped, and my stomach dropped at the familiar voice coming from across the room.

"Courtney, I'm not going to—"

"Shut up and watch it. Rewind it to the beginning and watch it."

I swallowed as I gathered my nerve to start at the beginning.

"I bet you wonder what I'm doing here all by myself?" The crowd hollered and whistled but was much more subdued than I had ever heard it during a live show. "I was having a conversation one day with someone special to me, and we were talking about reputation. She asked if my reputation or my music sold tickets." A few more whistles in the background made her smile, and my heart started beating very, very fast.

God, I missed her. I missed her smile, hearing her laugh, seeing the way her music connected with those that others had forgotten. The way she respected her neighbors and her band. The way she lit up the room when she walked in, and the way it felt like she was singing only to me in a stadium filled with tens of thousands of screaming fans.

"I didn't have an answer for her," Tobin said. "I wanted to say it was the music, because to me it's all about the music, but at times, and quite frankly more and more lately, I wasn't so sure." Tobin strummed her guitar quietly as she spoke, and I realized that she was the only one on the stage. No Russ, Jones, Cindy, or Charity. She was sitting on a high stool, a mug to her left, a microphone in front of her. She was wearing a pair of pressed jeans and a green, long-sleeve button shirt. Her hair was a little shorter, and she looked thinner and tired. She fidgeted on the stool. Was she nervous? Apprehensive? What was going on?

"I wasn't good enough for that someone special, but more importantly I wasn't good enough for me. I got caught up in being Tobin Parks and lost my way from the music. She helped me find my way back. I'm working on being a better person. Not for her, but for me. I want to be someone *I'm* proud of, someone *I* can look up to, because it's not about me. It's about the music."

"So I decided to find out. Would people come just to hear me play without all the fanfare and mega production? No video screen, lights, or souvenir T-shirts and key chains for sale in the lobby. Would anyone want to hear *my* songs, ones I've written but never sung before, at least in public? So, for the next hour I'm going to do just that. Just sing. Just me and my guitar. If you stick around you'll hear some familiar lyrics, but you won't recognize the melody. You'll hear some songs you've never heard and, depending on your reaction, maybe never will again."

I could tell Tobin was nervous, very nervous as she spoke to the crowd. The camera panned the audience for reaction to her words, and everyone was on the edge of their seat. This was a very different Tobin Parks.

"So, this is my, ugh, deal for you." Tobin strummed a few more chords and fidgeted on the stool before she spoke again. "If you don't like what you hear, I will double the price of your ticket and give you a refund at the door." The murmurs in the crowd almost drowned out her words. "No questions asked. If this isn't what you came to hear, then please feel free to leave at any time. I understand. If it is, please sit back and enjoy the show."

Tobin exhaled, and she smiled at someone in the audience in front of her. The camera over her shoulder zoomed in, and there in the very first row sat Mr. Justin and Mrs. Foster, both looking slightly uncomfortable but beaming.

The crowd was absolutely still as Tobin began. Song after song she told a story. Her story, my story, a single father's story, a struggling rancher's story, the story of loss, the joy of young love, old love, and new love. This was the Tobin that played in the senior centers, the burn wards, and the Alzheimer units. The Tobin that played in the middle of the night, on a tour bus countless miles from nowhere. This was the Tobin I had given myself to. I sat there in stunned silence.

Chapter Forty-eight

I was nervous and the car was going too fast and not fast enough. Mile after mile I repeated what I was going to say. I had written it all down and practiced it in front of the mirror in my bathroom and the lavatory on the plane. I knew what I wanted to say and hoped she'd give me the chance to say it.

The driver stopped in front of number 214. The sun was shining, and it was a beautiful spring day. Before I could change my mind I paid the driver, grabbed my bag, and opened the door. I exited on shaky legs and looked around. Memories flooded back to me. The afternoon we planted the flowers that were in full bloom along the walkway. The morning we sat in the chairs on the deck and watched the birds fight over scraps of paper for their nest. The evenings we sat close watching classics and laughing over silly comedies. The way Tobin looked at me, like I was the only woman on earth. The way I felt when she was near. The way my body tingled when she touched me. The way my body hummed with anticipation and burned with desire just thinking about her.

"It's about time you came back."

I turned around, not surprised that Mr. Justin would be the first to greet me. Tobin said he often sat by the window, a sentry watching from his post.

His welcome surprised me. I knew he liked me but was afraid he might be jealous of the time Tobin spent with me and not him. "It's good to be back."

"She's inside," he said, tipping his bald head toward Tobin's front door. "But she's not herself. She doesn't hardly come out anymore, and when she does it's more out of obligation than anything else."

"Why do you think that is?" *Please, please, please say it's because of me.*

"She misses you. Mrs. Foster thinks so too."

I looked from him to Tobin's front door, then back at him. I stepped toward him and kissed him on the cheek. "I hope to solve that." I stepped forward, more sure of this than I'd been for days.

I had to knock three times before Tobin opened the door. She was dressed in a pair of ragged cargo shorts, a faded Def Leopard T-shirt with the sleeves cut off, and untied Nike running shoes. Her hair was messy, and she was the most beautiful thing I had ever seen. Her shocked expression clearly indicated I was the last person she expected to see on her doorstep.

"Hi," I said shyly. So far so good. That was the first word in my well-rehearsed statement. When she didn't say anything my stomach churned, but I pressed on. "May I come in?" She didn't say anything but opened the door wider and stepped back, allowing me inside.

The room was dark, and Tobin opened a few shades to let in the natural light. The air was dank and stuffy, indicating the windows had not been opened in some time. Papers, takeout, and delivery containers were scattered around. Several beer bottles were balanced precariously on the top of an overflowing garbage container.

"Why are you here?"

No offer to sit or have a beverage or any other sign she was even remotely happy to see me. Determined to see this through, I placed my bag on the floor and sat down on the couch. I watched as Tobin debated whether to join me until she finally sat in the chair across from me.

"I saw your show on Phoenix City Limits." I didn't add that I'd replayed it from the channel's website at least a dozen times since then. Tobin didn't say anything, just looked at me suspiciously.

"I loved it."

She didn't respond.

"I thought it was the best you've ever done, and the audience loved it too."

Silence.

"The reviews of the show raved about it."

Finally she spoke. "Tell me something I don't know."

Her eyes were hard and her body stiff, the beat of the pulse in her neck the only reaction to my being here. I knew what that pulse tasted like and how it felt beating under my tongue. It gave me the strength and courage I needed.

"I was wrong," I said. "I was stupid, blind, and afraid." I was looking her in the eyes and didn't stop. It was important that she believe me. I detected a slight flicker in them before she blinked it away.

"You were not what I expected. Not at all. I had a preconceived notion of who you were and had prepared myself for that. I couldn't see anything other than that, and when I did, my reaction to you frightened me." I chuckled. "No, that's not right. It scared the holy hell out of me. I'm thirty-six years old, and I felt like a schoolgirl with her first love. You see, I never had that. Never felt the twitter of excitement of being with someone and that someone liking me, wanting me. And when I finally did, it was with you." Another flicker in her eyes that hadn't moved from mine.

"And I couldn't handle that," I admitted. "It was the most difficult thing I had to come to grips with. I have a reputation that I've worked my ass off to grow and achieve. I'm a shrewd businesswoman with impeccable timing of a deal and business savvy. I know when to back off and when to go in for the kill, or so a few business articles say about me."

"My family, although a bit screwed up, are prominent in the business and philanthropy community. My father owns the top law firm in the city, my brother-in-law is a world-renowned pediatric surgeon, and my baby brother is a missionary in some of the most dangerous, awful places in the world.

"How could I fall for a singer? A singer who sleeps around and is the topic of every gossip rag and website in the country."

"I would be the laughingstock of my friends, family, and business associates. I would lose everything I'd worked for, including my self-respect. All because I fell for the first person who rocked my world. The first person I allowed to get past all my defenses. Who made me feel confident enough to just let go. And the worst part? She didn't even know. She'd never given me any indication that I was anything other than the next one or the one before the one after that. If I went stupid over this…this girl, and if I can't control my personal life, how can I control my professional one?

"I'm smitten by a girl eleven years younger than me. I want to be with her, spend time with her. Hear her laugh and sing and play cards with the lonely old man next door. How funny is that?" I asked again. "And how sad and pitiful. I would be compared to a middle-aged man having a middle-aged crisis who goes after the fountain of youth with a younger woman. That's all I could see. In that moment, that special moment when I should have been and wanted to reach out for more, I didn't. I couldn't. And because of that I couldn't look you in the eye and could barely look at myself."

"Then what are you doing here?"

"Because I don't care. Plain and simple, I don't care what people think. I'm done with that. The time I spent with you—at the reunion, on tour, here in your home—were the happiest I've been in my life. And I want to feel that again. If not with you, then with someone else. I'll wait until I find it, but I will not be afraid of it again."

"Then what are you doing here?" she repeated.

"I came to give you a chance to finish your sentence."

Her eyebrows rose, the first sign of any emotion or interest in what I was saying.

"The morning after," I explained, "when you started to say that what happened between us was special. I didn't want to talk about it, couldn't talk about it, but I'm ready now if you'll give me the chance to listen."

Still nothing. My heart was pounding, and I clenched my hands in my lap to keep them from trembling. Tobin hadn't moved the entire time I poured out my soul. Funny, not one word after

"Hi" had been what I rehearsed. I knew coming here had been a mistake. Deviating from my script had been a colossal blunder. I'd completely misjudged this scene.

How much longer should I wait for her to comment? Did I even want to hear what she was going to say?

Seconds ticked by, the only noise in the room coming from a lawn mower somewhere in the distance. I wanted to run, I wanted to stay. I wanted to beg and plead, and I was determined to remain strong.

Without warning, Tobin stood and walked over to me and extended her hand. I searched her eyes and found what I'd been praying I'd find. Strength to weather the storm that will surely come, passion, desire, hope, and joy. I placed my hand in hers. I was giving her my past, my present, and my future. She locked the front door as we headed for her bedroom.

EPILOGUE

Her hands, fingers, lips, and tongue caress every inch of my body. I feel the touch of this woman, inhale the scent of her arousal, and hear the pulse of her desire. I'm lost in sensation, shut out from the world around me, and am swept over the edge in waves of release in her arms.

I bury my hands in her thick blond hair, touch her soft skin, travel over her curves and valleys, and sink into her warm wetness. She makes me have to remember to breathe, forget my name, and lose my inhibitions when I'm with her. I need to know her life history, her favorite color and her name, and I do. Her name is Kiersten Fellows. I am hers and she is mine.

THE END

About the Author

Julie Cannon divides her time by being a corporate suit, a wife, mom, sister, friend, and writer. Julie and her wife have lived in at least a half a dozen states, traveled around the world, and have an unending supply of dedicated friends. And of course, the most important people in their lives are their three kids: #1, Dude, and the Devine Miss Em.

With the release of *Wishing on a Dream*, Julie will have fifteen books published by Bold Strokes Books. Her first novel, *Come and Get Me*, was a finalist for the Golden Crown Literary Society's Best Lesbian Romance and Debut Author Awards. In 2012, her ninth novel, *Rescue Me*, was a finalist as Best Lesbian Romance from the prestigious Lambda Literary Society, and *I Remember* won the Golden Crown Literary Society's Best Lesbian Romance in 2014. Julie has also published five short stories in Bold Strokes anthologies.

www.JulieCannon.com

Books Available from Bold Strokes Books

Amounting to Nothing by Karis Walsh. When mounted police officer Billie Mitchell steps in to save beautiful murder witness Merissa Karr, worlds collide on the rough city streets of Tacoma, Washington. (978-1-62639-728-6)

Becoming You by Michelle Grubb. Airlie Porter has a secret. A deep, dark, destructive secret that threatens to engulf her if she can't find the courage to face who she really is and who she really wants to be with. (978-1-62639-811-5)

Birthright by Missouri Vaun. When spies bring news that a swordswoman imprisoned in a neighboring kingdom bears the Royal mark, Princess Kathryn sets out to rescue Aiden, true heir to the Belstaff throne. (978-1-62639-485-8)

Crescent City Confidential by Aurora Rey. When romance and danger are in the air, writer Sam Torres learns the Big Easy is anything but. (978-1-62639-764-4)

Love Down Under by MJ Williamz. Wylie loves Amarina, but if Amarina isn't out, can their relationship last? (978-1-62639-726-2)

Privacy Glass by Missouri Vaun. Things heat up when Nash Wiley commandeers a limo and her best friend for a late drive out to the beach: Champagne on ice, seat belts optional, and privacy glass a must. (978-1-62639-705-7)

The Impasse by Franci McMahon. A horse packing excursion into the Montana Wilderness becomes an adventure of terrifying proportions for Miles and ten women on an outfitter led trip. (978-1-62639-781-1)

ight Kind of Wrong by PJ Trebelhorn. Bartender Quinn happy with her life as a playgirl until she realizes she can't feelings any longer for her best friend, bookstore owner ett. (978-1-62639-771-2)

Wishing on a Dream by Julie Cannon. Can two women change everything for the chance at love? (978-1-62639-762-0)

A Quiet Death by Cari Hunter. When the body of a young Pakistani girl is found out on the moors, the investigation leaves Detective Sanne Jensen facing an ordeal she may not survive. (978-1-62639-815-3)

Buried Heart by Laydin Michaels. When Drew Chambliss meets Cicely Jones, her buried past finds its way to the surface—will they survive its discovery or will their chance at love turn to dust? (978-1-62639-801-6)

Escape: Exodus Book Three by Gun Brooke. Aboard the Exodus ship *Pathfinder*, President Thea Tylio still holds Caya Lindemay, a clairvoyant changer, in protective custody, which has devastating consequences endangering their relationship and the entire Exodus mission. (978-1-62639-635-7)

Genuine Gold by Ann Aptaker. New York, 1952. Outlaw Cantor Gold is thrown back into her honky-tonk Coney Island past, where crime and passion simmer in a neon glare. (978-1-62639-730-9)

Into Thin Air by Jeannie Levig. When her girlfriend disappears, Hannah Lewis discovers her world isn't as orderly as she thought it was. (978-1-62639-722-4)

Night Voice by CF Frizzell. When talk show host Sable finally acknowledges her risqué radio relationship with a mysterious caller, she welcomes a *real* relationship with local tradeswoman Riley Burke. (978-1-62639-813-9)

Raging at the Stars by Lesley Davis. When the unbelievable theories start revealing themselves as truths, can you trust in the ones who have conspired against you from the start? (978-1-62639-720-0)

She Wolf by Sheri Lewis Wohl. When the hunter becomes the hunted, more than love might be lost. (978-1-62639-741-5)

Smothered and Covered by Missouri Vaun. The last person Nash Wiley expects to bump into over a two a.m. breakfast at Waffle House is her college crush, decked out in a curve-hugging law enforcement uniform. (978-1-62639-704-0)

The Butterfly Whisperer by Lisa Moreau. Reunited after ten years, can Jordan and Sophie heal the past and rediscover love or will differing desires keep them apart? (978-1-62639-791-0)

The Devil's Due by Ali Vali. Cain and Emma Casey are awaiting the birth of their third child, but as always in Cain's world, there are new and old enemies to face in post Katrina-ravaged New Orleans. (978-1-62639-591-6)

Widows of the Sun-Moon by Barbara Ann Wright. With immortality now out of their grasp, the gods of Calamity fight amongst themselves, egged on by the mad goddess they thought they'd left behind. (978-1-62639-777-4)

18 Months by Samantha Boyette. Alissa Reeves has only had two girlfriends and they've both gone missing. Now it's up to her to find out why. (978-1-62639-804-7)

Arrested Hearts by Holly Stratimore. A reckless cop with a secret death wish and a health nut who is afraid to die might be a perfect combination for love. (978-1-62639-809-2)

Capturing Jessica by Jane Hardee. Hyperrealist sculptor Michael tries desperately to conceal the love she holds for best friend, Jess, unaware Jess's feelings for her are changing. (978-1-62639-836-8)

Counting to Zero by AJ Quinn. NSA agent Emma Thorpe and computer hacker Paxton James must learn to trust each other as they work to stop a threat clock that's rapidly counting down to zero. (978-1-62639-783-5)

Courageous Love by KC Richardson. Two women fight a devastating disease, and their own demons, while trying to fall in love. (978-1-62639-797-2)

Pathogen by Jessica L. Webb. Can Dr. Kate Morrison navigate a deadly virus and the threat of bioterrorism, as well as her new relationship with Sergeant Andy Wyles and her own troubled past? (978-1-62639-833-7)

Rainbow Gap by Lee Lynch. Jaudon Vickers and Berry Garland, polar opposites, dream and love in this tale of lesbian lives set in Central Florida against the tapestry of societal change and the Vietnam War. (978-1-62639-799-6)

Steel and Promise by Alexa Black. Lady Nivrai's cruel desires and modified body make most of the galaxy fear her, but courtesan Cailyn Derys soon discovers the real monsters are the ones without the claws. (978-1-62639-805-4)

Swelter by D. Jackson Leigh. Teal Giovanni's mistake shines an unwanted spotlight on a small Texas ranch where August Reese is secluded until she can testify against a powerful drug kingpin. (978-1-62639-795-8)

Without Justice by Carsen Taite. Cade Kelly and Emily Sinclair must battle each other in the pursuit of justice, but can they fight their undeniable attraction outside the walls of the courtroom? (978-1-62639-560-2)

21 Questions by Mason Dixon. To find love, start by asking the right questions. (978-1-62639-724-8)

A Palette for Love by Charlotte Greene. When newly minted Ph.D. Chloé Devereaux returns to New Orleans, she doesn't expect her new job, and her powerful employer—Amelia Winters—to be so appealing. (978-1-62639-758-3)

By the Dark of Her Eyes by Cameron MacElvee. When Brenna Taylor inherits a decrepit property haunted by tormented ghosts, Alejandra Santana must not only restore Brenna's house and property but also save her soul. (978-1-62639-834-4)

Cash Braddock by Ashley Bartlett. Cash Braddock just wants to hang with her cat, fall in love, and deal drugs. What's the problem with that? (978-1-62639-706-4)

boldstrokesbooks.com

Bold Strokes Books

Quality and Diversity in LGBTQ Literature

SCI-FI

E-BOOKS

MYSTERY

EROTICA

YOUNG ADULT

Romance

W·E·B·S·T·O·R·E

PRINT AND EBOOKS